The Hunters of Infinity have been protecting the Daharian galaxy for years, but there has never been a female Hunter—until now.

In a seedy bar in the shadowy corners of Daharia, Jessop comes to the rescue of young Hunter Kohl O'Hanlon. Impressed by her remarkable sword-wielding skills, the Hunters invite her to their training facility, the Glass Blade, though not all are pleased with the intrusion. But they soon discover that Jessop learned to fight from the rogue leader of the Shadow City of Aranthol—and escaped. Now they want to use her intimate knowledge of their enemy to destroy him.

As Jessop grows closer to this elite brotherhood, their leader succumbs to a mysterious ailment, and Kohl learns that Jessop is hiding dark secrets, raising suspicions about the enigmatic woman who saved his life. Has the Hunters' security been breached—or do they have a traitor in their ranks?

Allegiances will be questioned.
Loyalties will be betrayed.
Vengeance will be brutal.

The Glass Blade

Hunters of Infinity

Ryan Wieser

REBEL BASE BOOKS
Kensington Publishing Corp.
www.kensingtonbooks.com

For the family I come from and for the family Sam and I have made together.

Always. Forever.

ACKNOWLEDGMENTS

I would like to thank Richard Curtis, first and foremost, for his unwavering patience and constant guidance; without his support this book would never have happened. I would also like to thank Martin Biro, for believing in the piece. There are so many people who have contributed to the successful completion of The Glass Blade. Zorro Duck, who read the first draft in a day and got back to me with notes—I have no words for how grateful I am to you. You've always dropped everything to read my work, and it means the world to me. Bird, the constant champion of my writing, your support means more to me than you could ever know. To my mother, who has always encouraged my writing, I thank you from the bottom of my heart. Nana and Ralph, your work has inspired me all my life. Claw, you are the kind of reader authors long to write for. And always, I thank Sam, who has endured the late night edits and hours-long plot line conversations with never ending support and patience.

CHAPTER 1

The tavern was dark and quiet, barring the muted voices that filled the corners with whispers of quiet corruption and deceit. Hushed sounds traveled on thick smoke to the ceiling and her eyes trailed over the dimly lit corners and over the musty cloaked patrons. Dirty exchanges took place everywhere, too-young girls being offered coins and despair by corrupt travelers, whose lies traveled like fire across the alcohol on their lips. This wasn't a typical bar, this dark, underground dwelling in the heart of Azgul where there were more shadows than light, more smoke than air. It was a seedy, unsafe locale where illegal exchanges could occur. A place favored by those in the city's most important positions, for in this underground dwelling they could act as they truly wished.

From where she sat, with her cloak draped low over her face, she could easily make out the group of Aren. They were more discreet than she had anticipated, but few could go unseen to her well-trained eyes. They were scattered about the bar, donning the civilian attire of common Azgul nomad passer-by. The Aren weren't common travelers though; they were fatalistic believers who waited anxiously for a supposed impending end. A doom and darkness that would swallow the entire Daharian galaxy whole—their belief in some unimagined state of horror for the universe made her certain that not a man amongst them had ever laid eyes on Aranthol.

She scanned the room, counting twelve of the zealots. Without their robes they appeared as normal men, barring their brand, which could be seen on the base of several of their necks. The tender nape of the neck was where all in Azgul had their brands. She knew that their mark was not well-known though, not as well-known as they would have liked it to be. Thinking of the brandings nearly had Jessop reaching for her own neck, certain she could almost feel the hot iron against her still. The smell of burning, blistering flesh unnaturally recoiling from heated metal filled her nostrils. She shivered at the putrid memory and forced it back to the depths of her mind, where she kept all her locked-away thoughts and all her darkness.

Suddenly, the oddest sensation roused her, overcoming her senses. She could feel silk running across her skin, dragging her fine hairs on end, exciting her cells. The energy of the room had completely changed, thickening the air more than any smoke or liquor could do. She had only ever been around one other of her kind, and to feel the changing electromagnetic charge in the room without *him* present was as compelling to her as it was terrifying. The draw was a beast's cry calling her in, feeding her need to find the one like her. It was a pull strong enough to grip her, strong enough to shoot adrenaline through her, to dilate her pupils and ready her muscles and tell her, without question, that Hunters were near.

She closed her eyes and narrowed in on their presence. She could smell the faintest scent of grease on one of them; it had an acidic air to it—like the oil slick found in the Western corner of the city. She could hear his voice though he did not speak. She could see the diminutive smudge of black slick over his boot though she did not open her eyes. Her senses—so refined—ensured she could see most of him without ever glancing his way.

And then she laid eyes on him.

She found herself staring at a silver star-shaped scar, a twisted knot of marred flesh the size of a plum carved into his cheekbone. He had a mess of blond hair that he wore pulled back and dark eyes that he scanned the bar with. His frame was large but he held one shoulder slightly higher—due to recent injury, she imagined. As one of his large hands curled around a drink, the other rested comfortably against the hilt of his blade. His eyes trailed over the room and for a moment she wondered if he sensed her presence too. His gaze returned to his drink, and he smiled with half his mouth, allowing the star-shaped scar to pull and glisten. He was beautifully flawed.

Her gaze fell to the man beside the young Hunter—an older man, another Hunter. The men dressed as she had expected. Their uniform consisted of black breeches and tunic, over which they wore a waist-length black leather vest, bound shut with the belt that carried their blade. The vest had their sigil imprinted over the heart. She watched as the older of the two pulled a stool out from the bar, slowly sitting as his well-trained eyes searched the corners of the establishment with practiced ease. His braid of silver hair rested down his back and as a rare flickering of light caught his face she saw his skin was mapped with the deep lines of worn scars. She had let her gaze hold him for less than a minute when she felt the whirring energy of his keen mind.

His age made him more attuned to the presence of those like him. He turned in his seat, searching the room—he could *sense* her. But Jessop didn't worry—he wouldn't be looking for *her*; he would be searching for a man. Just to be sure, though, she forced her thoughts down, quieting her mind and turning her gaze away.

She concentrated on her hand, on drumming her fingers on the table before her. She could feel her blood coursing, warm and rapid, through her veins, and her heart quickening, all for feeling the presence of those so like her so near. Her foot bounced against the floor, pumping adrenaline through her long legs. The silent room seemed to be getting louder and louder, she could hear her beating heart, swelling under her breast, her green eyes straining to stay down as anticipation welled inside her...

Through her periphery she could make out the lone Aren, moving swiftly towards the Hunters. He held a blade. He needed to be quick. Her beating heart was pulsing rhythmically, deafening her thoughts. Someone—a girl—seeing the knife, screamed, a shriek that set the room into motion. Jessop finally let herself look up. The Hunters moved quickly in the shadows, swift to unsheathe their weapons. The Aren formed their pack quickly; there were thirteen, not twelve. For a brief moment, she was surprised at how one could have passed under her sight. She threw her hood back, finally able to watch the scene unfold. As the zealots formed a semi-circle around the Hunters, backing them up against the bar, the tavern crumbled into pandemonium.

The young girls cried with an adolescent fear that nearly overwhelmed Jessop. But she had learnt long ago how to ignore pain—hers and theirs. Her eyes stayed set on the Hunters as the travelers and girls and workers all fought for the exits. The dark space that had offered them such safety from prying eyes minutes before now offered them danger and isolation from help. Quick to come for pleasure and quick to escape pain—Jessop had many criticisms for those who came to be in this part of Azgul.

The sound of a man dying refocused her attention. An Aren fell to the ground before the Hunters. Jessop watched the young fair one, his strong arm wielding his blade about him like an extension of himself. Something about his flesh appeared silvery to her, somehow reflective. She couldn't quite make it out. He spun low and struck with ease. He *was* good. Despite his well-rehearsed steps, he was still exciting to watch. The older Hunter had his fight memorized, a veteran warrior with a trusted blade, faster than one would have prepared for—*he* was exactly as Jessop had expected.

They were good—better than most she had ever seen. But there were simply too many Aren and she was uncertain what odds the Hunters, especially the young one, had fought against before. With every deflection and assault a new attack came down upon them. It seemed two against thirteen was an impossible fight for them to win without suffering serious harm.

The young Hunter was flung back against the bar as two Aren wrestled his strong arms back, a third moving towards him with a blade. Jessop knew she had little time to make her move.

She leaped from her seat, charging swiftly toward the Aren set on impaling the young Hunter. To the cloaked disciple's shock, she hooked her arm under his neck and kicked his feet out from underneath him. As he stumbled, she wrenched the blade from his grip. With a heavy throw, she lodged the small weapon expertly into the chest of one of the assailants holding the young Hunter's arm back.

The Hunter tore his surprised gaze from her to the dying Aren clinging to him, gargling blood. He shoved his attacker to the ground before gruffly elbowing the other man holding him, bloodying the Aren's nose before striking him in the chest. The Aren fell forward as the Hunter grabbed a bottle from the bar and beat it over the man's head. As glass shattered and liquor spurted across the bloodied floor, Jessop couldn't help but think him resourceful.

He shot Jessop a grateful, if not confused, glance, before grabbing his blade from the ground and continuing his fight. She watched him as he clashed with the fanatics—he moved with skill and grace, his star glass blade travelling silently through the air. The Hunters' blades were forged with the pressurized sediment left over from star formations. The blades appeared as glass, each slightly different in color, but were harder than any material found in Daharia. The young Hunter's sword was entirely transparent, crystal clear from base to deadly tip. It was beautiful.

She kept her eyes on him, while still easily deflecting any attack against her. Thirteen Aren against two Hunters was too many, thirteen against two Hunters and *her,* was just fine. She grabbed the shoulder of one Aren and quickly spun him around. He stared at her with shock.

"*What* are you doing?"

She didn't answer him. To see a woman intervene in an Azgul fight would be a surprise to any. She grabbed his wrist and disarmed him with a forceful twist of his hand. He lashed out with anger, hurling his spare fist towards her small face. She ducked and caught his arm with both hands, twisted at the hip, and kicked him viciously in the abdomen. He fell from her, winded. She knelt beside him and offered a vicious strike to his temple, leaving him unconscious.

She was on her feet instantly, turning just in time to grab the neck of the next Aren. She grabbed his wrist, holding his hand back, and then, quickly, released her hold on his neck, recoiled her hand, twisted her fingers into a fist, and struck back at the exposed flesh forcefully, punching him in the throat. The Aren coughed for air, grabbing at his windpipe. She took a step towards him, darted her arm past his face, and jerked it back, hitting him with her elbow. He fell to the ground.

She stepped over his writhing body and caught the eye of the young Hunter. He too had been watching her. A look of distinct admiration was in his eyes, despite being embroiled in his own fight; it was clear she had impressed him. She turned from him and found the hands of an Aren grabbing at her, coiling tightly around her neck. He lifted her off the ground and slammed her back against the bar. She could hear glasses shattering behind her, stools knocking against her legs and falling to the side.

She brought her arm up and over his hands, jerking downward until she leveraged his grip off of her. She kneed him in the abdomen, and as he buckled forward, she kneed him again, breaking his nose. He stumbled back and she crouched to the ground, spiraling with one leg extended and kicking his legs out from underneath him. She was standing, already in mid-motion for her next assault before he hit the ground. She kicked him swiftly and leapt over his body, her hands landing on the shoulders of one of the three Aren surrounding the older Hunter.

She spun him around and struck. She got his throat and elbowed his cheekbone. Holding his collar as she struck at him again, she looked to the old Hunter. "Get out of here—I've got this!" she yelled to him.

His aged cobalt eyes widened with suspicion. "Who are *you*?" He kicked one of the Aren back, seeming more concerned about Jessop than he was about his attacker.

The guttural cry of the young Hunter drew their attention—the young man was wounded. An Aren fell fatally from the Hunter's sword, but he had left a dagger stuck in the fair Hunter's side. The fight had gone on long enough. As the older Hunter ran past her to his wounded comrade, Jessop took a deep breath and closed her eyes; she concentrated on the feeling of electricity running through her, deep within her. The unadulterated power that she had long since learnt how to lose herself in—how to stay safe within the boundaries of.

She slowly exhaled. And with expert skill, she snapped the neck of the Aren before her, opening her eyes as he hit the ground.

She flicked her cloak to the side and found the hilt of her weapon. She drew the blade from its sheath and spun about, skillfully wielding the sword. The lethal piece was beautiful. Made of star glass, it was the only one of its kind—forged to be entirely onyx in color; the blade was black as night. She ducked low and spun on her knee, moving the sword around her in a circle, and came up behind an Aren attacker. She struck him down and stood as he fell from her weapon's lethal edge, slicking the sword with his crimson blood. She bent her knees and quickly jumped atop the bar, dancing over glasses as she made her way towards the Hunters.

She flipped from the edge, curving her blade out as she spun in the air. She landed on one knee, the Hunters safely behind her, the Aren before her. She remained crouched down as she brought her weapon's point up into the diaphragm of the next assailant. He stumbled towards her and she spun on her knee out to the side, liberating her weapon from his dying body as she stood. The two remaining Aren descended upon her swiftly. She twirled, her cloak flying about her as she landed a roundhouse kick against one. He fell to the ground as the other, with surprising might, grabbed her from behind. His strong forearm locked around her neck and pulled her back tightly. Her leather boot slipped in a thick pool of blood and she struggled to regain her footing as the other Aren recovered, steadying himself before her.

She backed into the man holding her and thrust her sword outward, connecting with the second Aren's side just enough to sting. He lunged at her, snarling wildly. She leaned back into her captor and kicked at the wounded man. She got his chin and forcefully sent him flying onto his back.

The silvery glint of the dagger caught her eye just in time.

The Aren holding her held his weapon high above her; ready to bring it down on her chest. She closed her eyes, concentrating on the energy between them—on her *power*—and, just as she had anticipated, the Aren shrieked in agony, dropping his blade to the ground, loosening his hold on her neck. Jessop snaked her sword about in her expert fingers, curved her body to the side, and thrust her sword inward, past her hip, into his abdomen.

She spun out of his grip, pulling her blade loose. He coughed, blood dripping from his lip, pooling in his gut. She remained in position with her sword extended out, perfectly parallel to the ground, her feet steadying themselves in the still-warm blood of her slain victims. She stood at the ready in a circle of the dead or dying. None of the attackers moved and she took a cautious breath, mentally assessing her body for injuries—she was mostly unharmed and the battle was over.

She cleaned her blade swiftly on her cloak and sheathed it before turning to the Hunters. The older was supporting the younger, applying pressure to his wound and they both stared at her with wild-eyed confusion, though the young one looked on through fluttering eyelashes.

The blue eyes of the old Hunter narrowed on her. "Tell me who you are," he ordered.

She looked away from him to his wounded companion. She could see the blood shining over his leather. His paling face and slowing breaths were poor signs. "Your friend needs treatment," she advised.

The silver-haired Hunter nodded, more concerned with his young friend than her identity. "Then help me get him some, girl."

Jessop flinched at the word, but nodded. She took a step towards the Hunters, and eased the young one's arm over her shoulder, slowly pulling him away from the bar. It was only once she was close enough to support his weight did she understand why his skin seemed to shimmer like silver to her—he was covered in hundreds of scars.

"You saved us," he whispered, his hazel eyes studying her. She smiled tightly at him, uncertain of how to respond, and then watched as he lost consciousness; his heart slowing caused her own to speed up.

* * * *

"This one," the old Hunter barked, practically dragging them towards what Jessop believed could quite possibly have been the oldest Soar-Craft she had ever seen. She had no time to question the safety of the ship, as the silver-haired Hunter had already begun to push his wounded comrade into the vehicle.

She crawled over the door and into the back, trying to avoid the precarious metal prongs poking through the old vinyl seat cover as she awkwardly continued to help support the weight of the Hunter. The older man pushed his unconscious body at her gruffly, and she coughed as his young heavy frame collapsed against her, pinning her down. She freed her arms from underneath him, readjusting her sheath before fixing his head against her shoulder and pressing one hand against his wound. His hair had fallen loose from its knot and covered his face like a veil of gold. Without thinking, she stroked it back, smoothing it away from his soft skin. And then quickly retracted her hand.

She forced her attention onto the older Hunter as he leapt into the control seat. He fiddled with a compartment door and when it wouldn't give under his rough grab, he let his hand hover slightly above it, and then—like *magic*—it popped open.

Jessop took a deep, controlled breath; this was her cue to confirm her beliefs about the Hunters. "You're one of *them*?"

"Yes, I'm one of the Hunters of Infinity, girl. Can't you see our sigil? Now here, take these," he barked, tossing a pair of worn out leather goggles at her. She pulled the goggles over the young Hunter's head, securing them over his closed eyes. The older man handed her a second set, and despite their frayed leather and browned screens, she pulled them on. She studied the sigil on the leather vest of the unconscious Hunter—she had seen the mark, she knew it well.

The older Hunter hit a button on the dash several times before another compartment opened up and a yoke ascended from it. As he grabbed hold of the yoke, a blue light emitted, scanning his hands.

"Welcome back, Hanson Knell," the automated Soar-Craft voice crackled.

Jessop had heard the name many times before and she was actually somewhat shocked that of all the Hunters for her to have found, it was Hanson Knell. And if *he* was Hanson Knell, she could be certain that the fair, scarred young man lying unconscious in her lap was his mentee Kohl O'Hanlon. She could have mused over the knowledge further, but now was not the time—she was a nervous flyer in the safest of ships. She anxiously looked the vehicle over, and squeezed against Kohl O'Hanlon a bit tighter under the sputtering of revving engines.

"Is this thing sky-worthy?" she yelled up to Hanson Knell.

"It's been safely navigating the Daharian skies since before you were born," the old Hunter called back. He pulled on the yoke and the Soar-Craft began to shakily hover off the ground.

"That's what I'm worried about," she grumbled, closing her eyes as they took off at a surprisingly quick speed for the old machine.

Hanson Knell navigated the Soar-Craft through the underground maze, where those who wished to go to such a bar had to park their ships. It didn't take long for the old machine to gain a terrifying break-neck speed and soon they were whirring through the dark space, taking sharp corners and diving down steep descents. Jessop held the young Hunter tightly, pushing her cloak against his wound.

As they finally emerged from the labyrinth, the unmistakably red sky, where hundreds of other Soar-Craft zipped around them, blinded Jessop. It took a minute for her eyes to adjust to the unfamiliar crimson atmosphere of Azgul.

She wasn't from Azgul, though she had been there for several days, preparing for *this* moment, where she would find the ones like her. She couldn't help but think, as she looked down at the young Hunter's blood, staining rivers into the lines of skin on her hand, that with all the violence that had already ensued, she was exactly where she was supposed to be.

As quickly as the sense of certainty materialized it had disappeared, wrenching from her gut as the Soar-Craft dropped some sixty-feet in the sky to undertake a row of oncoming ships. Hanson Knell was either a brilliant or superbly dangerous pilot. He tore the old machine through the skies, weaving through organized lines of Soar-Craft, cutting off other pilots, making unsanctioned cuts and dives around Levi-Hubs, where other pilots, busy recharging their ships, yelled and cursed at them. Jessop didn't care about the dangerous flying, the precarious Soar-Craft or the angry slurs of other pilots—all she cared about was the direction they were travelling in. She had confirmed who they were and she knew they were going to a place she had envisioned entering for many years.

Jessop could see it nearing in the red horizon, the building that mirrored the crimson light of the city, refracting red rays in every direction. The building that appeared like a needle in the skyline; slender, tall and reflective. The Glass Blade was the training center and home to all the Hunters of Infinity there had ever been, and all the Hunters of Infinity there ever would be. She narrowed her eyes at the architectural spectacle that she had only ever known through the thoughts of others and she wished she could remove her stained goggles to get a clearer look. The sickly sensation of fluid slicing her fingers drew her attention away from the nearing Glass Blade and back to the wounded Hunter.

She cautiously drew her cloak back and pulled at his leather vest. His tunic was saturated with dark blood. She pulled the hem up, narrowing her eyes on the injury as the wind whipped around his garments. The sheer amount of blood made it difficult to assess the actual injury, but with focus, she could see the small pocket of a wound, tucked in between the mounds of his red-stained muscular ridges. It amazed her how humans, Hunters or otherwise, were kept safe by the integrity of this fine skin, and one small slice was all it took…

The wound was bad, the blood loss potentially fatal. She covered the injury back up, pushing a handful of material hard against it. The abilities of the medical team at the Glass Blade were renowned, known of even where she came from. If anyone could save the young Hunter, it was the team residing within his own home. As if on cue, the gleaming reflection of the red sky against the glass-paneled building nearly blinded her and she looked down to the pale face of the Hunter, silently willing him to hold on just a little bit longer.

She looked ahead as they sped towards the glass, with no signs of slowing down, and no visible entrance. She knew the Hunter trick, but she could not pretend she was not put somewhat on edge by the nearing building. As her heart sped up, the old Hunter threw his hand, fingers extended and palm out, in front of him, making the mystical mark in his palm visible to the glass walls. And just like that, the glass seemed to melt, rippling as though burning, and a black hole, barely large enough for the Soar-Craft to fit through, opened up to them.

With a sudden sickening drop, the Soar-Craft ducked into the mystical entrance, enveloping them in darkness. The preternatural mark, burnt into the hand of the Infinity Hunters, was the only way to gain entrance into the Glass Blade. A building that housed the protectors of Daharia, and the Blade of Prince Daharian, or the Blade of Light, as they called it, needed such security measures. Although, Jessop knew, such measures had only been put in place after what had happened with Falco Bane all those years ago.

They soared down a pitch-black tunnel and it was clear that Hanson navigated the ship through such darkness by memory alone. Jessop, on the other hand, pulled her goggles off, able to see in the darkness just fine. She had been raised in darkness. It was more soothing to her than any source of light could ever be. Just as she thought it though, a light did appear. A white glow in the distance illuminated a docking bay. Hanson zipped the Soar-Craft forward, bringing them in for an abrupt landing on the parking zone. Almost immediately, a team of white uniformed techs and engineers began yelling, angry, as they circled the ship.

"Knell, if we've told you once we've—" one began, but froze, his voice caught in his throat, as he saw Jessop and the fallen Hunter.

Hanson leaped from the craft, wrenching open a side door so that Jessop nearly fell out onto the hard floor. "Help me get him inside!"

Hanson and a group of the white uniformed men lifted the young Hunter from Jessop and quickly began to haul his unconscious body down the bay, leaving her, bloodstained, in the back seat. She quickly leapt out of the ship and ran after them, barely getting through the sliding automatic glass doors in time. She stared as Hanson Knell watched over his young mentee with fear, applying pressure to his wound and whispering under his breath to him. She could feel the combined concern of all of them, who clearly knew the wounded man and feared for his life. The second thing for her to learn about the young Hunter was that he was clearly beloved. The first had been that he was a half-decent fighter.

But her attention was torn as she lurched forward, unsteady on her feet as the floor beneath her began to rise. The steel metal platform on which they stood flew up a transparent chute, travelling through the Glass Blade, like a bead in a crystal clear tube. While she dug her heels in, the surrounding men seemed quite accustomed to the force.

They passed floor after floor of training rooms, engineer docks, labs, and workplaces, each one containing groups of men, all in the same uniform— black if they were a Hunter, white if they were not—all conducting different business. After several more levels were passed in which Jessop had seen a handful of young boys, some barely old enough to talk, undergoing martial training, the glass bullet came to a sudden halt, opening its doors to a medical floor.

Jessop nearly fell out, stumbling to the side as the white uniformed men and Hanson Knell carried the young Hunter out. "Let's get some help over here!" Hanson yelled, and immediately, under his vicious growl, a flock of medics and nurses swarmed them. Jessop stepped back and watched the team as they moved like an efficient flight of birds, swooping in, opening the young Hunter's vest, removing his blade, and carrying him away, disappearing down the corridor without any hesitation or questions.

The room fell quiet as all of them stared at the slow swinging doors the medics had taken Kohl O'Hanlon through. Jessop took a deep breath, looking around slowly, amazed by the building she found herself in.

One of the men from the docking bay turned to Hanson Knell. "Do you want us to wait with you, Sir?"

Hanson shook his head, staring down at the young Hunter's sword in his hands. "No, go on."

The man nodded, slowly clapping Hanson Knell on the shoulder as he walked past, leading his group of techs back into the glass chute. Jessop studied the old Hunter's face, the smattering of blood flecked across his cheek, the way his cool eyes fixated on the blade in his hand. He was old and he was weary, and likely in need of a medical inspection. She knew better than to suggest it though. Instead, she let her gaze fall from him, slowly taking in the brilliant opal lights that surrounded her, the pristine ivory floors and glass furniture. It was the brightest and cleanest room she had ever been in.

Suddenly, Jessop was choking. Without warning, a terrifying grip had locked around her small throat, closing around her jugular and flinging her body against the glass doors. Hanson Knell's grizzled fingers tightened around her windpipe and in his spare hand was the blade of his comrade, pointed directly at her face. She was pinned between the blade and the door behind her, his rough fingers grinding at her neck.

She didn't stir, her startled heart slowing as she studied the hardened eyes of Hanson Knell. Being startled was not the same as being afraid— true fear was something that had long since been beaten out of her. She took shallow breaths between his vice grip. "*What?*"

"Who are you, girl?" he growled.

She slowly raised her hand to his and pulled gently at his wrist, willing him to release her throat, but he resisted, inching the blade closer to her eye.

"I don't know what answer you want," she spoke hoarsely, her voice straining against his hold.

"Don't toy with me, *girl*," he barked, jerking her by her throat and slamming her body hard against the glass door again.

"Do not call me girl, *old man*," she growled back, narrowing her eyes on him.

He brought his angry face closer to her. "I want a name, *girl*. And once we have that, then perhaps you'll tell me why you fight with Falco Bane's sword?"

She slapped at his hand, urging him to loosen his grip on her throat... before she forced it loose. Slowly, he acquiesced.

She coughed, swallowing hard against her bruised windpipe. She held his gaze as she ran her fingers slowly up and down her neck. "Because I took it from him when I escaped Aranthol."

CHAPTER 2

"You're lying," he snarled, once again grabbing her throat.

Jessop had had enough. She grabbed his hand, twisted it outward, and before he could stop her, she had pulled the young Hunter's blade from him. But Hanson Knell wasn't some half-trained Aren; he was a well-seasoned Hunter. In an instant he had removed his own weapon and directed it at her, prepared for a fight. She stepped to the side and slowly lowered the sword, showing she meant no harm. She had not come so far to fight Hanson Knell.

"Bane trained you," Hanson hissed with disgust, following her slow steps with his sword. "I knew Falco Bane, I helped train *him*, I would know his style anywhere, and I saw it in the tavern as clearly as I see it now."

She continued to make slow steps to the side, keeping the old Hunter moving. "There is nothing you have seen that I could not explain." She watched him study her, looking over her face with a keen eye, as if he were searching for signs of Falco.

He shook his head at her slowly. "Earlier, in the bar, *you* used Sentio. But no woman has ever been taught the ways."

She thought back to the bar, when one of the Aren had her by the neck and was ready to kill her. She had pained him to free herself from his grasp. *Sentio*, the ancient training of the Infinity Hunters that combined telepathy and telekinesis, was, like the role itself, reserved only for men. It had been decided long ago by the Hunters' Assembly Council that females did not possess the necessary strength to wield Sentio to any great extreme.

She shook her head at him. "I can communicate the odd thought, push if I need to—if my life depended on it, like today—but no, I cannot wield Sentio."

The old Hunter shook his head. "He taught *you*—a woman—our greatest gift."

"No—after thirteen years of having him rifle around my mind and watching him move objects as though they were connected to strings on his hands, I finally learnt just enough to say 'stop' or force a door closed when he came after me," she explained, her voice low and serious.

He continued to shake his head, his blade still at the ready. "A woman who fights as well as you has had formal training."

"A woman who fights as well as me has been forced to learn. Falco Bane taught me—he taught me by savaging my body for half my life," she hissed at the old man. The words felt like oil in her mouth, disgusting and dark.

Finally, he lowered his blade. She could see his imagination working; she watched him envision the life of horrors she must have suffered. While he maintained his dispassionate glower, she knew she had subdued him with her words.

"I need to take you to the Assembly Council."

She stepped away from him. Although Jessop had anticipated being taken to the Council, she knew it best to show fear at his words. It had been soon after she had first realized that she no longer felt true fear that she had learnt it was best to let others think she still did. "And what will they do with me?"

"Ask you as many questions as I have... more."

She nodded slowly, unsurprised by his vague answer. "You should see something then, before the rest of them do. So you can know I'm not trying to keep secrets."

Jessop knew that the more she volunteered, the less they would forcefully take from her.

Hanson nodded, waiting. She reached to her throat and gingerly undid her cloak, lowering it as she slowly turned her back to him. Jessop pulled her dark braid over her shoulder and revealed the nape of her neck to the Hunter—revealed her burn to him. She could feel his eyes boring into her, staring at the image of the intricate sword centered in a perfect circle, burnt into her flesh many years ago. It had been done with the smallest of wires, slowly and repeatedly, until the scar accurately depicted a beautiful encircled blade.

It had been hell.

The old Hunter cleared his throat before speaking. "Bane did this?"

Jessop nodded, slowly readjusting her cloak back into place. She turned around to face him. He was touching the back of his neck, as though checking that his own burn was still fixed in place.

"Did he tell you why? Why would he burn you with our mark—with the Hunter's sigil?" As he spoke, he lowered his hand from his neck to his chest, where the identical sigil was engraved into his leather.

She could see the disgust in his eyes. He stared at her as though she had permanently captured a part of his identity and he couldn't figure out how to take it back. "Of course he told me why."

He waited on her answer, his silver brow furrowed.

She shrugged, as though the answer were obvious. "He told me it was *his* mark."

* * * *

The Glass Blade appeared to be made of almost entirely diaphanous materials, translucent chutes and glass floors and walls, with clear tubes connecting rooms; see-through bullets that zipped upward and downward through transparent shafts that weaved through crystal glass walls and floors. Every few paces a refracted ray of red light struck across the floor, but for the most part, the building seemed near impenetrable to the outside elements. Jessop thought of Aranthol—the Shadow City where she had come from—and all of its blackened corners and darkened halls. It was a place where secrets hid well. Yet, something about the intentional transparency of the Azguli fortress where the Hunters lived made Jessop think that it was perhaps even a better hiding place for secrets to dwell.

Jessop followed Hanson Knell through a glass corridor, looking underfoot into labs and offices and training centers. She saw men writing scripts and forging weapons, young boys fighting with staffs, and even a room where a group bowed down in prayer towards a glass mantle holding an effigy of a Hunter's sword, their sigil proudly displayed on a banner behind it. The Glass Blade was more than Jessop had ever imagined it to be. It was a city within a city.

She had asked Hanson Knell if she could wait to see the young Hunter recover before being taken to the Assembly Council, but the old Hunter had refused. He had reminded her in no uncertain terms that her presence was entirely unwelcome. The Glass Blade was a sanctuary for Hunters—and Hunters were male.

"You have a light step." His voice startled her. He hadn't said a word to her since leaving the medical floor.

"As do you," she said. Jessop had spent more than half her life with Falco Bane, and she was finally in the Glass Blade with the renowned Hunter, Hanson Knell, who dragged her to *the* Assembly Council... the

Council that would undoubtedly want to know every small detail about Falco. She didn't have time for chitchat with the old Hunter—she needed to concentrate on what was to come.

"Bane taught you that quietness?"

Jessop stopped walking at his question, only a few feet away from the room she was certain the Council resided in. The old Hunter came to a stop and turned to her.

She eyed him up slowly. "Survival taught me that skill—and a great deal more. I saved *your* life today, Hunter, because of such skills." She kept her voice low, her green eyes locked on to him.

"Well, they are skills you need to explain knowing. They are not meant—" he began, flustered.

Jessop shook her head, interrupting him. "If you want to hear stories about how I came to be the way I am, it's not going to happen. I will walk out of here right now and I'm fairly certain you know I'm capable of it."

He narrowed his gaze, but remained silent.

"But, if you want to hear about Falco Bane and Aranthol, if you want to possibly learn something that could help your hunt, then stop wasting time demanding answers I won't give and lead me to your Council."

His blue eyes held her stare with contempt. "There are no questions that will go unanswered if asked by the Council—your truth will be forced from you and it will not be pleasant."

Jessop slowly shrugged her shoulders. "There are no horrors your Council could present me with that I haven't survived before."

"If you're thinking you can resist—don't. No matter the suffering you've undergone I would advise compliance," he spoke. His tone had changed from threatening to worrisome, as though he truly didn't want to see anyone endure the Council's methods.

"Ensure your Council asks the *right* line of questioning and you will find me to be most compliant."

He nodded at her slowly and took a deep breath before speaking. "I don't know if you were just lucky today or if you're one of the best damn fighters I have ever seen. Maybe it's both. I don't know you, I don't trust you and I am too old to pretend I like you being in my home. But I know enough about the scum we hunt to know what they do to women like you—so I'm going to offer this just once."

The old Hunter lowered his voice, leaning close to Jessop. "Because you risked your life for ours you can leave Falco Bane's blade with me and leave this place, I'll explain away your disappearance, and you can start your life over elsewhere. But if you stay… well, I have only ever seen one person wield *that* blade with such proficiency, he nearly brought ruin to us all… and you're about to meet the man who mentored him. The man who has hunted him for over a decade."

She nodded slowly. "Hydo Jesuin." Everyone who knew anything about the Hunters knew the name of Falco Bane's mentor. She had heard it cursed a thousand times. Hydo Jesuin, in many ways, was the man responsible for so much of what had happened to her.

"*Lord* Jesuin, Leader of the Assembly Council of the Hunters of Infinity, Lord and Protector of the Blade of Light and the Daharian Galaxy," Hanson corrected.

"I don't fear your Lord seeing what my life with Bane has made me. I'm not leaving," she answered firmly.

He shook his head at her, hissing his disappointment. "This may surprise you but I am one of the more pleasant Councilmen. I fear what some of the others will do when they see a woman who has learnt a role no woman is fit for. The Council does *not* train females."

Jessop slowly crossed her arms over her chest. She could see Bane in her mind clearly. "The Council didn't train me."

Hanson shook his head at her. "No, we didn't. You were trained by the only man to ever nearly bring the Council to its knees."

Jessop stared up into his determined eyes. "That's not my fault."

Hanson arched his brow at her, his lips tight around his teeth as he spoke. "No, but it will be your problem."

She glared at him, refusing to voice what she had immediately thought— *no, it won't be.*

"I choose to stay."

Hanson Knell scoffed at her. "I am trying to help you. You're an idiot— and I will not be indebted to an idiot."

"And I won't be intimidated by a fool," she hissed back.

"What do you want, girl? The Glass Blade does not house women; this is a sanctuary for a brotherhood of men."

"The Glass Blade is the one place I am safe from those who would seek to drag me back to Aranthol," she answered.

"You seem capable of protecting yourself."

"I need to be here. Only Infinity Hunters can gain access to the Blade. I am safest here. And you will need me."

"There is not a woman alive who is needed by the Hunters of Infinity."

"Oh, I think not long ago in a local tavern two such Hunters might have felt greatly in need of me," Jessop snapped at the old Hunter.

"Under your wounded eyes I can see your true self. Perhaps from too many years with *him* and too many years in the Shadow City, there is a darkness in you, girl," Hanson Knell growled down at her, his hot breath sticking against her pale cheek as one of his strong hands wrapped tightly around her arm.

Jessop slowly inclined her head, so that her own words barely needed to travel before falling over his ears, as she slowly, forcefully, pulled his hand off of her. "Indeed there is. And don't you ever forget it."

* * * *

The room was entirely dark barring a single sphere of white light, emitting from a glass circle in the floor. Heavy curtains were drawn across all of the walls, though Jessop suspected she wasn't supposed to be able to see that they were just curtains. In the blackness the glass circle in the floor cast a globe of light shooting upwards, forming a matching circle on the high ceiling. Jessop understood the purpose of the room. It was designed so that the one could be seen by the many, without ever seeing the many in return. A room shrouded in darkness with one fixed light, so that she felt isolated, vulnerable, and exposed, so that she fixated on who sat in the darkness as they sifted through her mind. She had known the purpose of the room as soon as Hanson had disappeared into the shadows. He seemed pleased to be leaving her in the dark, hoping she would feel alone. But Jessop knew that they were not alone.

Hidden in the shadows were the members of the Assembly Council. She glanced around the dark space, forcing herself to conceal a smile. She knew that until she stepped into the white beam of light, they could not see her. But she, unbeknownst to any of the Councilmen, could see them perfectly well. She was of the Shadows—this tactical room had no effect on one who saw better in darkness than any nocturnal beast could.

She could see them all, cloaked, sitting at a silver panel desk, staring at her with tense apprehension. They did not reveal much, restricting their movement and using Sentio instead of spoken words. She knew better than to attempt to pick up on any of their communications—she didn't know the full extent of their abilities and she did not wish to start this meeting by alerting them to her own ability to pry.

She took a reluctant step forward, her boot illuminating, and her shadow disappearing into darkness. It took a minute for her eyes to adjust under the ray of light. The Councilmen did not know she could see and hear them, or that she could *sense* them entirely—they were not prepared for one of the Shadow City. Jessop found it odd that their room was designed to interrogate an Azguli—whom the Hunters rarely hunted—and not for an Arantholi, whom they *always* hunted.

She pushed the thought away, knowing their unpreparedness worked in her favor today. The most famous of Hunters sat on the Assembly Council, led by none other than Hydo Jesuin. *Hydo.* She had to fight to keep her gaze off of him, to keep her heart steady. The mere thought of his name filled her with too many memories. She could still close her eyes and hear Falco cursing his former mentor. But Jessop couldn't be thinking of Falco Bane, not with the Assembly Council looking her over for signs of him.

Finally, a voice filled the room. "Hunter Knell tells us you fought to save his and his mentee's lives in an encounter with Aren insurgents. That you bear *our* mark and that you wield our one true enemy's sword and fighting style—or, as it were, *my* fighting style."

Jessop looked around the dark space, intentionally allowing her gaze to trail despite being able to follow the voice to its source easily—Hydo. She didn't need him to know she could see him perfectly through the darkness. "These things are true."

"Why?"

She glanced to the floor, forcing her stare away from the Council Lord. "Why what?"

"Why did you help them?" His voice was tight and pressing. The perfect voice for quick and grueling interrogations.

"They were under attack," she began, but she had barely finished answering before being pressed with another question.

"How did you help them?"

Jessop glanced over the Council, knowing that averting her gaze too much would be just as telling as if she watched them intently. "With my blade."

"You're mocking me," he scoffed.

She glanced about the room. "Is that a question?"

The Hunter Lord carried on, ignoring the digression. "Tell me, do you fight with Falco Bane's blade?"

Jessop flicked her cloak back to reveal the blade's hilt. They could see her, from their position of power, where they sat shrouded in darkness, so certain that whoever stood before them couldn't see them too. But she *could* see them. She could see them staring at the blade on her hip, with complete astonishment. They pushed their thoughts amongst one another, whispered bewilderments and questions, all of them wielding Sentio, certain she could never follow the telepathy of men.

And then Hanson told them.

"Fellow Hunters, I believe I witnessed the woman use Sentio this morning, mind your thoughts," he warned.

The room went silent.

Jessop readjusted her cloak tightly around herself. She waited until Hydo Jesuin's voice once again filled the darkness. "Is this true?"

"As I already told Hunter Knell—many years with Falco Bane taught me how to understand the smallest aspects of Sentio, I could close a door, hear a trace thought—but *no*, I cannot do what any one of you could do," she repeated her explanation.

"You understand we can—and we will—verify these claims, girl? We can enter your mind and check the stories you tell," Hydo Jesuin threatened.

Jessop forced her gaze downward to stop herself from staring him in the eye.

"Of course I understand." Jessop couldn't help but wonder if the Council had even been listening—of course she would understand having her mind brutally ransacked. Falco had spent years pushing through her thoughts, bringing forth recollections, disappearing certain memories, and speaking to her without ever making a sound.

"And, apparently you wear *our* sigil—who is your true kind?" Hydo Jesuin carried on, his voice travelling around her. Jessop understood his tactic, he overwhelmed his subject with the darkness, the quick voice, the never ending line of questions that he asked so swiftly—certain he would be able to catch someone out in a lie. Every living being in Daharia received a mark of their heritage on their ten and third birthdays—except for Jessop. She had lived many years with no such brand.

"Bane gave me the mark—he said it was his brand and I was…" she struggled over the words that she had practiced, knowing one day she would need to say them.

She took a deep breath, staring at her leather boots in the white light. She crossed her arms defensively over her chest.

"He said the brand was his and that I too, was his." She took a slow breath before continuing. "I knew his Hunter past, as everyone knows, and that the Glass Blade had become impenetrable to anyone except an Infinity Hunter after what happened with Falco Bane, so I knew if there was one place I would be safe from him, it would be here." She pictured the mystical mark on Hanson Knell's hand, the mark that acted like a key to the Glass Blade; the mark that Falco did not have for it had been made to keep him out of the Hunters' fortress.

She felt the lone tear travel over her cheek.

"How old were you when he took you, girl?" The soft voice was that of another Hunter, neither Hydo nor Hanson. Jessop kept her gaze down to avoid finding the man's face in the shadows.

"Twelve," she whispered, wiping the tear away. She could hear the man breathe disgust.

"While what she has endured is most regretful, there simply is no place in the Glass Blade for a woman," another Councilman began, but another quickly interrupted him.

"We cannot release her into Azgul, Hanson has told us how dangerous she is."

"Hunters, *please.*" The voice, which silenced them all, belonged to Hydo Jesuin. "She is an ally to us here."

The room remained silent, waiting for him to explain. Jessop held her breath, as anxious as the Councilmen.

"Girl, you understand that we do not train women to be Hunters, and yet, here you are, already trained, according to Hunter Knell, and while we have no tolerance for this, we might have *use* for it. We have hunted Falco Bane for over a decade. After his dissent, we made the Glass Blade an impenetrable fortress, but Falco followed suit, didn't he? He forged the Shadow City, and through rare and dark magics, he made it as impenetrable as our Blade. So, girl, if you wish to stay here, under our protection, then you must agree to help us. Help us find entrance into Aranthol," he offered.

Jessop suppressed a smile. "Of course."

"Don't sound so eager—we will need to verify your story, and you will need to be here for some time, to have your loyalties confirmed, before any venture back to Aranthol occurs. Your pains did not end, unfortunately, when you escaped the Shadow City," he cautioned.

"I can handle it," she insisted.

"Expect the worst, girl, and know not everyone has survived," he warned.

She glanced up through the darkness, "I've already faced your worst," she reminded them, resting her hand on her hilt and turning the sheathed blade in the light, "And I took *this* from him."

* * * *

The enormous mirrored room offered never-ending repetitions of Jessop's reflection. She could see her own appearance, and that of the Councilmen's, reflected all around, dozens of the moving black uniformed figures angled down the long room until they obscured into darkness. She moved and fifty reflections of the same movement occurred. It pained her eyes greatly, so she focused instead on the vat of shining crystal fluid before her. The focal point of the nauseating mirrored room was a single drop-in pool. A rectangle, barely longer than her own height, half that in width, carved into the glass floor, with the Hunter's sigil etched into the ground beneath. Were one walking without paying much regard, they could fall straight off the edge of the floor and into the crystalline liquid.

"You will need to change and step into the pool, girl," Hydo ordered. Jessop eyed the glass tub before her, confused by its liquid contents. At first look, it appeared as water, but upon closer inspection she found it to be thicker and containing small shining specks of... glass? The sludgy matter was so reflective she could see, once again, her own face staring back at her.

She held in her hand the white linen robe one of the Councilmen had handed her upon entering the room. She ran the thin material between her fingers and took a deep breath. She may have not known what substance the pool was filled with, but she understood the purpose of it. Once she was within the liquid, the Council members would all be able to simultaneously use their Sentio to explore the depths of her mind, searching as a unit; the fluid would bind their powers together and lead to a more efficient search. Were they to all rifle through her mind as individuals it would take days, and were they to try to do it at the same time without syncing their abilities through the liquid, one of them could push at a memory whilst the other pulled and they could refract her mind. They could accidentally kill her, or drive her insane. And having seen someone with a mind corrupted by Sentio, she would have preferred death.

Jessop knew it would hurt. She knew it would take all the power she had to control the pain, to control her mind, to hold on while they twisted and racked and sifted through her. She was not afraid of what they would find, for she had everything in order, and she was not afraid of the pain. She was only concerned because she did not know the extent of her own resistance—how long she could suffer without fighting back.

Jessop knew what she wore in the vat of crystalline fluids did not matter—stripping was simply another tactic formulated by Hydo to break his subjects. She rolled her shoulders, loosening up the tension she felt building between her thick muscles, and then she undid her cloak. It fell to the floor and billowed about her boots, which she stepped out of. She would never let them think she cared. She had learnt that no matter who saw or maimed her form, her body would always be *hers*.

She hooked her fingers around her tunic and pulled it up over her head. She ignored their shadowy forms and uncomfortable gazes, knowing they stared at the intricate scar between her breasts, if not just at her breasts. For a second, she thought she caught a pair of glowing eyes watching her—but she couldn't bring herself to look back through the group. She released her belt and slowly lowered her blade to the floor, keeping it near the pool edge. Finally, she hooked her thumbs into the waistband of her breeches and shimmied out of them. She stood and with her shoulders back, she took a slow breath. She stared straight ahead as she undid her already loose braid, ignoring the images of her naked body mirroring her around the room. She could hear one of them breathing heavily as her long hair fell loose around her form. And with slow, deliberate movements, she pulled the thin linen robe on.

She exhaled silently and crouched down to the floor, sitting as she twisted, and lowered her feet into the pool. The liquid was freezing, its icy embrace sending shivers through her body. It was gelatinous; the shimmering specks were suspended in the congealed translucent fluid. She glanced up to the Councilmen as they began to slowly inch closer to the pool's edge in silence. Jessop knew that the cold was intended to shock her system and ultimately weaken her mind—making it harder to conceal thoughts and memories from the Council. Hydo Jesuin really had thought of everything. She put her hands on the glass ledge and slowly lowered herself in, resisting the urge to hiss as the icy slush enveloped her.

The Hunters formed a semi-circle around the pool. She took a deep breath as she moved to the center of the tub. The liquid was hard against her chest and soaked her robe. Her dark hair began to travel slowly about her shoulders in thick black ropes, collecting the crystal flecks.

"Submerge." Hydo's low, tense voice carried around the room.

Jessop took a deep breath, then another, and with her third, she immersed herself. She kept her green eyes open and used her arms to force her body down. As soon as she was fully under, it seemed as though the unknown liquid came to life. With mystical abilities it tore around her, no longer slow and thick. It ripped through her robes and encircled her strong torso. It lapped against her back and attacked her eyes and ears, forcing a white-hot pain through her. The crystal flecks *were* shards of glass, tearing through her robe, ripping the linen and scratching her taut skin. She grabbed at the garment and ran her hands over her body, trying to wipe the specks away, but no matter how hard she fought, they clung to her. She struggled to stay under, to keep her eyes open despite the pain. Through the icy liquid, she saw their hands enter the pool, all of them showing her their palm, and the inverted *F* scar that was carved into each, and then—

Jessop is twelve years old and looking into the gray eyes of a teenage Falco Bane. He examines the charred marks under her eye and across her neck; her frayed hair and marred appearance...

She's fifteen and someone is nursing bleeding wounds on her back. The wounds will scar, she's told. She hisses as the ointment is applied, the cuts are deep—she was lashed hard. She bites her lip and dreams of vengeance. She bites her lip, and she sees the flames.

She's seventeen, and intimately alone with Falco. The long silver scar runs through his brow, over his eyelid, down his strong cheekbone. His hands move over her slowly, trailing across her thigh, gripping her bare hip.

Jessop couldn't breathe. She looked around the pool, her heart racing. The pain was otherworldly and the claustrophobia too much to bear. She felt trapped, as though the possessed liquid was somehow holding her down while her mind was forcibly lit up with a thousand memories, all of them being searched for something unique, something the Councilmen wanted to see. She closed her eyes and saw flashes ripping past her; faces, names, words, screams, and certain memories began to form but rippled into entirely different ones, ending in mismatched recollections.

Her skin sizzles under the hot wires and her neck is on fire. She's eighteen, and her brand is nearly complete. And now she's older—maybe twenty—she is fighting with a man... he attacks her brutally, she doesn't waste time in her defense—she kills him swiftly.

Jessop clapped her hands over her mouth, silencing a scream. The unnatural fluid crept between her slender fingers, clawing through her thick lips and searching through her mouth. It felt as though a thousand knives were carving away the layers of her mind—of her sanity—in search for Falco.

She's twenty-three and Falco is yelling, she's crying. He throws a glass, it shatters against the wall, and with a swipe of his hand, shards are flying through the air.

Twenty-four and a dead woman lies on the floor between her and Falco. They are silent as the blood pools out between them. She watches as his gray eyes fixate on the lifeless corpse.

Jessop cried out and choked on the liquid as it cut her throat and tongue. She grabbed her face to fight the pain. She tried to keep her thoughts organized, reminding herself that she had survived worse. As if on cue, her body began to shake violently. She could feel her nails digging into her cheeks, tearing at her neck, ripping at her robe. She curled deeper down and into herself, tucking her face into her chest. She wished she could drown in this mystical pool, but it was not possible. This was a pool for torture, not death.

Falco is sleeping... she reaches over his broad body, her hand coming around the blade's hilt, she is twenty-five, and finally ready to disappear into the night.

The liquid had filled Jessop's throat, providing the sensation of choking as she swallowed large gulps. She knew she needed to emerge. With a forceful kick, she rose from the liquid, her hair flying back from her face over her back, sending a trail of crystals across the room. How gruesome the sound of her own guttural coughing was, her body fighting to expel the liquid and find oxygen, startled her.

And the Council, hands still in the pool, continued to try to read her.

"Sto—op—Stop!" Jessop coughed. But none of the men retreated.

"I—*arg*—can't—brea—" she choked and still they ignored her. She tried to force herself towards the side of the pool, but her feet slipped on the slick glass. Her muscles ached and tears ran down her cheeks as her throat burnt with each hacking cough.

"WHAT IS THIS?"

The booming voice caused the Council to yield, allowing Jessop the moment she needed to catch her breath. The fluid immediately returned to its thick, gelatinous state and she trudged through it, her legs on fire until she reached the edge. She leant forward, coughing still as she pushed herself onto her toes and flung her weak arms out before her. Her fingers pulled at the glass floor with a squeaky cry, and she forced her diaphragm onto the ledge. As she had hoped, it pushed the liquid up her esophagus, and she threw up a mouthful of the vile fluid. It traveled unnaturally, with life, from the glass floor back towards her, sliding over the ledge and back into the pool.

Jessop ignored the horror and let her face rest on her extended arm. It took her a moment to realize her head was rattling because her entire body was shaking, covered in thousands of miniscule cuts. The remnants of her robe twisted around her. Through the distorted glass she could see her bare body, glistening under the trace remains of the material. She could see the linen was ripped to shreds. Few strips of the fabric clung around her hip and thigh as she shook violently.

The Councilmen moved away from the pool slowly. One came around the pool. "Kohl, how have you been released from the medics so swiftly?"

She recognized the voice immediately. It was Hanson Knell.

Jessop followed him with her eyes as he passed her, slowly trailing her gaze over them from her weakened position. Her head rolled between her tired arms, watching the Councilmen retreat from her as the young Hunter approached.

"*Swiftly*? They treated me with lasers yesterday. It's been an entire night—how long have you had her in there?" he demanded, crossing the room. His hazel eyes fell onto her and he looked at her with such apology.

Jessop clung to the side of the glass ledge. She couldn't believe his words—it had been an entire night? She had stepped into the pool minutes ago—how had night already passed?

"Time does pass differently in this room—you know that, Hunter Kohl. It is easy to lose track of the process." This time it was Hydo Jesuin speaking.

The only thing that gave away the time-passed was the pain she felt in her own strong muscles. She could feel it in her limbs, the ache of survival, the hours that had gone by.

Jessop clawed at the glass floor but she was physically exhausted. She bit her lip as she struggled to push herself out of the pool. The remnants of the robe tugged at her legs as they fell from her, trailing down her calves and off her feet. The pain and cold rippled through her bare body. It felt as though her arms would collapse and she would slide into the dangerous pool once again. Her fingers fought against the wet glass, twitching violently as they scratched at the floor, and her forearms, despite their muscular form, shook precariously under her.

She didn't care that she fought to liberate herself from the pool naked. Her breasts shook between her strong arms and the curve of her bare thighs tensed, more pronounced as she got a knee onto the ledge. Every inch of her skin glistened as the glass flecks clung to her, making her shimmer iridescently in one hundred reflections of surrounding glass. What was a body, even one that was naked and glistening, compared to all they had seen? Whether they eyed the curve of her form or the white lash scars on her back, or the Hunter's sigil on her neck, or the bizarre scar between her breasts, it did not compare to the wounds they had already witnessed in her mind. The scars were not what she tried to hide, the histories behind them were.

She kept her eyes down, ignoring their speculative, haunting gazes. She was in pain, and she was weak, and their torture had nearly broken her—she was exactly how she needed them to see her. She fell forward, finally entirely out of the pool, and collapsed on the glass floor.

Suddenly, strong arms curled around her. Her muscles froze under his tight grip and her breath caught as he lifted her, curling her body into his embrace. Her own strong form finally felt a forgiving sensation of relief—no longer needing to fight. The Council had been resilient—but they had seen nothing of Jeco. That was what mattered most.

She turned her gaze up into the hazel eyes of the young Hunter. He looked her over with his golden eyes and shook his head apologetically. He readjusted her in his arms and she heard the clinking of metal as he picked up her sheathed blade. He laid it over her shivering chest and Jessop wrapped her hand around the hilt.

He stood with her in his arms, holding her tightly against his chest. Her dripping mane of dark hair clung between them, soaking his tunic. She could feel their eyes on her still. She may have been weakened by their tortures and to their eyes was beautifully female in her shapely design, but Jessop had constructed her body into armor; she was a moving muscle, as deadly as any man who dared ever try more than stare.

And they all stared but him. Not the young Hunter, whom she had saved in the tavern. His eyes stayed unwaveringly concentrated on her face. He held her tightly against him and she realized he was attempting to shield as much of her body with his large arms as possible.

"I'm sorry," he whispered.

Slowly, with a heavy breath, Jessop relaxed in his arms, trusting his strong body to hold her weakened one safely. The thick muscles of her back and thighs ached, having been wildly overexerted. She felt her neck tighten up and she had to rest her head, cautiously letting it ease against his large shoulder. She closed her eyes and she could feel wisps of his pale blond hair dancing across her face.

"She saved us, Hanson," the young Hunter hissed, his quiet voice filled with disappointment as it traveled, breathy, over her cheek.

"Kohl, we had to verify her claims."

Jessop kept her sore eyes shut, but she listened keenly.

"And? Did you?"

The young Hunter's anger surprised her. She fought off a yawn, tucking her face deeper into the curves of his broad chest.

"What the girl says is true, she was tortured and held captive for some thirteen years… she escaped and found us." Hydo Jesuin answered, his voice sounding almost embarrassed. They had hoped she was lying. She almost smiled.

She could feel the young Hunter shaking his head slowly. "Then you'll excuse me if I liberate her from this torture chamber."

"Kohl, remember your place," Hanson warned.

Jessop could feel the young Hunter shaking. "My place is far away from men who would torture a hero for information."

"KOHL!" Hanson erupted.

"You're Hunters—you should know better!"

Jessop was astounded. His intrepid criticisms of his mentors, his unbridled tone—he seemed fearless. He held her firmly against his body, his grip on her tightening with each angry word. She had expected him to be subservient—the Hunters ruled with might—and yet Kohl O'Hanlon did not fear castigation. He was outspoken and temperamental and simply not whom she had expected him to be.

"Kohl—" Hanson growled, but the young Hunter had already pivoted tightly on his heel, turning his back on the Assembly Council. He tucked his chin over the crown of Jessop's head, and she could feel his thumb gently running back and forth on her arm as he carried her from the room—he was trying to soothe her.

Let him go, Hanson, let him calm down, Jessop heard Hydo Jesuin push the thought to his comrade.

The young Hunter readjusted his grip on Jessop and carried her weak body out of the room—saving her as she had saved him.

CHAPTER 3

It took three attempts before the biometric scanner pad would read her water-beaten handprint and unlock the door to her new quarters. "It needs to be set to your print, so that only you can secure the room," he explained to her. She stood shivering beside him, with his black vest draped around her shoulders. The glass hall was empty and an icy breeze traveled through it, chilling her bare feet against the smooth floors.

Kohl rubbed her hand with his tunic, trying to dry the skin back into its recognizable form. She watched him as he tenderly dabbed at her palm and couldn't help but notice the scar in his own palm, the inverted *F*. The scar that gave him entrance to the Glass Blade. He was a fully-fledged Hunter, trusted by the Council he had just chastised on her behalf.

She shivered as he slowly turned her hand over in his and pushed it up against the biometric scanner pad. The silver pad vibrated softly under her skin, and with a *ting*, the door slid to the side, opening.

"Welcome." The automated voice startled her as the heavy metal door began to slide to the side.

"Say your name, so it can register you as the tenant," the young Hunter instructed.

She cleared her throat and fought against her shivering lips. "Jess— *Jessop.*"

She looked up to the young Hunter, and he nodded approvingly. "Perfect."

As the door fully opened, Kohl swung his arm out, directing her to enter. She stepped into the room slowly. One whole wall was made entirely of glass, a window over Azgul, but the others were painted gray, even the floor beneath her. Beside the window was a small bed, with a black cover and pillow, and beside that, a glass side-table with a carafe of water and a drinking beaker. To the left there was a metal door. The young Hunter followed her gaze and as he stepped up to the door, it automatically slid open, revealing a gray and glass bathing room.

Jessop turned from the bathing room and approached the bed. She slowly lowered Falco's blade onto it, running her weak fingers over the metal slowly.

"I will have clothes brought to you," the young Hunter spoke, watching her. She eyed Bane's blade and turned to him.

"I have clothes," she answered softly, thinking of the pile of her belongings in the mirrored pool room.

"Nonetheless, I will have new ones sent."

She nodded at him slowly as he held her stare.

"We actually haven't formally met," he half-smiled at her, awkwardly. She was surprised by his ability to navigate his emotions, turning from such rage to such kindness. It reminded her of another she knew.

She looped her arms around her body, pulling his vest tighter, trying to forcibly stop her shaking. "You're Kohl O'Hanlon." Her words were still shaky, distorted by the quivering of her jaw.

"And you're Jessop... ?" he pressed, waiting for a surname.

She let him wait a moment longer. He didn't try to search her mind for the answer. Again, he surprised her.

She shook her head at him, eyeing the twisted knot of a scar that was tucked into his cheekbone. "I don't have a family whose name I could inherit," she answered.

He nodded, casting his gaze downward. "I'm sorry about that," he said, his voice soft.

She turned from him and looked over Falco Bane's blade. She lifted the silver hilt slowly in her trembling fingers. The black glass was as singular and beautiful as it was treacherous. "You're not the Hunter who has to be sorry."

She turned back to him and found the blade was shaking in her hand, aimed loosely at him. She was too weak to wield a weapon and she meant him no harm. Slowly, Kohl O'Hanlon outstretched his hand and touched the tip of her sword, lowering its point down from him. His fingers slid down the blade until his hand rested atop her own, and with a small tug, he took it from her and rested it back on the bed. He looked her over slowly. "What *happened* to you?"

Jessop lowered herself to the ground and leaned against her bed, holding the leather tightly to her chest to stop shaking. She noticed the vest had no knife hole or blood stains—he had obtained a new one. "Haven't you seen what all the Council has now seen? Surely you heard their thoughts or saw mine... I escaped Aranthol," she sighed heavily, sick of the story herself now. Slowly, the young Hunter lowered himself to the floor beside her.

"I might have heard a thought or two, but I prefer different methods of learning things about people than reading minds," he shrugged.

Jessop arched her brow at him. "Torture?"

He shook his head at her, shocked by the dark remark. "*What*? No! I just ask them."

She shrugged, almost laughing at his response. "I lived under Falco Bane in the Shadow City, and now I'm here, in the Hunters' Red City. You know everything there is to know about me."

She looked up to him and found his hazel eyes studying her. He shook his head slowly. "Somehow, I highly doubt that."

* * * *

Jessop woke early the next morning and quickly dressed in the fresh clothes the young Hunter had sent to her before beginning the task of braiding her long hair. He had stayed with her late into the night, asking her questions and continuously apologizing for the way she had been treated by the Assembly Council. He had arranged for food and clothing to be brought to her and assured her that her room was well protected, so that she could sleep soundly. "You're safe here, I promise; no one can hurt you," he had told her before leaving her side.

She hadn't told him that, sweet as his sentiment was, she already knew that. She had slept better than she had anticipated. As morning broke, she thought of the young Hunter. He had a kindness that Jessop was quite certain she had never encountered before. It was different than anyone she knew—*he* was different than anyone she knew. His sweetness was disarming and he lived by a simple moral code, so certain of what was right and wrong. Jessop wouldn't admit that a part of her envied that level of moral simplicity. She had lived too dark a life to believe in a black-or-white world. Her life, as it had always been in the Shadow City, was darkly gray.

She pulled her thick mane over her shoulder, her fingers working expertly on the plait. As she began to tie it off with a leather band, the automated door operator's voice filled the room. "*Hunter Kohl O'Hanlon.*"

Jessop finished with her hair and checked her appearance once more in the mirror. She wore all black, from her tunic to her breeches, and the young Hunter had even sent a new pair of boots, but she refrained. Hers were worn leather, fitted perfectly to her step. She had been prepared to go back for the clothes, but when she had awoken she found her belongings outside her door. She was dressed exactly like one of the Hunters, barring the leather vest.

She reached for her sword, knowing it was the last thing she needed to be ready for the day, and, blade in hand, she opened the door for Kohl O'Hanlon.

"I see the clothes fit," he said and smiled as he stepped into the room.

She turned from him and began the process of pulling her sheath around her belt.

"But you didn't like the boots," he noted, staring at her worn footwear.

Jessop fixed her belt, her blade steady, and turned to him. "Mine know my fight, they know my steps," she explained.

He leaned against the wall, crossing his arms as he regarded her with a somber expression. "Of course, you've had to defend yourself for so many years."

Jessop looked him over slowly. His golden hair was pulled into a tight knot at the back of his head and he had a shadow of a beard, which drew more attention to the silver star-shaped scar under his hazel eye than he probably intended. A scar that on another's face would have been hideously overpowering, but on Kohl's was oddly appealing.

She looked over his massive frame, his broad chest and wide shoulders. She wasn't blind; she knew that the Hunter was both young and handsome. While she had expected the former, she had been surprised by the latter. He had golden eyes and silver scars; he was undeniably striking... but that didn't make his sympathetic stare any less critical.

Or any harder to face.

"Please don't do that." She shook her head at him.

"Do what?"

She snaked her sheath onto her belt. "Pity me."

He pushed away from the wall, letting his arms fall from his chest, and stood before her. "I'm sorry for whatever happened to you that made you what you are." He took a slow step towards her. "But you saved my life and for that I'm grateful."

She felt uncomfortable under his pensive gaze. His candor felt near palpable. Honesty was so important to Kohl that it was an extension of his very being, a code he lived by—armor he wore. Jessop's armor was more in line with his mentors, and she felt almost embarrassed by that fact. She stepped away from him. "I did what any would do."

He nodded slowly. "What not many *could* do."

She didn't want to speak about it further. She had saved him, but she didn't need to be thanked for it. She had entered that bar with the intentions of meeting a Hunter and ending up in the Glass Blade, surrounded by those Falco Bane most hated and most feared. She had been successful and Kohl O'Hanlon had just been… collateral damage.

"Many can fight," she said, making her way towards the door.

"Not women," he argued, following.

"Hunters don't let women train in the Red City—that doesn't mean women can't fight. They fight often, and well, in Aranthol," she argued.

"Well, women in Azgul don't seem to have the temperament for it," he explained, stepping out into the hall.

Jessop eyed him over slowly. "Or maybe the men in Azgul simply fear what would happen if women *did* take up the sword."

He stared at her bold claim, looking over her with serious eyes, and then his lips pulled back in a half-smile, "I suspect you're right."

She froze in the hall. Though he wore a completed uniform, she knew she had his leather from the night before. "I forgot your Hunter's vest. Let me get it for you."

He rested his hand on her forearm, halting her. "You keep it."

* * * *

"What do you mean Hydo cancelled the Assembly Council meeting?" Kohl pressed, staring at Hanson with confusion.

"He said he had an urgent matter to attend to, that he would return to the Glass Blade soon and we would deal with Falco Bane and the girl then," Hanson relayed the message for a second time to them, his voice dull with repetition.

"Jessop," Kohl corrected—for the second time.

Hanson shot his gaze to her. She didn't care if she made the old Hunter uncomfortable. He alone couldn't dictate her presence in the Blade; he couldn't force her out now. Hanson eyed her over critically, seemingly certain the time spent in the pool would have worn her out for longer, and yet, she had recovered fully. Even the minute cuts had nearly vanished overnight. His suspicion and dislike for her could become troublesome, but she did not fear the old man. Hanson wasn't her concern.

Jessop thought of Hydo Jesuin. While he tortured her it had seemed that nothing mattered more than information on Falco Bane, and yet, when the opportunity had finally arisen to see what information she could volunteer to him, he found he had more important places to be. Jessop briefly wondered if there was any way he had seen more than she could recall from her time in the pool…

Impossible, she thought. She knew what he had seen and it wasn't enough to take action, especially against Falco, without her. Wherever Hydo was, whatever he was attending to, it mattered not; it simply set her timing back. He would return soon enough and then they could begin their mission for Falco Bane.

"Jessop?"

She stirred at the sound of her name, looking up to Kohl.

He looked down at her, his amber eyes flicking over her. "I said, would you like to train with me today?"

Jessop looked from him to Hanson. "I don't think that would be a good idea."

Hanson shook his head, "We don't train women, Kohl."

Kohl scoffed, "We aren't training her—she's clearly damn well-trained. It's just practice."

Hanson looked her over, his eyes narrowing. Jessop knew what the old man thought—he was afraid of losing the hold he had on his mentee; between the outburst before the Assembly Council and the notion of training with a woman, he was beginning to act too independently. Jessop could see more than just control though—Hanson Knell loved his student. He viewed Kohl O'Hanlon as a son. She looked over the old Hunter's eyes—he had no idea how much he revealed to her.

Jessop turned to Kohl, "It's not a good idea."

Hanson crossed his arms over his broad chest, staring down at her with a critical eye. "Women have no place in the Hollow, Kohl."

Jessop held the old man's gaze. She knew he was resisting using Sentio on her; he didn't want to anger Kohl further. She held his stare, challenging him to break into her mind… but he looked away.

"Women aren't meant to be in the Glass Blade at all, but here she is, and I need someone to practice with," Kohl insisted.

"I will practice with you," Hanson answered but Kohl already had an argument resting on his lips.

"Please, Hanson, we have fought together too long—I need something different, to ensure I don't get injured again."

"Then I will call upon another Hunter—"

"I have already bested them all!"

Jessop turned from the old Hunter to the young, and finally spoke. "Kohl, I wouldn't want to worsen your wound, you are still recovering."

"Please, I have recovered just fine," he insisted, turning to her and lifting his leather and tunic to reveal his side. Jessop was amazed to see that where the wound had been was a freshly formed scar—but that wasn't all Jessop saw.

Kohl's abdomen was covered in hundreds upon hundreds of small silver lines and marks, all trailing off in different directions, exactly like his arms. They were faint, several years aged at least, but plentiful. She returned her gaze to his, her eyes trailing over the goring star-shaped scar on his face. One thousand silver scars. Horrifying but not unique; Jessop had seen such endlessly marred flesh before.

Were they truly the marks of a Hunter's life? Had she misinterpreted what that explanation had meant, when she had first heard it years ago? She looked to Hanson, whose worn and wearied skin glistened with several scars too deep to fade, resting on hundreds of smaller, much older ones.

"You'll train with us then?" Kohl pressed, his hopeful smile distinct in her periphery.

Hanson held her gaze for a moment longer before turning from her, as if knowing her thoughts and attempting to conceal his own.

"Sure, I'll train with you."

* * * *

"Consider it helping," Kohl explained as he led the way through the Glass Blade. "Hanson grows tired of spending his days in the Hollow with me." As they curved through narrow corridors and traveled down the Blade in glass bullets the rooms began to appear darker and darker to Jessop.

She watched the passing floors flick past as they made their descent. "I'm glad my presence has given your mentor a reprieve from his usual scheduling." Her tone was more sarcastic than intended. She could hear Hanson mumble something behind her.

Kohl looked her over apologetically, lowering his voice. "I'm sorry for how he's been with you… He's suspicious. All of them are—since… everything."

Jessop nodded up to him, knowing he meant since Falco. She followed him down a narrow hall that had a low incline. She hadn't meant to sound so derisive—it was Hanson. The older Hunter's presence irked her. "The Hollow, you said?" she asked, changing the subject along with her tone.

"The Hollow is the Hunters' training room," he smiled down at her, "Every truly great Infinity Hunter has been trained there." As soon as

Kohl said the words his face contorted apologetically towards her—he had once again accidentally made reference to Falco.

"I'm sor—" he immediately began, but Jessop raised a hand to stop him.

"It's fine. Everything here reminds me of *him*, I know you don't mean to reference him. It's impossible not to in this place."

In the bullet, standing behind her, Hanson scoffed heavily. She wrung her fingers tightly around the hilt of her sword, refusing to acknowledge him.

"Everything?" Kohl asked, looking down at her with big eyes.

She looked away, staring through the thick glass at the darkening rooms they passed. "Everything."

They continued further down into the depths of the Glass Blade and, eventually, whether they were still travelling through glass chutes or see-through spaces became unknown to Jessop, even with her advanced visual abilities. She kept her hand on her hilt, certain Hanson stood not inches away from her, his breath on the back of her neck.

When the doors finally opened, it took Jessop's eyes a moment to readjust. Ahead of them was a gray corridor, with several dull bulbs of light hanging from the ceiling in small metal cages. It was as treacherous as it was familiar to Jessop... but she was unsure why anything in this place would feel familiar. Even if she had experienced traces of a place through another's memory, it rarely felt familiar to her upon seeing it herself; perhaps somewhat recognizable, but not as though she had been there before. Yet, this place, with its stale, thick air and cold, gray walls, felt... familiar. It felt like Aranthol.

"Here we are," Hanson spoke, pushing gruffly past her to step out into the dark corridor.

"After you," Kohl spoke, staring at her apologetically.

She looked him over and then cautiously stepped out, following Hanson. She eyed the damp walls and dirt floors. Jessop could easily recall Falco's memories of this place. Moss grew in the creases of the stone slabs. She could hear, in the distance, sloshing liquid, lapping at an unseen edge. The smell of fire, scorched rubber and something else... something Jessop was familiar with—the smell of spilt blood. She closed her eyes and she saw flames. She felt as though she were choking on smoke once more, screaming, swallowing fire...

Kohl accidentally brushed against her as he overtook her, excitedly rushing ahead, bringing her back to the moment. Jessop followed after him with trepidation, her eyes darting over the corridor, keeping Hanson in her periphery as she wondered what other unknown dangers skulked about in the depths of the Glass Blade. She tightened her hand around her hilt, scanning the space ahead of her.

Such quiet footsteps, girl.

Hanson forced the thought into Jessop's mind but she refused to acknowledge it. He was too concerned with whatever grasp on Sentio she might have, and she wasn't going to help aid his fascination.

She carried on, silently walking down the corridor, acting as though she had heard nothing.

"This is the Hollow," Kohl called out from the end of the corridor, his deep voice echoing around her. Jessop came up behind him and found herself looking into the depths of a colossal stone pit. Just ahead of her boot there was a steel beam, one of several, reaching out and bridging the landing they stood on with the mossy cave wall across the way, fixed some thirty feet above the cave pit's dirt floor. Dangling from the beams were old, frayed ropes that hung at varying lengths to the ground—a way to enter and exit the Hollow, Jessop imagined.

She looked to the far end of the pit and saw steel platforms, some wide enough to lay across, others just small enough to fit a boot on, levitating at different heights in the air. On the ground, far beneath the floating platforms, Jessop could see mounds of scrap metal, rusted cages, and old tires. All of the metal junk was scattered around tar pits—several large craters carved out in the ground filled with boiling, black oil. As if on cue, the pits spontaneously ignited and jets of fast-burning fire traveled the edges. Jessop couldn't deny that it was quite the training arena.

No fancy weapons, no easy escapes, and no ideal hideaways... the Hollow was designed to replicate as realistic a fighting scenario as could be imagined. And as the fire flickered in the darkness, dancing an amber light over the twisted steel, casting great shadows up blood stained walls, she could easily recall her life in the Shadow City. She could recall Falco's kingdom of darkness, and a thousand easy memories rushed to the forefront of her mind. She fought to force Jeco's face back into the depths of memory, needing to concentrate on the young Hunter before her.

Jessop watched as Kohl stepped out onto one of the steel beams. After taking several paces out, he spun on his heel, turning his wicked smile onto her. He continued to cross the beam backwards, one foot carefully finding its place behind the next. He let his dark eyes trail up to her, proud of his precarious poise so high above the ground. "Ready?"

The young Hunter was showing off for her. Jessop offered his attempt to impress a half-smile.

She looked Hanson over. "You watch from up here?"

He nodded slowly. "Today, I watch from up here." He spoke each word slowly and deliberately, letting her know he would be watching *her*.

She resisted engaging further. Instead, she turned and stepped quickly out onto the beam. She kept her eyes up, trained on Kohl, confidently closing the distance between them. She didn't need to watch her feet. Not only did Jessop have impeccable balance but thirty feet was not a drop that concerned her. One hundred feet was not a drop that concerned her. But the young Hunter didn't know that—she was quite certain he didn't even know what heights his own abilities could conquer. He watched her quick movements with surprise, hastening his own steps, extending his arms out for balance.

"You're not afraid of heights," he remarked, his half-smile reappearing as he found his footing.

Jessop unsheathed her blade with ease, bringing her black star glass sword out in a quick, clean movement, continuing to gain on him. She thought of her dislike of flying. It wasn't the height that scared her, but the reliance on the machine. "No one is afraid of heights—they are afraid of their own inability to navigate them."

"I suppose that's true," he answered, looking down to his feet as he shakily continued back.

Jessop twirled her wrist and her blade, glinting a reflection of the far below fires, cut a circle at her side. "Did we not come here to fight?"

The young Hunter seemed as surprised as he was impressed by her easy footwork. He paused briefly and, with a daring smile teasing at his mouth, he stepped off the edge of the beam, disappearing off the ledge.

Jessop quickly looked over the side and found that he had caught himself on one of the ropes that hung from the steel. She watched as he shimmied down, the rope stopping about fifteen feet short from the ground. Once he reached its end, the young Hunter let go and fell. He landed firmly on his feet, kicking up a cloud of dust, and slowly looked up to her. He smiled smugly as he unsheathed his blade.

"Come and fight me then," he called up to her.

Jessop couldn't help but look over her shoulder at Hanson Knell. He wanted to see how much of her was the product of Falco Bane. Aranthol was the most dangerous place any would ever find themselves in and she couldn't hide how she had managed to survive it. If the abilities Falco had instilled in her reminded the old Hunter of his enemy, then so be it. Fighting like Falco had gotten her into the Glass Blade and she knew it would also be what *kept* her there.

She looked forward, steadying her body, controlling her breathing. With graceful precision, she sliced her weapon upwards and held it out to her side, the blade singing as it cut through the air and formed an extension of her arm, a perfect line parallel to the ground. She took an easy breath and, with a slight bend of the knee, she dove head first off the steel beam. She brought the sword across her body as she spiraled through the air. She twisted through the fall, tucking her head low and turning her body out, and, just as she saw the floor approach, her eyes transformed the world into beautiful slow motion. She turned her arm out, extending her blade once again to the side, and found her feet beneath her, her knees bent and feet ready. She landed, one foot flat as she kneeled, her head low, and her sword held up high to her side.

Slowly, she looked up, her green eyes travelling to meet Kohl's. He stared with shock, his lips apart as he looked from her up to the beam above. She followed his gaze and found Hanson looking over the edge, his critical stare locked on to her. She slowly rose from bended knee, turning her gaze back to Kohl. "Are we doing this?"

He cocked his head, flicking a strand of golden hair out of his eyes. "Definitely."

Jessop brought her blade up, taking a confident step forward, as Kohl made his first move. He closed the gap between them quickly, expertly crossing his crystalline blade from either side of his body. He descended on her with precision, executing an expert strike at her. She parried and sidestepped. He pivoted around, swinging his blade out across his body, aimed at her neck; she ducked, rose and hit his sword away with the *ting* of forged star glass.

She already knew that Kohl, as an Infinity Hunter, was a good fighter. He moved with control and grace. He had been trained extensively, but Jessop could see the negative side of such thorough training—perhaps, as with her and Falco, Kohl's mentor had influenced his style too much. As a man, the young Hunter seemed to have an easy confidence and natural flair, despite his serious training and rigid beliefs, but it did not come through in his fight. He moved with textbook deliberation instead of fluid intuition. He executed his regimented attacks so efficiently it was as though his body didn't know there were other options.

She weaved around him, bringing her blade over her back to block a blind assault. She pivoted and squared off with him, holding his blade off with her own. The brilliance of his transparent blade connected with the dangerous edge of her black weapon, two entirely distinct edges ringing out. She smiled at him wickedly. "Getting tired, Hunter?"

She could feel Hanson's eyes on her from above. She knew that he wouldn't be able to deny her uses to the Council having seen her hold off his own mentee with such ease. She thought of hunting with them and she could imagine a hundred scenarios where Hydo Jesuin and the Councilmen could see that she was *more* than a battered escapee, more than—

Umph!

Kohl's fist connected with Jessop's chest so hard that it sent her flying through the air. With luck, she grabbed hold of one of the hanging ropes and quickly regained her footing. She had provoked him and then allowed herself to be distracted by her thoughts—she may have been the superior fighter but the young Hunter was no amateur. His blade came straight at her and she couldn't help but notice that being incited had loosened Kohl up—had brought out his aggression.

To be a good fighter you have to be hungry for the fight. The memory of words she had heard so many times before filled her mind. She ducked back as Kohl came for her. She slid to the side, pulled on the rope, and as he cut just past her, twisted it swiftly around the hilt of his blade. With his hand temporarily trapped, she kneed him in the side. She grabbed his hilt and kicked him hard in the chest, sending him flying back and forcing his grip free. She arched her brow at him, his blade now in her hand.

He recovered swiftly and with anger. He came after her quickly, eager to retrieve his weapon, and she backed away from him, watching as he hit the ropes out of his way. And then he stopped.

He extended his hand out in front of him and pulled his fingers tightly in the air, as though grasping an invisible hilt. Within seconds, Jessop could feel his blade shaking violently in her hand.

Sentio.

She knew better than to resist. She let his blade go and watched as the sword flew through the air, back into the grasp of its master. He caught the hilt easily, spinning it in a full circle about himself and as the crystalline star glass caught the light of the burning tar pits, creating the appearance of a circle of shimmering fire around him.

He took quick steps towards her and executed a strike with great force against her. She blocked and began to step back, keeping the momentum of their fight moving. She found her feet easily, stepping back again and again as she blocked and attacked. She defended against his sword with ease, but remained wary of his willingness to use Sentio.

In her periphery, she saw they were beginning to pass through the levitating metal platforms. Without delay, she crouched down swiftly and flipped back into the air, recalling where the next floating metal board would be. She landed smoothly atop the edge of the platform and, just as quickly as she had landed, she flipped back off, leaping behind Kohl. Before he could turn on her she had kicked him in the back. He fell forward, rolling right onto the precipice of one of the tar pits.

Before Jessop could say anything, the fire of the pit traveled its periphery, and leapt onto Kohl's tunic, burning around him with an angry blue flame.

She felt her hands twitch at her side, her eyes widen at the sight. She wanted to help him extinguish the flames, but she was frozen in place. He leapt to his feet and ripped the vest and burning tunic away from him, cursing at the discarded material as it lay in a smoldering heap on the ground between them. Jessop looked from the burnt tunic to Kohl. Her eyes traveled across his exposed stomach, his body rippling with adrenaline and might. She looked across his abdomen and wide-set shoulders. The marks she had previewed earlier had alluded to a much more grave sight.

Every inch of Kohl O'Hanlon was scarred. Some of the scars were deep, some slender, some carved out in circle formations, others had been clean cuts—all silver and all old. The scars were so old it made her wonder how young he had been when he suffered their creation. His entire body was made of muscle and scarred flesh. He had the formidable size of a prime Hunter, but the flesh of a torture victim. It was horrifying to simply imagine such pain, even for a woman as scarred as herself... But Jessop had seen the same devastation before.

On the body of Falco Bane.

CHAPTER 4

"Your body…" The whisper fell from Jessop's lips before she could stop it. She knew *what* had happened; she knew *how* someone got scars like that. What she didn't know was *who* was responsible—for Kohl's or Falco's.

"It's the Hunter life," Kohl shrugged, picking up his leather vest and leaving the burnt tunic on the ground.

"It's the Hunter's life," Falco shrugged, noting her stares as he undressed…

The memory vanished as quickly as it had emerged—the same words, the same scars, but a different man, a different time and place. Jessop shook her head, clearing her mind.

"We're done here." Hanson's tense voice carried over them. Jessop had nearly forgotten he was there. She looked up, just in time to see a flick of the old Hunter's long silvery braid as he disappeared down the corridor above.

Jessop turned her attention back to Kohl. She had experience ignoring grotesque things—beauty was uncommon in the Shadow City—but this was different. To be so reminded of Falco Bane… she forced her eyes to concentrate on Kohl's face, to know that he wasn't Bane.

Kohl watched her carefully, and she could see that where there had been fight and anger in his eyes just a moment ago, there was pride and discomfort. He *knew* what she saw when she saw his body. He crossed his arms over his marred flesh. "Want to get out of here?"

She watched as his blonde hair fell in front of his dark eyes.

"And go where?"

Without thinking she reached up and pushed the hair back, tucking it behind his ears. She slowly pulled her hand away, catching his hazel eyes, entirely unsure of what she had just done.

He slowly smiled down at her. "Anywhere."

* * * *

Instead of taking her out of the Glass Blade, Kohl had decided to take her up it. They traveled through one of the many glass chutes, in a small, translucent bullet, and as they rounded another floor Jessop couldn't help but show her amazement. They had been ascending the building for some time and she couldn't help but stare at how the floors beneath her feet disappeared into blurry, distant dots and details as they climbed higher and higher. She wondered, having been to the depths of the Blade, and now seemingly to its very top, where did they house the famed Blade of Light?

"The height can be daunting to some." Kohl's voice surprised her, pulling her attention back. She slowly looked away from the disappearing floors beneath her feet and up to his hazel eyes.

"It's more the building that fascinates me," she said. He nodded at her slowly, and she found herself studying the star-shaped scar carved into his cheekbone. It made her think of his marred body—and of Bane.

He arched a brow at her. "A wound from my first serious fight."

She nodded. "You left a larger mark on him that day."

He studied her face, running his hand over the stubble of his jaw line, his fingers just grazing the old wound. "On who, exactly?"

"I think you know the answer to that."

His lips fell into a weak smile and his gaze dropped for just a moment. "How did you know it was Bane I fought that day?"

"Several things have given me the impression that you and he would have been trained together, not least of which is that he mentioned his former best friend over the years," she answered. She couldn't help but picture Bane's face, his gray eyes, and the scar that cut through his brow and down his cheekbone, a perfect silver line down his face. It had nearly robbed him of his eye—the blade that marked him.

"He mentioned me?"

She nodded, trying to read his expression. "In passing."

"You're right, I did give Bane that scar," Kohl spoke, answering what she hadn't needed to ask.

The Hunter took a step towards her and for the first time Jessop noticed how *tall* he was, how intimidating—how similar to Bane. A fight between the two would have ended in devastation at one point in time. Before Bane had become unstoppable. She looked up into his amber eyes and found the intensity of his stare surprising.

"Earlier, you said everything here reminds you of him. I don't want to remind you of such pain," he spoke. His voice was soft and sad. It surprised Jessop, to hear such emotion in his speech, but she knew they were bonded forever now.

You're responsible for the lives you save—another lesson from the shadows of Aranthol.

She took a deep breath and touched his arm softly. "You don't remind me of such pain."

He smiled sadly, "You're sweet to lie."

He stepped away from her and Jessop couldn't help but stare at him. "I'm not lying—feel free to check."

He looked over her darkly. "You know I wouldn't do that."

She cocked her head to the side. "You had no issues using Sentio earlier in the Hollow—to get your blade back," she reminded him.

"That's different, I wouldn't use my abilities to invade your mind," he answered, his voice low and his expression serious.

Jessop leaned against the glass, crossing her arms over her chest. "Then you're the sweet one. Your fellow Hunters feel differently."

He stepped back to her slowly, "I'm sorry for what they did to you... for what *he* did to you. Since meeting you, all I could think about was that I could have saved you so much pain, had I known things sooner. Had I been able to tell there was something off about him—"

"Stop." She held his intense gaze as she cut him off. At his concerned expression, she elaborated, softening her tone. "You can't keep apologizing to me, Kohl. What has been of my life has not been your fault. You were just a boy when you knew Falco Bane."

He nodded, "I know. It's just that you saved me—and that means something to me." He rested a hand on her shoulder and Jessop couldn't help but stare at his fingers. And then he pulled her into a hug. "I just want you to know that we *will* get the man responsible for your suffering," he whispered.

Slowly, she wrapped her arms around him. Jessop didn't *like* to be touched; she didn't like to be embraced. But she understood Kohl O'Hanlon's attempts at comforting her. She nodded against his broad chest, picturing the face of the very man. "Oh, I know we will."

* * * *

While the view was undeniably incredible, Jessop was certain she would never get used to the color of the sky in the Red City. Everything around her shone crimson, like the world was on fire. They were on a large ledge outside of an empty training room. Kohl had said it was his spot, that whenever the training or Hanson or the Council had gotten to be too much, he would come to sit on the ledge. He said it was a reminder of why they trained, of the importance of the Blade of Light and the Daharian galaxy, and of themselves.

"As a child, I wondered if the fall would kill me. I had been raised seeing Hunters move—the way *you* moved today—and I never knew how high was *too* high," he mused, looking down at the miles of space beneath them. She had been right in her earlier assumption; perhaps he still didn't know the extent of his own abilities.

She looked over to him, arching her brow. "You were raised here? In the Glass Blade?" She knew those chosen throughout Daharia were selected young, some perhaps too young to remember a different home, or parents.

He nodded slowly, still looking down over the ledge. "For as long as I can remember this has been home."

She turned slightly in her seat, forcing down thoughts she did not wish to think. "Well, you can move the way Hunters can now."

He turned to study her face. "I know *I* can. I'm amazed that *you* can. That kind of power, it's what's needed for Sentio."

She shrugged; uncertain of what more she could say about her abilities. "Is that what the Council fear women wouldn't survive—if they trained them—is wielding that kind of power?"

Kohl nodded slowly, "Yeah, either they wouldn't survive that or the…" his voice trailed off quickly, dying out on the passing wind.

"Or the what?"

He smiled at her brightly. "Nothing."

Jessop knew not to press him. He had been open with her; she felt he would continue to be if she didn't push him. It would be a topic for another time. Instead, she found herself, once again, meditating over his star scar.

He arched a brow at her. "What?"

She shrugged slowly. "Was *he* always so—" she began, but he cut her off. "Terrifying?" he finished.

She said nothing. It wasn't the word she would have used for Bane. But she remained silent.

"I grew up with Falco, until we were just about fourteen. And yes, he was always that way." Kohl began, his gaze locked on the crimson skyline.

"We were close… for a time. But Falco was different. He felt nothing, no pain was too great, no wound too deep, nothing could hurt him… nothing could break him. Not even… Well, you've seen the scars. He had all of these ideas about changing anything, changing everything, and it was so easy to want to follow him… until you realized that he was bound by nothing, loyal to no one, entirely uncontrollable. He was born dangerous," Kohl sighed, turning to her. "But surely you already knew that."

Jessop nodded. Talking about him *was* too hard. "I shouldn't have said anything—it's too many memories for both of us."

She looked out over the Red City, at the Soar-Craft that zoomed past and the levitating engineer blocks and buildings that rested a thousand feet up in the sky on slender foundations, like giant heads on sinewy scrap-metal bodies that wove down to the ground below. She smiled as she noticed, from this view, that all the buildings that had foundation on the ground, in the Red City skyline, looked somewhat like humans. Compiled of rusted metals, additions haphazardly added here and there, odd offshoots with Levi-Hubs connected to them… and all about them, more buildings, and ship-docks, levitating in the sky.

"I know why you're here, you know." Kohl's voice broke her concentration.

She turned slowly, her eyes trailing over the steep thousand-mile drop below them, before reaching his dark eyes. "What do you mean?"

"The Council thinks you're here for your safety, but I know you're here because you know you could be a Hunter—that you're the *only* one who could possibly hunt down Bane, show us a way into Aranthol."

Jessop shook her head slowly, taking in his words, his interpretation of her. "There are no female Hunters, Kohl."

Even as she said the words, she could feel the brand on the back of her neck tingling.

Before she could say anything further, Kohl had leaned in to her, his eyes narrowing on her. "I'm pretty sure I'm looking at one."

She smiled under his compliment. "I'm *not* one of the Hunters of Infinity. I am a fighter because I spent my life thus far needing to fight a trained Hunter."

He shook his head at her. "Titles are titles. I've been in the Hollow with over a dozen men who couldn't do what you did in there today."

"And what's that?"

He smiled, surprised at her. "Beat me."

His words were so comfortable, even in admitting defeat.

She looked over his calm face slowly. "You were undefeated?"

He nodded. Jessop didn't know men like Kohl O'Hanlon. He was unassuming and humble, a bizarre combination for the truly capable, and yet, he was kind. He had no qualms admitting she had bested him and no reservations in offering her praise.

She thought of his scars, his marred body and the star carved into his cheekbone. She pictured his skilled fighting abilities and the way he wielded Sentio. Kohl O'Hanlon was both nothing, and everything, like the infamous Falco Bane.

* * * *

"It's getting dark," Kohl's voice carried over the icy air. Jessop had been watching the horizon for nearly an hour but she hadn't noticed that it was beginning to darken. The red sky was beginning to turn not into a night sky, but a hazy crimson one.

"It never seems to be truly dark here," Jessop sighed, but got to her feet nonetheless. She turned to find Kohl staring at her pensively. She shrugged. "What?"

He shook his head, as though dismissing a thought. "They say it's a perpetual night in the Shadow City."

At his words she grew concerned at her own comments—she should not criticize his home. "What they say is true… it is a forever night. Your Red City has much more to offer in terms of skies," she added quickly.

Kohl led the way back from the ledge, pushing aside the glass window for her to crawl indoors. "Some people prefer the darkness, I suppose."

Jessop couldn't fault his astute mind. She had made one comment and he had leapt on it—he didn't need Sentio when he paid this level of attention to others. "I suppose some do," she answered, standing upright and stretching out in the warm indoors. She watched as the young Hunter followed in her stead, crawling through the window and latching it shut behind him.

"You've figured me out then," she stared up to him.

At her words, his smile faded and she watched the growing concern creep through his warm eyes. She had unnerved him.

"I prefer a black sky to your red one," she smiled at him sheepishly. She touched his arm and he immediately relaxed, smiling back at her.

"Promise you'll keep my secret? I wouldn't want to offend anyone else in the Red City," she pressed, brushing a strand of dark hair out of her eyes.

He watched her keenly, his amber eyes darting over her lips.

"I would keep all your secrets, if you let me," he whispered, leaning closer to her.

His hand found the back of her head softly, and she could feel his thumb brushing against her affectionately as he tilted her face up to him. The intensity of his golden stare nearly made her forget… everything.

Just before his lips found hers, she remembered herself. She rested a firm hand against his chest, stopping him from kissing her. "Maybe one day you will," she whispered.

* * * *

Jessop rolled over, pulling the blankets tight around her. She was restless, too warm and then too cold, unable to sleep despite having spent hours trying. She couldn't get the image of Kohl leaning in to kiss her, out of her mind. She would be lying if she said she hadn't thought this would be a possible eventuation of her entering the Glass Blade. She had thought out every scenario and *that* had definitely been one of them.

But not the way it had come about with Kohl. He was handsome and kind, but he wasn't… he was too… it was too soon. She had been the object of an Infinity Hunter's attraction before, she knew that life and she wasn't going to simply forget it now that she was in the Blade. Every time she closed her eyes she could see Bane's face and her life outside of the Blade would come rushing back to her.

So she kept her eyes open.

* * * *

Jessop pulled the blinds to the side and cursed the red sky. She had been raised in the dark—in the perpetual night, as Kohl had so aptly put it. She was certain she wouldn't grow accustomed to the angry scarlet glare of Azgul. She knew she hadn't slept; maybe she had gotten an hour in, but it felt like less. She turned from the window, pushing the covers off of her as she reached for the silver control panel beside the bed. She fiddled with several metallic knobs and switches before she found the right button to command her bedroom lights on.

She stepped out of her bed, hissing at the cold floor beneath her feet. She quickly crossed the room, pushing her hand against a silver panel, and opening her bathing room door. She was thankful for the heated floors that welcomed her as she made her way to the washing stall. With a flick of her hand, the glass doors slid open and a waterfall of scalding water erupted from the roof.

She undressed quickly and stepped under the water, closing her eyes and fighting off the sickening feeling of utter exhaustion. She cleaned her long hair and stared at the slate floor beneath her feet. She could feel Kohl's hand on her still… and then, to her surprise, she could see the look in his eyes as he watched her from the bathing room doorway.

An apology was already hanging on his lips. Kohl was standing, his eyes wide as he tried to look away, his hands outstretched in an apology. But she had already reacted to his presence in the room, frightening her. She swung her hand, and with a force she didn't intend, she sent Kohl flying out of the doorway. The sound of his head cracking against the floor startled her further and Jessop leapt from the water.

She grabbed a robe and pulled it over her wet body, rushing across the room. "Kohl, *Kohl*, are you alright?"

She had no idea what he had been doing in her room but she hadn't meant to hurt him—she absolutely hadn't meant to use Sentio in front of him, let alone *on* him. She fell to her knees and pulled his face into her lap. He was unconscious. "Kohl…" she whispered. She was as mad at him as she was at herself.

Jessop took a deep breath and rested her small hand over his cheek, her thumb atop his scar. She closed her eyes and concentrated. The sensation was similar to running—sprinting through someone's mind. She saw thousands of images and heard millions of sounds, but she needed to find the exact image and pair it with the exact sound in order to find the *exact* moment she was looking for.

She tried to be quick with it, she tried to work whilst ignoring as much of the content as she could, but she couldn't help but see that within the flashes there was a girl, with long blonde hair and hazel eyes… she was crying… Jessop pushed on, intentionally ducking away from images of Hanson or the Council. She *couldn't* do that. She couldn't betray his trust like that.

And then she saw her own body, naked in the washing stall. She saw herself turn, wave her hand, the look of sudden anger in her eyes… Jessop concentrated on the image, and, then watched it disintegrate. The sounds were the first to fall away, and then the colors—they began to fade out, until she saw a silent, black and white of the memory. Then the image became distorted, shattering, and then, it disappeared entirely.

Jessop opened her eyes. He was beginning to stir, turning his head in her lap. "Kohl," she spoke, stroking his temple to help him wake. Slowly, his eyelids began to flutter, and he glanced around calmly—until he realized *where* he was. He rushed to sit up, but she restrained him, urging him to remain still.

"Jessop—what happened?" He asked, raising a hand to his head, noting his injury.

She looked him over closely. "You tell me—what do you remember?"

He looked from her, to the bathing room, and sat up slowly. "I don't know. I came to see if you were awake and wanted to get an early morning training session in... I couldn't sleep. I came in and—"

Jessop waited but he seemed stumped.

He looked up at her with a perplexed expression. "I don't know what happened after that." he admitted, his voice tense with confusion.

She nodded, smiling softly down at him. "You accidentally saw me bathing, you slipped on my clothes and hit your head pretty hard."

He ran his hand over his head once more, as if trying to recall her story. He nodded slowly. "Jessop, I'm sorry. If I saw you... I'm an idiot. Forgive me?"

She smiled at him, nodding. "Don't be ridiculous, there's nothing to forgive." She stood and extended a hand to him, helping him get to his feet slowly. "Do you forgive me?" She asked, watching him as he steadied himself.

He looked down at her, confused. "For what?"

She kicked her tunic out from under her foot, demonstrating to him that her clothes were strewn all about the floor dangerously. "It's my fault you're hurt."

"Of course, that's not your fault... I should have never been in here," he shook his head at her. He looked around the room, as though the entire situation were a mess he was responsible for.

He leaned against the wall, rubbing his head, and looked her over with his golden eyes. "Can we... can we just forget this ever happened?"

She took his hand in hers and nodded slowly, "I'd like that very much."

CHAPTER 5

It had been a fortnight and still Hydo Jesuin hadn't returned. Word of Jessop's presence in the Blade had gotten out and her training sessions with Kohl had begun to draw quite a crowd. Kohl hadn't mentioned the incident in her bathing room since that morning, and she had followed suit, pleased that he only remembered what she needed him to. She felt bad for what had happened, but he had given her no choice.

"On your left, O'Hanlon!"

The warning had come from one of the captivated young Hunters above. Jessop had grown used to it—they came in throngs to see her best Kohl twice a day. She sighed, dropping to the ground, extending a leg and spiraling, kicking Kohl's legs out from underneath him. She leapt up and flipped, executing a backward somersault through the air and landing on a levitating platform. She extended her blade and waited.

But Kohl did not move. He normally would have leapt to his feet and been midway through his next attack. Had he struck his head too forcefully?

She leapt down from the platform and slowly approached him where he lay still and silent. "Kohl?"

He didn't stir. The audience of young men quieted down, concerned for their friend. She took another step, coming up on his side. "Kohl—"

"*Ah ha!*"

He lurched up and grabbed her around the thighs, wrenching her off her feet. She fell on top of him, and rolled to the side, laughing.

He leapt to his feet, sword ready, and stood above her, laughing at his own ploy. "Admit defeat," he laughed.

Jessop laughed as she rolled to her knees, brushing her sword off on her tunic. "The Hunter cheats!"

He patted her on the shoulder, "Of course—I had to. You kept beating me in front of my friends," he teased, gesturing up to their spectators. Jessop laughed, glancing up to the amused group.

It was obvious to them both that she was the more advanced fighter. Training with her was making Kohl an excellent fighter; he was already better than his friends and working with her gave him practice with a faster, more experienced opponent. But she didn't feel as though she was training him—she was enjoying working with him.

Jessop had become a skilled fighter for all of the grotesque reasons that violence came about in nature. It had been a survival skill and she, living with the most violent of them all, had become most adept at survival. No matter how jovial their sparring sessions were, she did not tell Kohl that with every move she made, she heard Bane's voice correcting it, with every errant foot, she felt Bane's anger. He didn't need to know that. He didn't need to know there were worse things than being reminded of Bane. Like being reminded of the others still in Aranthol. Like being reminded of Jeco.

* * * *

It was unsurprising to Jessop that Hydo Jesuin moved so quietly. He was, after all, the Lord of the Hunters of Infinity. She saw him step out onto the docking bay. She watched as he slowly closed the door to his obsidian Soar-Craft, as he tightened his black vest and glanced about the dimly lit docking zone. There were no engineers or techs on duty at this late hour, and he wouldn't see her at her vantage point, so high above, in the darkest of the few shadows.

With a silent step, she crouched farther out onto the ceiling beam. Like a spider, she kept to the scarce shadows that the remarkably well-lit Glass Blade offered, keeping a hidden eye on the Hunter Lord. She scurried down the dark beam, following him as he began to cross the abandoned docking bay. She wondered why he would return at such a time, to no welcome reception. She wondered where he had been for so long—although she had a vague idea of what that answer might be. The Hunter Lord looked less than pleased—he almost looked afraid, watching his back as he moved.

Which told Jessop all she needed to know.

She leant far over the beam, keeping her narrow eyes on Hydo Jesuin as he stepped into the glass bullet. As the bullet began to travel up the transparent chute, she retracted, ducking back into the safety of the shadows. She studied his slow-approaching gray form. And then he looked up, as if he could sense her.

She wondered if what she had heard about the Hunter Lord was true. His mind was strong—she had felt that much already. Her abilities—the ones she had used to fix the situation with Kohl—they might not work like that on Hydo Jesuin. Not if he was as strong as she had been told. But she would need to rely on more than herself to prevent her situation from unraveling. She closed her eyes and saw Bane's face.

She *needed* to do this. She wouldn't fail—she wouldn't be hurt by him again. She rocked back on her haunches, and with a low hiss, she leapt from the beam, flying through the air—landing silently on the roof of the transparent chute Hydo traveled in, watching him fall to the ground, afraid.

* * * *

Jessop pounded on the silver door for the third time, banging her small hand against the cool metal. She could hear the automated voice announcing her presence quietly on the inside of the room. Nothing happened. Slowly, she let her hand fall from the door. She could return in the morning… or not at all. She turned on her heel, ready to leave, to return to her own quarters. But then she spun back around, facing the door again.

She thought of Hydo, and what tomorrow would bring, and she continued to convince herself that she was making a necessary decision. She was about to turn back, for a third time, when the smooth *shhhh* of the metal door sliding open froze her. Kohl stood in the doorway, running a hand through his loose golden locks. She couldn't help but look him over, as he stood before her in nothing more than breeches. His scarred, muscular form filled up the doorway. His golden eyes readjusting in the light, pulling a confused look across his face as he eyed her up slowly.

"Jessop? It's… it's the middle of the night," he complained.

She knew what she was doing; she just didn't know if she knew *why*. "I… I know. I'm sorry."

He let his hands fall from his tired eyes, from his flaxen hair. She let her gaze travel over his star-shaped scar—but she couldn't look at that. She looked at his body, his strong, broad, scarred body. She looked at the silver lines that disappeared between his muscles. She looked at the hook-shaped marks, the thin whip lines, and the thick, raised scars, longer than her hand. His scars were horrifying, just like hers. But his body was beautiful. She thought about what she was going to achieve, about the decision she was making.

"I… I needed to talk to you," she whispered. She saw a small silver line cutting into the bow of his lip. More scars.

She thought about him, and her, and why she was standing in his doorway at such an hour. And then her eyes fell on his newest scar—the one he got the day she had saved him.

He looked her over, concerned. "Jessop, are you—"

Her hands tucked easily around his face, her fingers messing into his soft tendrils. Her lips found his and he took her in his arms without hesitation or surprise—he had wanted her from the moment he met her.

His hands traveled down her back, rolling over her hips, tucking around her, and with an easy turn, he lifted her into his bedroom. He lowered her feet softly to the ground as the door slid shut behind him. Jessop pushed his strong body back against it. She knew she should leave. She knew this could solve only as many issues as it could create. But for whatever reasons she was there, or should have been there for, even in the darkened room of his quarters she could see the hunger glowing in his amber eyes.

And she wanted him to want her.

She ran her hand over his chest. She could feel his heart in her fingertips.

His lips pulled softly at hers as he tore at her tunic, the material ripping mercilessly under his grip, turning the top into a thin vest. She leaned against the wall and watched him watch her. His fingers ran softly over her lips, her chin, down her neck. He drew his hand across her bare chest pulling her torn tunic to the side. He ran a line down her with his hot fingers, moving from the base of her neck, between her bare breasts, down to her navel, stopping at her waistband.

She had expected him to be… different. He leaned his face back and watched her with dark, confident, eyes. He was hungry for her, but experience had taught him his measured, controlled, movements. She hadn't needed to teach him that satisfaction, like a punishment, was best when drawn out.

He turned her, one arm softly holding her body near him, her back tucked against his chest. With his spare hand, he pulled her long braid out from between their bodies, draping it over her shoulder. He kissed the back of her neck, her sigil, and ran his hand over her tunic-covered back. She rested her hand against the wall. She could feel his fingers at the back of her collar.

She froze under his touch, concerned. "Kohl…"

He immediately stopped. "What is it?"

She thought of her back.

He began to retract. "You don't want…"

She ran a hand over her face. "No, I do. It's just…" She took a deep breath, leaning her body back against his hot chest, running a hand over his strong arm, wondering for the first time how much of her he had seen that first night. She looked over her shoulder, finding his soft golden eyes. "I have scars."

She felt his heavy breath against her shoulder. And then he kissed her neck.

"Who here doesn't?"

* * * *

Jessop had begun to roll away when his strong arm pulled her back, locking her in his grasp. "Where are you going?" His breath was hot against her cheek and she could tell he was smiling.

She turned in his arm, resting her hand against his chest. "I thought you were asleep."

He rested his forehead against hers, shaking his head slightly. His warm hand rested on the curve of her hip, her breast softly tucked against his sternum, his legs wrapped up around hers. "I thought you didn't want this... *me*." He spoke, and Jessop realized it was the first time she had ever heard him sound insecure.

She shrugged against his body. "I thought I didn't either..."

She thought about her night. She held her breath and fixed her stare on one particularly grueling scar on Kohl's chest. And she began to cry. She bolted upright but it took Kohl less than two seconds before he had pulled her into his lap, locking his arms around her, as though he was protecting her from something unknown.

"Jessop, what is it?"

She sobbed heavily, rocking against his chest. "H—Hy—Hydo's back," she cried. The tears came much easier than she had thought.

She felt his stare on her; she could hear his thoughts, trying to understand how she knew that and why it would upset her this much.

"He—*they*—hurt me. I don't want him to hurt me again. Him, Hanson, they *hate* me."

And, under the grip of realization, his hold tightened around her. He brushed her hair out of her face, pulling it away from her wet cheeks. He rocked her back and forth softly in his arms. "You're with me now. I won't let them hurt you again."

"Hanson hates me... he's going to tell Hydo to send me away," she cried, holding on to Kohl tightly. "I don't want to leave you," she whispered against his warm skin.

"You aren't going anywhere," he answered sternly.

She wiped her face on the back of her hand. "Kohl... they're your mentors, I can't have you involved."

"I'm already involved," he answered softly.

She crawled out of his lap, searching for her clothes as she stepped off the bed. Kohl was in front of her in an instant, his broad, naked body blocking her path. His hands locked around her arms. "Where are you going?"

She blinked away her tears, staring up into his amber eyes. "I should just leave now... before they put me back in that pool. They don't want me here, they'll never let me hunt with you, they'll just rake through my mind until they find a way into Aranthol," she explained.

His grip on her tightened, "I would *never* let them do that to you. Not again."

She nodded slowly, brushing her damp cheek against her shoulder. "I'm afraid." She noted the tremor in her voice.

He nodded down at her, lowering his hands until they fell loosely around her exposed back. "Haven't you heard me, Jessop? I've got this. I've got you."

She smiled softly at him, and tilted her head back, offering him her lips. He kissed her deeply, and, eyes closed, she blindly guided him back to the bed.

* * * *

Jessop watched Kohl's back expand and contract under quick breaths. He didn't sleep peacefully and she respected him too much to learn whatever it was he dreamed of that he so feared. She ran her finger slowly over one of the thousand silver lines on his body. She traced the scar up his spine, into his hairline, where she felt the faint ridges of another. She brushed his hair to the side and saw the scar of the Hunter's sigil—identical to her own.

"Hunters need to know pain... they're just scars..."

Bane's voice filled her mind with such ease that it startled her. She pulled her hand back from Kohl's sleeping body and sat upright.

"Hunter Hanson Knell is here." The automated voice from the door just about gave Jessop a heart attack.

She scanned the floor of Kohl's bedroom and grabbed his tunic, pulling it over her head quickly. She didn't have time to dress further as the sliding metal door began to open. She leapt back onto the bed and covered her body with the blanket, roughly hitting Kohl on the arm to wake him.

"Ow—what the—" he began, but quickly turned his tired gaze from her to the doorway, hearing Hanson's entrance.

As Hanson fully entered the bedroom, Kohl pulled at the blankets, covering Jessop's body as much as possible. "Hanson, get out of here!"

Jessop looked from Kohl's desperate attempts to shield her, to the old Hunter who stared at the scene of the room with disdain.

"You've got to be kidding me." He shook his head, kicking at Jessop's torn tunic from its spot on the floor.

"Hanson, get out!" Kohl ordered, crawling off the bed and grabbing his trousers.

The old Hunter crossed his arms, his critical stare travelling over Jessop. "I didn't come here to question your poor decisions, Kohl."

"Hanson—"

"I have plenty of time for that later."

"Hanson, that's—"

"Lord Jesuin was attacked last night."

Kohl froze in the process of getting dressed, a fresh tunic half-tucked into his breeches. Jessop held the old Hunter's severe stare, remaining still.

Kohl looked to Jessop, staring at her with a perplexed gaze, before turning his attention to his mentor. "Hydo? Is he alright?"

Hanson let his arms fall to the side, finally turning his stare from Jessop to Kohl. "He's unconscious, in some sort of sleep from which he cannot wake. There is nothing the medics can do at this stage..."

Jessop shifted in the bed, her long dark mane falling over her shoulder. "Surely you can wake him with Sentio?"

Both men turned to her, the younger with a hopeful look in his amber eyes. But Hanson shook his head slowly. "Not this time. It appears whatever injury our Lord Hunter has endured has trapped him in his own mind, and we are locked out. The Council has yet to find a way in."

Jessop nodded, somewhat surprised by the old Hunter's admission. The great Assembly Council wasn't quite omnipotent after all. She pushed the cruel thought from her mind—she still felt anger from her time in their pool.

"Get dressed and meet in the Assembly room in fifteen minutes," Hanson ordered.

Kohl nodded, "Of course."

Hanson turned for the door but froze, looking over his shoulder. "And bring the girl."

* * * *

Jessop stared at her hands, unmoved from her position in the bed. She played Hanson's words over and over in her mind and wondered why the Assembly Council would want her present. Surely they believed she wouldn't be of any help…

"Jessop…"

She needed to bathe, to clear her mind, and then this would all be easier to address. She pushed the blankets off of her legs and rolled off the bed. She looked for the rest of her clothes.

"Jessop."

She thought of Hydo and wondered if he was with the medic team still, or if he had been moved to his private quarters. She wondered if the Assembly Council had tried to correct his mind as a collective, or one by one. They would have better luck if they tried collectively.

Cold hands around her arms startled her, and she looked up into Kohl's amber eyes. "What?"

"I was talking to you," he explained, letting go of her.

"Sorry."

"I need to ask you something," he continued, his stern voice tight with concern.

She waited. And then she knew what he was about to ask.

"Earlier, you said you knew Hydo was back… *How* did you know he was back?"

Jessop took a deep breath. She thought of their night together, of his mouth on hers, his hands, the way he had given himself over to her.

"I saw him. He was in one of the glass bullets, when I was coming over here," she explained, studying his face for any indication of concern.

He nodded slowly, and then his expression relaxed. "Did you see anything else? Anything suspicious?"

She held his gaze, wondering the depths to his inquiry. His wide eyes gave him away—he was asking her in the same manner he would have asked anyone. He had no insights; he did not push into her mind. She shook her head. "I saw nothing."

"Alright, I wouldn't normally advise this, but I don't think we should tell the Council. I don't want them to have any more reason to persecute you," he explained. Slowly, she nodded, knowing this loyalty was a result of their shared night.

He pulled on her hand, directing her towards the bathing room. "I just don't understand how this could happen—to *Hydo Jesuin*," Kohl spoke as he prepared the shower. "He's one of the most powerful men in Daharia—if not *the* most powerful. What could leave him trapped in such a sleep?"

He pulled his tunic off, turning to face Jessop as he continued. "A sleep so serious that the most experienced of Infinity Hunters can't pull him back..."

Jessop nodded along. "It will be alright, Kohl. He'll be fine."

He stepped into the water. "You don't know that."

Jessop followed in suit, closing her eyes as the hot water cascaded down her bare body. "Yes. I do."

"I really don't like this," he complained.

"What?"

"Whatever or whoever did this to Hydo—he's something the rest of us cannot deal with... something worth being afraid of."

Jessop turned under the water and stared up into his concerned eyes. She ran her hand over his strong jaw and pushed back the wet tendrils of his golden mane. She shook her head. "You don't know that."

He cupped her hand with his, "Yes. I do."

She said nothing, and slowly, his gaze traveled down her body. With his spare hand, he drew his finger across her collarbone, and down between the valley of her breast, touching the intricate woven lines of her scar. She recoiled immediately, letting his hands fall from her.

He looked at her with confusion. "I'm sorry."

She pressed her own hand over the scar, and she could feel her heart. "It's fine. I just don't like people touching it."

CHAPTER 6

Jessop had never seen the Assembly Council members so riled and, from the look on Kohl's face, she wagered he hadn't either. They were pacing, speaking in hushed tones; some seemed aggressive, and others anxious. They were afraid.

The room was different from the last time she had been in it. There were more lights than just the one they had used to interrogate their persons of interest. It was bigger than she had first believed it to be. It drew out narrowly to a back wall made entirely of windows, letting in the red light of day. It took Jessop a long moment to realize what was different about this room than all the others… It was not entirely made of glass. Behind the heavy curtains, the room had slab walls and gray floors. It seemed transparency was not a requirement for the Assembly Councilmen.

And yet, the Councilmen were entirely visible to her. As they walked around, afraid, whispering their concerns, they paid her no attention. She studied their different faces quickly, recognizing many from her first night in the pool. She was unsure when they would notice her presence or how they would respond to it.

Most of the Councilmen were like Hanson and Hydo—grayed and suspicious. They were the same older generation of Hunters, scarred and distrusting of the world around them. Some she recognized for their accomplishments: Urdo Rendo, who killed Elias Rahut, the founder of the Aren, and Balk Tawn, who saved the Eastern Sand's emissary from a raider invasion. Others she knew nothing of. Some were younger than Hydo, Hanson, and Urdo. One in particular, a younger man, stood at the back of the long, gray room. He had dark skin, a shaved head, and eyes more yellow than Kohl's, a kind of golden shade that softly glowed as they traveled slowly across the room. Seeing the glow is what gave those from beyond the Grey away. She forced down a smile, remembering the glowing eyes from her first night. And she immediately knew that he was a man she was meant to know.

She watched him watch the room, and for the second time since she had been in the Glass Blade, the unmistakable feeling of familiarity overcame her. He did not simply look like a people she was so familiar with—the dark skin and golden eyes were trademark characteristics of a tribe well known throughout Aranthol—but he personally felt familiar to her.

She softly let her hand fall on Kohl's arm. "Who's that man over there? With the yellow eyes." She did not add what else she saw about him, that his yellow eyes glowed, mystically bright, like lights. The ability to see the eyes of the tribe's people as they truly were indicated one possessing tribal heritage as well. Somewhere inside her she had Kuroi blood, and she knew enough about Azgul and the Hunters to know that was another secret she would keep close to her chest.

He followed her gaze, quickly looking through the older Hunters. "That's Trax DeHawn, the youngest on the Council. He's Kuroi, the tribe from *beyond* the Grey Mountain."

Jessop turned at his words, pleased to hear the name and know why he felt familiar to her. Mistaking the source of her surprise, Kohl nodded, shrugging, "I know, who would have thought anyone who lived beyond the Grey Mountain would be on the Council."

She turned from him, scanning the long room for Trax DeHawn, who had seemingly disappeared into the group of men. "Who would've thought…"

Suddenly, Kohl was frozen at her side, his hand tightly wrapped around hers with such *affection* that it drew her attention immediately and she had to fight the urge to withdraw from him. She stared up to him, but he was looking across the room, where the Councilmen had been huddled in their group, speaking. She followed his gaze and found that on the other side of the worried, whispering men, there was a small silver platform. It stood about four or five feet off the ground and looked about seven feet long. It reminded Jessop of a medical trolley, although somehow more clinical, colder, as though it carried more dangerous cargo than surgical instruments. And it appeared it did. As the gap in the group widened, Jessop laid eyes on the resting body of Hydo Jesuin.

He was laid out on the silver platform, his Hunter's blade resting over his body as though he were some effigy of a fallen warrior. But he was not dead. She could see the slow rise and fall of his animated breast—Hanson had been right, their Lord was simply trapped in a sleep. As Jessop moved to take a step closer to the crowd, Kohl remained frozen in place.

He stared ahead, his hand tight around her. "I've never seen him like *this.*" Jessop couldn't ignore the cramping in her chest; she felt bad for Kohl. He was angry and upset, and however different he was from the Councilmen, he felt the same as them.

She tugged him forward gently. "It's okay, Kohl. He will be fine." He hesitated, slowly turning his gaze to her.

Softly, he let go of her. "I just need a minute." He walked away from her, heading towards the door. Leaving her with the entire Assembly Council and a handful of younger Hunters.

Hek'tanatoi, Oray-Ha?

The voice pushed into Jessop's mind like a warm stream of welcome waters. She listened to the Kuroi language, and knew, before turning, that it was Trax DeHawn standing behind her, asking in the tongue of the Kuroi how she had come to be so far from home, affectionately calling her Green Eyes.

"I could ask you the same, *Hasen-Ha,*" she answered, turning slowly and looking up into the glowing eyes of the Councilman.

His mouth pulled into a broad smile. "*Hasen-Ha*—Golden eyes. Yes, this is what they would call me there."

She smiled in turn. "And here they call you Trax DeHawn."

He stared at her intently, with the same bewilderment in which she had regarded him.

"You're from beyond the Grey, *Oray-Ha?*"

Jessop shook her head and pictured Koren'da's face—the last Kuroi tribesman she had been close to. She ignored his question. "I have always been fond of your Kuroi tribe."

"You see our eyes as only one from beyond the Grey sees them, *Oray-Ha,* and you yourself have the glowing green of one beyond the Grey. You lie when you say you do not come from where we come from," he whispered, pulling his dark robes tighter around himself. His words were not accusatory, but musing.

"I was once cared for by one of the tribe. He meant a great deal to me." She offered him information, but no answers.

She pushed a thought across his mind. Slowly, Trax DeHawn nodded down at her. *We should speak, later, Oray-Ha.*

But before she could answer him, Kohl had reappeared at her side. "DeHawn," he greeted Trax, extending his arm.

Trax pulled him into a quick embrace, "O'Hanlon."

"I see you have officially met Jessop," he smiled, looking from his Councilman to her.

Trax nodded. "Yes, officially."

"What does the Council think about Hydo? What can *we* do?" Kohl pressed, anxious to somehow help his Lord. Jessop didn't think him wrong for caring, but she couldn't quite reconcile the young man who had pulled her from the Council's pool of torture, and this concerned Hunter beside her, desperate to help, as the same Kohl O'Hanlon.

Everyone and everything comes second to the Lord Hunter, before all else comes Hydo Jesuin. Falco's voice filled her mind and nearly caused her knees to buckle. She remembered all he had said about Hydo, and for every wrong Falco Bane had ever done, about this he seemed most right.

"We think that more discussion is needed—whoever did this is beyond our conception at this time," Trax answered diplomatically, but his deep voice was heard by more than just Kohl and Jessop.

"Whoever did this?" An older man, one Jessop did not recognize, approached, his loud voice drawing the attention of the room. Jessop stood up straighter, feeling the narrow eyes of the old man burning against her as he approached.

"There has only ever been one man capable of touching Lord Jesuin, and here we stand, in the presence of that man's escaped slave!"

He pointed his wrinkled finger at Jessop, with accusation.

"Councilman Bevda, you can't possibly think Jessop—a *woman*—could do this to the Lord?" Kohl queried. She knew he meant her no insult; he used the sexism of the Hunters to advance his defense of her.

She looked Councilman Bevda over slowly. She did not know him for any famous accomplishments, but she had heard his name nonetheless. He was the one who was known simply for being more fanatically loyal to their Lord than the others combined.

"Of course not! But she must have something to do with it! First the Lord takes his leave of us, to research pressing matters, and before he can report back this attack occurs? The first attack within the Blade, the first against the Lord, in over a decade!" Councilman Bevda exclaimed, his voice growing louder with each word.

"Coincidence?" he barked, his loud voice raspy. "I think not!"

Jessop stared deep into the old man's eyes. She could be in his mind in an instant. She could throw him entirely off course, and force him to see reason. He was too weak to fight her. She could do it without anyone even noticing...

"She's brought evil into this sacred place!" he rambled, nearing her slowly, his finger still extended out angrily. She could see in her periphery the other Councilmen and Hunters slowly approaching, listening to their old comrade as he stirred suspicions.

"Councilman Bevda, please, you said it yourself, she couldn't have done this, and only one with the mark could gain access to the Blade," Kohl reasoned, turning his palm out in reference to the F-shaped scar, but the older man wasn't through with his tirade.

"You brought her here, to see our fallen Lord, to let her bask in the damage she helped create."

"Councilman!"

Jessop began to push. She didn't need anyone else hearing any more. It would take her a matter of seconds to fix his opinion of her. She just needed to find the right spot. She could see first his perception of the room, and then herself through his eyes, standing between Trax DeHawn and Kohl. Then she saw the face of unconscious Hydo Jesuin. And then—

Jessop fell from his mind, forcefully expelled. At first, she thought it had been him, the old Councilman, stronger than she had anticipated. It took her a second to recognize the glazed expression that came along with death, as it plastered itself over the old man's face. Councilman Bevda, his jaw still slack with another accusation waiting on his tongue, fell to his knees.

His hand grabbed at his chest. Kohl leapt forward, falling beside the man to help him. "Councilman, what is it? Someone—call for a medic!"

But it was too late. The Councilman's fingers clung to the sigil on his snug leather vest above his heart. He stared up at her with shock, and she stared down at him as he took his last breath. He fell back in Kohl's arms—dead.

Kohl looked up to her, stunned. It had appeared the old man had succumbed to a heart attack. But Jessop knew better. A bad heart couldn't have flung her from his mind. Only one thing could have done that— someone else also using Sentio. She took a step back as the Councilmen and Hunters descended on their fallen comrade, circling him, shocked.

She searched their faces, looking past the few tears, the gaping expressions and wide eyes—searching for whoever had just murdered one of their own in a room full of his allies. All of them may have thought they had just witnessed a heart attack in motion, but she knew better. She knew someone in the room had found her in Bevda's mind, and had kicked her out just in time to kill the old man, to either save her from his accusations… or frame her for his death.

* * * *

The medics lifted the body, with the white sheet tucked tightly around it, onto the silver trolley. Jessop couldn't help but notice the eerie parallels between Bevda and his Lord, as they both lay still as meat on silver platters. She had felt too self-conscious to slip into anyone's minds. As the medics had arrived and futilely attempted to revive the Councilman, she had felt both helpless and alert, studying the face of every man in the room.

"Overcome by grief for his Lord—the stress took his heart," one Councilman guessed, shaking his head solemnly.

"I think it more likely that he was overcome by rage. He didn't want *her* here," his comrade hissed.

Jessop resisted the urge to speak back to them.

"He was right—she has no place here."

"She knows Sentio!"

"But she couldn't have done this—no matter how trained she is, she's still just a woman."

Jessop could feel the tension in her palms, her nails digging into her plump flesh as she held her tongue and braced her mind.

"She did not do this. I was in her mind as Bevda fell." The voice belonged to Trax DeHawn. Jessop twisted around to him, staring up as he calmly addressed his fellow Councilmen.

"Despite whatever doubts there may be surrounding the limited scope of her abilities—she could not have killed him without me seeing her thoughts."

Jessop was shocked. Not at his decision to defend her—but at his willingness to lie for her. The yellow-eyed Hunter had *not* been in her mind when the Councilman fell.

"What were you doing in her mind?" Kohl's angered voice traveled across the room. His eyes were swollen and his fingers curved around his jaw with pensive concern—he was upset.

"What I do is no concern of yours, young Hunter," Trax answered with more aggression than Jessop would have anticipated from him. Her being in his presence, sharing what thoughts and language they had shared, had brought out a side of the Kuroi Hunter that she was certain most of his brethren would never have seen before. The Kuroi were fierce and loyal people—loyal to their own kind before all others. Making them entirely similar to—and entirely different from—the Hunters of Infinity.

"Oh, I see," Urdo Rendo, the renowned Hunter, finally spoke. "O'Hanlon is sleeping with her."

Jessop was certain that if she had lived a different life—if all of these men had not already seen her naked and tortured—she would have been embarrassed. But she had no room for humiliation—simply rage.

"With all due respect, Master Rendo, you have no right—" Kohl began, turning on his Councilman with fiery anger.

"No right? I have no issue with women taking up the sword, but I do have a problem with you not using your better judgment." At his rebuke, the room erupted.

"Better judgment! What—"

"Falco Bane has killed thousands of men and this woman—"

"No better than an escaped pet!"

"*Enough!*"

The bellowing voice of Hanson Knell silenced the room and startled Jessop. She had entirely forgotten his presence there. They all turned to see where he stood, at the back of the room, leaning against the wall near Hydo.

"If Master DeHawn insists she is innocent, she is innocent. We all know my budding, albeit wayward, protégé is sleeping with the girl—but he did *not* bring her into this place, *I* did, and he would not compromise our way of life for her. She is here because she saved his life—and my life too. She is simply not capable of bringing anyone into our fortress, for she does not bear the mark, and who here truly believes our Lord was bested by this girl?"

He pushed off from the wall, taking a step forward to look over Hydo's still face more carefully.

"In fact, she is only here because Hydo deemed it so. Before he succumbed to his attack, he made it clear she would be directly involved in our hunt for Falco Bane. For his fortress is as impenetrable as our own."

At his name, all the men grew tense. Some cursed under their breath, others shook their heads, obviously certain of the futility of the task.

"Who here could overpower Hydo Jesuin?" he asked, approaching the group. "You, Urdo? Or you, Master Wale? How about you, DeHawn—youngest of any Hunter to ever make the Council?"

At her side, Trax shook his head slowly, his yellow eyes glowing as he looked to Hanson. "Not I, Master Knell."

"Nor I, Trax, nor I…" Hanson answered, nodding his head. He continued through the small group, nearing her. She hadn't seen it before, but Hanson had the ability to captivate his colleagues. Every eye rested on him, every ear peeled for an instruction.

"Nor she. However strong she may be, whatever Sentio the enemy has taught this young woman—do any here truly believe she could put Hydo— *our Lord*—into this dark sleep?" He asked, standing right before her.

"This shouldn't just be a question of who *could* do it, but who *would* do it," Kohl interjected, taking his mentor's eyes off of her and onto himself.

"Perhaps. But the fact remains; no one in this room could have done this. Our Lord has said it infinite times—there is, and has only ever been, one strong enough. Falco."

Urdo Rendo stepped forward slowly, his arms crossed. He was an imposing man, standing half a foot taller than the others in the room, with a full gray moustache. "You think Falco Bane was once again inside the Blade?"

Hanson shrugged, his eyes falling once again on her. "No. That doesn't mean his agents haven't infiltrated our fortress."

Jessop shook her head. "There's no way he has agents here. Hydo may have been poisoned, or attacked during his travels only to succumb to his wounds here—but none of the men within the Blade are loyal to Bane."

"And why's that?" Hanson pressed.

"Because I would know about it already."

"Bane may not know we have you here," another Councilman argued.

"I'm sorry—you are?"

The older man pressed his chest out slightly, his head tilted with offence. He had a mane of thick dark hair and small eyes. "Master Renaux."

Jessop turned to him slightly, her hand falling on her hilt. "Underestimating Falco Bane will lead to your death. I'd advise you correct your way of thinking."

At her words, several of the younger hunters actually chuckled, muffling their laughter.

"How dare you, you—"

"She's right," Hanson interjected.

Slowly, the old Hunter turned from her, facing his colleagues. "She's right." He reiterated. "We cannot underestimate Falco. We all saw what tortures this woman has undergone, we all saw her scars."

Jessop shivered, affected by his words for the first time.

"Falco would have had her killed or taken, if he could have done it… and we cannot underestimate his abilities or his knowledge. We must always assume he knows what we know, if not more. It's the only way we will find him, and a way into Aranthol."

"No," Trax DeHawn spoke, looking down to her. "*She* is the only way we will find him and a way into the Shadow City."

CHAPTER 7

Kohl reached for her hand as they brought their impromptu Council meeting to an end. "I was thinking we could go down to the Hollow? Train, talk about all of this," he offered.

Jessop squeezed his hand softly before letting it go. "Actually, I think I'm going to go speak to Trax for a while."

He cocked his head at her, his blond hair loose around his dark eyes. "Why?"

"Why what?"

"Why do you want to speak to him?"

She took a deep breath and tried to control her voice. "Because it's been a long time since I have gotten to speak to a Kuroi tribesman, I'd like to talk with him."

"You know many Kuroi then?"

She pursed her lips, unwilling to play the question game with him. She could trust him with more of the truth than she did the others. "Many Kuroi have thought I derived of their people… Look, we can train together later, Kohl."

He held her tense stare for a long moment before a smile broke across his face. "Of course, sorry. I'm just stressed. Speak with Trax and come find me when you're done."

She smiled back to him. Jessop wasn't one for explaining herself. With abilities such as hers, it tended to not be a requirement.

"I am sorry… for Bevda," she added.

He nodded at her slowly. "I know you are."

And then, with a slow smile, he turned from her and walked out of the room. She thought about his words, unsure about their meaning, but very aware of the uncomfortable feeling they had left her with. Did he suspect something? Did he know Trax was lying—unnecessarily at that, because, despite any intentions, she actually hadn't killed the old Councilman?

"*Oray-Ha.*" Trax's voice pulled her from her thoughts. She turned to see his gleaming yellow eyes staring down at her.

"*Hasen-Ha, huk-hananaimei?*" She asked if he would speak with her, offering a small smile to accompany the use of his native tongue.

"*Baruk,*" he nodded. *Of course.*

"How do you come to know the language of those beyond the Grey?"

"Many in Aranthol speak Kuroi—one in particular who cared for me, and we spoke near exclusively in his tongue," she answered. The account was the truth, even if it wasn't the honest answer.

Hanson narrowed his eyes on her. "I did not see any foreign tongue or Kuroi caregiver in your mind from the night you spent in the pool."

She took a deep breath. "Then you didn't look hard enough."

"Or perhaps you can conceal more than we initially gave you credit for."

Jessop looked from the old Hunter, to Trax, and back to Hanson. "You just said that I am here to help hunt Falco, that I need to be a part of this, that there's no way I attacked your Lord—and within minutes you are making new accusations."

"It's simply an observation," he shrugged.

"Then do me a favor, Lord Knell, and go back to observing me from afar."

* * * *

Trax DeHawn's room was similar to her own and Kohl's, comprised of gray metal and glass. It was slightly bigger. She regretted her words with Hanson immediately. She had heard too many accusations, too many disparaging comments against her sex—a man had died in the middle of berating her. She had run out of patience. He may have told the others to listen to Hydo and include her in the hunt for Falco—but he would keep pushing her, watching her, waiting for her to mess up.

"They won't like us spending time together. They think you're a snake in the grass… and the Council has very strong, very negative feelings, towards the Kuroi. It's common knowledge that there are many of my tribe loyal to Falco Bane."

"Yes. They believe him to be the rightful Infinity Lord, as he who could protect the Blade of Light most ferociously, would be the true Protector of the Blade and the Daharian galaxy…"

His golden eyes trailed over her. "He failed to take Hydo's title… but many of my people remain loyal still."

She crossed her arms over her chest, leaning against his dresser. "But not you?"

He stared at her. "Do I even have to dignify that with an answer?"

"I'm sorry, I'm tense from the day." She shook her head, raising a hand to apologize.

"Then let us speak and you can return to your boy," he answered curtly.

She arched a brow at his words but he was already closing the space between them with his long strides. He stopped short of her, his face not two inches from hers, his breath falling onto her lips, his yellow eyes so close she could see the way they held dancing flames.

Slowly, he raised his hand to her face, and cupped her cheek. His long fingers tucked into her hair, his thumb just touching the corner of her mouth, his massive hand covered half of her head. She raised her own hand, slowly touching his chin, letting her fingers travel slowly over his cheek, stopping just as they grazed his temple.

And then they shared all their thoughts and secrets.

* * * *

Jessop opened her eyes slowly, her lashes fluttering. She couldn't help but smile softly as she let her hand fall from his cheek. He opened his glowing gold eyes and smiled down at her. They now knew all there was to know. She patted his shoulder. "*Sevos, Hasen-Ha*," she thanked him for sharing.

"*Sevos, Oray-Ha*," he nodded down to her, finally lifting his large hand from her face.

She stood up a little straighter, stretching her back. "How long have we been?"

"Several hours at least," he answered, watching her intently.

"I need to go. Kohl will be wanting to see me," she explained.

Trax smiled down at her. "Ah yes, the boy."

Jessop crossed her arms, "Do you take issue with him?"

"Of course not—he's a good Hunter, he has a kind heart. I'm actually quite fond of him," Trax answered.

"Then what is it?"

He shrugged. "He *is* just a boy."

She understood his meaning… and knew it was time to leave. "I need to go, but we will speak again soon, my friend."

She turned from him and took a step towards the door. As she began her exit she felt him grab her hand, gently stopping her.

"You could stay, *Oray-Ha*," he offered, his voice soft and low.

She turned to him. "You have been in my mind for hours now... You know I am already in love."

He smiled with a slight shrug of his shoulders. "It was worth a shot."

She squeezed his hand. "Thank you for sharing all you have shared with me, but I need to go now."

He let her hand go and nodded slowly, escorting her to the door. "The offer is always there," he smiled down to her as the door slowly slid to the side.

"Good night, *Hasen-Ha*," she smiled, and left him standing in the doorway.

* * * *

"Did you enjoy speaking with Trax?" Kohl asked, stepping aside to let her into his quarters.

"Very much so." She smiled, walking past him. "I feel most at ease with the Kuroi." She turned and sat on his bed, offering him a small smile along with the truth.

"You've never mentioned it," he pointed out, crossing his arms as he leaned against the wall.

Jessop studied his expression, his furrowed brow and warm eyes. Was he suspicious—or was he just trying to learn more about her? Had she been wrong in assuming he was so different from the man who trained him? She could search his mind, but she thought back to the night in the bathing room, when she had removed his memory of her abilities, and resisted the urge to rummage through his thoughts. She felt different towards him... as though searching his thoughts, after how close they had become, would be a more intimate betrayal.

"We haven't spoken about everything with one another," she said.

"You know the Council has strong feelings towards the Kuroi—and those who align with them," he spoke, and his dislike for her decision to spend time with Trax became more apparent.

"Obviously not all of them—Trax is on the Council, isn't he?"

Kohl shrugged, staring down at her. "He is indeed. He leads all missions that take us beyond the Grey, and he coordinates with the Kuroi tribes to ensure our safe passage around the Mountain—his presence on the Council is very beneficial to the Infinity Hunters."

Jessop slowly stood from the bed. "What are you saying? The only reason he is on the Council is to deal with his people? You don't trust him."

At her words, his entire demeanor changed. He shook his head, running a hand through his golden locks. "No... I don't know what I'm saying. I'm voicing old, long-forgotten rumors."

Jessop nodded slowly. She didn't like how fickle Kohl was in his disposition, alternating jealousy and accusation with kindness and support so rapidly. What had seemed like an impressive navigation of distinct emotions now seemed like simple indecision. "You're jealous of my time with him."

"No... and yes. I dislike his interest in you. You two locked eyes and then he was in your mind, and you speak his language, and spent the remainder of the day together," he explained, looking embarrassed.

Jessop knew she needed to put his mind at ease. If her time with Trax derailed all the work she had put into building a relationship with Kohl—she would be most upset. She took his hand and squeezed it tightly.

"You know many of the Kuroi are loyal to Falco Bane. Many work within the walls of his abode—and one in particular, a man named Koren'da, went to great lengths to care for me. He, along with others, believed that I am of Kuroi descent. So he helped me whenever he could. I cared for him and Trax reminded me of him and others I once knew. That is all."

She couldn't think of Koren'da without also thinking of Jeco. She closed her eyes and forced the faces down into the depths of her mind. She took a slow breath, looking up at him only when it felt safe; when she knew her memories were neatly tucked away.

Kohl nodded slowly. "That explains your interest in him... not his interest in you."

Jessop leaned closer to him. "Is it so bad that one of the Councilmen doesn't hate me as the others do?"

His face softened. "Of course not. Forgive me?" He raised his hand and pressed her palm into his cheek, as if offering his mind to her. But Jessop knew it wasn't his mind he offered willingly, but his heart.

She thought of Trax's offer and all the Kuroi Hunter had shared with her. He was handsome, smart, and trustworthy, but he was *not* Kohl. She knew the inherent link she had to the Kuroi was not the same, and would never be the same, as the relationship forged with the young Hunter who felt as though he owed her his life.

Even if he would never be Kuroi, Kohl was attached to her, possessive already of her body, *truly* good to her. And in thinking it, she couldn't help but also think of what she had told Trax—that she was already a woman in love.

"There's nothing to forgive."

* * * *

She woke before him, pushing herself up slowly from the bed. She looked over the thick strips of marred flesh across his chest, shoulders, and stomach. Nearly every inch of him was scarred, and it reminded her so greatly of Falco that she couldn't help but stare. She knew that if she slipped into his mind, particularly in this moment of sleep where he was so vulnerable, she could see his history of pain… but regardless of her curiosity, she couldn't do that to him.

The thought of caring for him in such a way bothered her so greatly that she leapt from the bed. She couldn't *sincerely* have feelings for him—she wasn't capable of it. It took her a minute to dress in silence, another to fix her dark hair back into a plait. As soon as she was dressed, she escaped the small room, winding her way down the glass hall. She knew where she needed to go.

* * * *

Jessop could hear her name through the automated voice as it announced her presence. She waited in the hall a moment longer before the door finally slid open. He stood there, staring down at her with an arched brow, his arms crossed over his chest, wearing his black uniform.

She glanced down the hall to her side before looking back to him. "Can I come in?"

"If you must," Hanson grunted, slowly stepping to the side and allowing her entrance. She walked past him quickly but didn't roam far into his quarters. The room was quite large, but similar in style to Kohl's.

She spiraled on her heel and locked eyes with the old Hunter. "We need to stop this… this feud we have. You care for Kohl, and so do I. You have plans for Falco Bane—so do I. We will get more done working together than apart."

Hanson leaned against the wall, his arms still crossed over his chest. "I agree with you… but I don't trust you."

"Isn't it enough that Kohl trusts me?" She knew the answer to her own question, but thought it worth reminding the old man that others he had faith in trusted her… then she thought of her earlier conversation with Kohl and his dislike of her time spent with Trax DeHawn. Maybe he didn't trust her implicitly, maybe only to an extent…

"Absolutely not. You've got him bewitched," he scoffed, jerking his chin at her like she was something untouchable.

She crossed her own arms, leaning away from him. "What do I have to do to prove myself to you? You said it yourself, I couldn't touch your Lord Jesuin, your own mentee has faith in me, your colleague Master DeHawn trusts me, I saved your life, and I let you all ravage my mind, freely, searching for whatever you wished—and you found nothing. What else can I do?"

"*Nothing!*"

Jessop was unsure if she had heard the old man correctly, he had spat the answer out with such vehement frustration.

"What?"

He took a step towards her, lowering his arm, narrowing his cobalt gaze. "I said nothing. You can't do anything. I know all you have said is true, I know you saved my life, I know you had nothing to do with Hydo or Bevda—but that doesn't mean I trust you. The Blade is no place for a woman."

"Let me hunt for you then. Let me show you that I would risk my life to stay here."

He stared at her with clear apprehension. "You can't be serious?"

"Of course I'm being serious. Send me out on a hunt—you've seen me train in the Hollow. You've seen me in real action. I can help you; I can help the Blade, especially during this time with Hydo. Plus, if I die out there, that will fix all your problems concerning me."

"No," he answered immediately… but Jessop could see his mind turning. "The other Councilmen would never stand for it. A female Infinity Hunter? It's never been done."

"Then don't title me as one of your Hunters of Infinity… send me with Kohl, his comrades, all of your Councilmen's mentees—you know I have seen more fights than most of those I bested in the Hollow. Call me their assistant, their guide, their comrade for all I care. Just let me help. Let me show you what I know to be true—that given the chance I can change *everything* here for the better."

He eyed her over with his blue gaze. "You speak Kuroi fluently?"

"Yes, fluently," she nodded, unsure where he was going with the line of questioning.

"Then I give you the title of translator. Trax DeHawn has mentioned for some time there are too many missions past the Grey for just him alone to handle, and he has another mission coming up soon. Report to him in the morning as his official assistant translator, you'll travel with him."

Jessop didn't know how to react. In many ways, this was the perfect opportunity; Hanson had conceded. But she knew it was also a test, pairing the least trusted guest in the Blade with a representative of the least trusted tribe. She also knew Kohl would not be happy about it.

"A translator?"

"A translator… who will wear a tracking device, paired to none other than he who has such faith in you—my protégé, Hunter O'Hanlon, who will mission alongside you."

Jessop nodded slowly, watching the bemused expression cross over the old man's face. He knew this was the perfect opportunity for the Council—they could test her loyalty, and if she died, it was of no great loss to them. He was agreeing to *her* idea, so why wasn't she happy about it?

Afraid of upsetting Kohl by spending more time with Trax? She pushed the niggling voice out of her head, focusing on Hanson.

"What kind of tracking device?"

"Does it matter?"

She had seen tracking devices before that were quite invasive and she had a feeling that if the Council had the opportunity to hurt her just a little, they would take it. "I don't want Kohl hurt on my behalf."

"He can take the pain," Hanson said, shrugging his shoulder nonchalantly.

"Is that what you told yourself when you scarred his entire body?"

As soon as she had said the word *body*, the back of Hanson's hand had struck her. She was astounded by the lightning speed with which he had hit her, more so than the strength of his strike. She tasted the metallic flavor of blood and raised the back of her hand to her lip, gingerly patting it.

She could kill him where he stood.

Instead, she slowly brought her hand away, looking at the kiss of blood she had left on it. His reaction had confirmed her suspicion. She raised her head to him and forced down her urge to retaliate. She had gotten what she had come for—she would be on the next mission and she would gain the trust of the Council. "I'll report to Trax DeHawn in the morning then."

His eyes were wide and he stared at her with shock, his lips parted. Despite all his vitriol, it was clear he was not accustomed to striking women. Slowly, she turned from him, making her way for the door.

"I—I'm sorry," he called after her, his raspy voice sounding small.

Jessop pictured the scars. The layers of marred flesh. Scar atop scar, where blades and whips and maces and fire had carved him up in an attempt to kill him. She saw his body… and she saw Falco's too.

"I'm not the one you have to apologize to."

CHAPTER 8

"Wait, wait... so, you're going to be an Infinity Hunter?" Kohl interrupted, waking quickly, looking at her with excitement from where he sat upright in his bed.

"No... I am going to be a translator," she clarified, running his bed sheets through her fingers.

"Translator is just a fancy word to mean you're a hunter beyond the Grey, just like Tra..." but Kohl let his voice trail off, his sentence unfinished.

"I know. It wasn't my idea, Kohl. Hanson needs to test my loyalty to the Blade, and we all know there is no way I could be called an Infinity Hunter, so 'translator' it is... under Trax."

He nodded slowly. "And I have to have a tracking device installed, so it can be paired with yours?"

Jessop reached across the bed and rested her hand on his knee. "You don't have to do it."

Slowly, he rested his hand on top of hers. He took a deep breath and she watched him carefully. His gold locks were loose around his tan skin; his dark eyes seemed thoughtful as he took in all that she had said.

"Let's get them installed in the morning."

"Really?"

He looked up to her. "Really. This is the only way to prove your loyalty, so let's do it."

She let a small smile pull at her lips. "Thank you, Kohl."

He began to smile at her—but froze. His gaze homed in on her mouth and slowly he reached over and touched her full lip. As his finger grazed her, she retracted, feeling the sting of Hanson's strike.

"What happened?" His tone was instantly different, deep and angered.

"Nothing," she shrugged, raising her own hand to her lip.

"Don't lie to me, Jessop. Not after everything."

His voice was filled with an urgency that surprised her. She had never seen this part of him—and she was beginning to think there were more layers to Kohl O'Hanlon than she had ever thought possible upon their first meeting.

She dropped her gaze, staring at her hands. "Hanson."

Kohl was off the bed in an instant, reaching for his clothes. "Hanson? *My* Hanson? Struck you?"

Jessop followed suit, jumping from the bed. "Calm down, Kohl. I made a comment to him…"

"I have had it with him, with his disrespect and now his abuse."

"I said something—"

"He shows no regard for me, for those I care for!"

He fastened his trousers and fiddled with his tunic, desperate to dress and deaf to her voice. So she reached to his face and locked her hands onto his cheeks, forcing into his mind the picture of her with Hanson.

"*I don't want Kohl hurt on my behalf.*"

"*He can take the pain.*"

"*Is that what you told yourself when you scarred his entire body?*"

Jessop lowered her hands from Kohl's face, letting them rest on his broad shoulders. She waited for him to open his eyes, her heart racing. She had used her abilities with him… She had no idea how he would react to her, or why she had even used them. Or perhaps, that was a lie… She did know why, she had done it because some part of her *needed* to know the truth; she needed to know how he would react to her, the real her.

Slowly, he opened his hazel eyes and stared down to her. "What *else* can you do?" His voice gave him away—low, full of betrayal and accusation. He was enraged. She knew the emotion well.

"A lot. I don't want to lie to you, Kohl, because I care for you, truly. But I need to know I can trust you to not tell the others. If they knew what I was capable of… they would kill me."

He leapt back from her, his eyes dark. "Trust you? I have defended you since your arrival and you have lied to me."

"Kohl—"

"I sided with you…"

"Kohl, please—"

"I held you in my arms. I trained with you."

Jessop took a step towards him but he moved out of her reach.

"I made love to you," he whispered, his voice thick with disgust.

"Kohl!"

Unable to listen to any more, Jessop threw her arm out, her fingers outstretched, her palm aimed at Kohl's chest. His knees buckled as she forced him to fall before her. He stared up at her but she didn't need him to speak—so she did not permit him to.

She touched his face slowly, ignoring the horror in his eyes. "I should have never let it come this far, for us… I should have never felt anything for you. But I did… I do. I wanted you to know, to see me for *me*. But it appears I can't do that."

She stroked his cheek and brushed his hair back, as he stared up at her, paralyzed by her abilities.

"I'm sorry… for everything, but I can't have you remembering any of this." He made muffled sounds against his closed lips, his wide eyes staring at her with fear, and he twitched in her grasp, as though all his might was being used to break free from his own body—his skin a cage, trapping him inside by her will.

She closed her eyes, ignoring his resistance, and made her way into his mind easily. She navigated the memories, the older ones she had seen before, and the newer ones, which included images of her body, her scarred back and sleeping face. And she moved faster and faster, ignoring all the thoughts of love and lust he had for her, of hope for their future. She sped through it all, until she found them standing in his room, just one-minute prior.

And just like that—she destroyed the memory. She could feel the single tear as it trickled down her face.

* * * *

She wiped the tear away and helped Kohl to his feet, and within an instant, he had regained a sense of reality. He looked disoriented for a moment, as if he did not know why he was standing up.

He stared down at her with a look of peculiarity. "Wh—what was I saying?"

"You were saying Hanson shows no regard for you… but Kohl, I said something to him." Jessop grabbed his hand in hers, taking a slow breath. "I told him I didn't want you in pain, he said you could take it, and I made a comment about him finding that out through scarring your body, the way it is…"

His eyes widened. "You said *what*?"

"I'm sorry. But I *know*. I know he did all of this," she spoke, pointing to his chest. "I know he gave you all these scars." She had thought on it enough; she had spent many years figuring it out. The scars, the vague excuses—even Falco, who leapt at any opportunity to disparage the Council, had remained tight-lipped about the marks. She knew they must have been the product of more than violence, but of betrayal, and ritual.

He shook his head at her. "You know *nothing.*"

"Tell me I'm wrong," she challenged sadly, wishing she were.

He took a step back from her. "This was a rite of passage. This is what it means to be a Hunter, a protector of Daharia. *This,*" he growled, running a hand over his scarred flesh, "is why we don't train women."

Jessop felt her breath catch. She could see the regret in his eyes immediately—he had seen her scars, he had heard of her past. He knew what torture she too had survived. She had found it so easy to bond with the disfigured Hunter—they were a pair of survivors who shared a silent understanding. Apparently she had been wrong to think that.

"Jessop, I'm sorry," he began, but she raised a hand to silence him.

She didn't want to hear his apology—she had taken enough from him, his body, his anger, and his memories. She took a deep breath and forced herself to look him in the eye.

"The scars… the fighting, the Sentio, the torture. If I were capable of *more*, if I were stronger, would it scare you? Would you hate me for being afraid to show anyone?"

His shoulders slumped over slowly; he was upset with himself for inferring she hadn't survived equal tortures, that she couldn't survive his pain. "No, of course not."

She nodded, her lips tightening before she could say anything more. She turned, making her way for the door, comforted by the fact that she wasn't the only liar in the room.

* * * *

"I can't pretend I'm not somewhat pleased," Trax smiled, his glowing eyes looking her over in the morning light. She had slept in her own chambers that night, not wishing to be so near Kohl after everything that had transpired between them. She had woken early and found Trax eating breakfast in his chambers. He invited her to join, and despite initially resisting, Jessop found that she was seated at his small desk sipping a warm beverage.

"It's a test. They don't trust me. Or you, for that matter," she reminded him, watching him from over the lip of her cup.

"Of course it is. They never have. They never will." He shrugged, pulling a stool out from around the corner and sitting at the desk opposite her. "I became a Hunter many years ago, and before Hydo first began training Falco Bane, before Hanson first began working with Kohl, before either showed any promise, the Council believed me to be the future of the Glass Blade. That changed of course, as Falco Bane's abilities grew. And as Falco's grew, so did Kohl's, and so did their rivalry."

Jessop nodded along, listening as Trax told her a new perspective on an old story. She sipped her hot drink and leaned back in her chair, captivated by the Kuroi's glowing eyes and deep voice.

"While their rivalry lasted, Kohl's ability to keep up with Falco did not. Falco surpassed the boy, and then me, and then his own mentor, our Lord Jesuin. It was not lost on him that he had become the greatest of us all—that he had become untouchable. He would have been destined to protect the Blade of Light.

"It was around then that the trips began. The Lord Jesuin had frequented beyond the Grey many times with his young protégé. Hydo said it was rougher terrain, better training for the future Protector of Daharia and the Blade of Light—but whispers traveled, and we knew the real reasons. Hydo was hopeful Falco would become more like him." Trax sighed.

"What the Lord didn't foresee was that during these trips to my homeland, while the Kuroi grew weary of him and his maltreatment of my people, they saw the strength of his mentee, young Falco. You know his charisma, his power over all those he comes across. It did not take long for able bodied tribesmen to promise themselves to his path, to his future leadership of the Blade."

Jessop put her cup down on the table slowly. "This is a part of the story I know well. The Kuroi have historically disliked the leadership of the Infinity Hunters."

"For good reasons. While the Hunters were known for taking power and keeping the realm safe, they treated the land beyond the Grey as a playpen. They hunted our people, tortured us for insights into the powers we drew from the mountain, they feared our wild nature and bloodline of power. But the Hunters have always been the law… and while they had stopped the hunts and torture, and had even begun to train a few of us, myself included, it wasn't until one captivating young student began talks of a different future, that the Kuroi did really believe a change was coming."

Jessop knew what Trax said to be true; she knew it all very well. She pictured Falco in her mind. He was as Trax described... beyond charismatic, and more than intimidating. He spoke and people listened, and any who didn't knew without question that the gray-eyed Hunter was more powerful than any who had come before him. She had felt his power, even without his touch; his was an ability that you could sense just by being near him.

"And I was here... hearing whispers of a coming coup, trapped between those who had raised and trained me, and those who were my blood, my family."

Jessop nodded slowly, leaning closer as Trax revealed more of his past to her, in a way that they hadn't done when they first met. Thought sharing, with Sentio, was like watching flickering images; you had to concentrate to get a sense on one's retired emotions. The difference between the process and speaking were quite literally the difference between being shown and being told.

"I can imagine that put you in an impossible position," she sympathized, reaching once again for her cup, remembering where she was in her own life at the time of these events. Remembering the others—remembering seeing Falco appear from the sky.

Trax cocked his head down at her, watching her with his bright eyes. "Not really."

Jessop stood. "I'm sorry, I didn't mean to question your loyalty."

Trax followed suit, slowly rising from his stool. "My loyalty is beyond question."

"Then let us not mess up this partnership, let me show the Council where *my* loyalty lies," Jessop declared, placing her cup down before crossing her arms.

"Agreed. Go find your boy. The sooner your tracking devices are fitted, the sooner we can plan your first hunt."

"Trax—don't call him that," Jessup ordered, sick of the epithet.

He raised his hands innocently, but a wicked smile pulled at his face. "That scar on his face, the one shaped like a star. Did he ever tell you how he got that?"

Jessop sighed. "Falco Bane has a scar that travels through his brow, over his eye-lid, over his cheek, and stops just before his mouth. He nearly lost an eye to the blade of his former friend, Kohl O'Hanlon, whom he scarred on the face as well," she summarized the story she had been told many times before.

"Indeed. Your *boy* got a slice of Bane—but just a slice. Falco carved the crooked scar into Kohl with deliberation. He had offered his childhood friend a position at his side, and upon rejecting Falco, the two fought. Falco bested him, without surprise, and carved the star into his face as a reminder. Were Kohl ever to travel to a place where the stars shone in the sky, such as Aranthol, or beyond the Grey, Falco would find and kill him."

Jessop didn't move, nor did she drop his golden stare. To her surprise, she *hadn't* known those details before. She had figured the extent to which the twisted scar resembled a star in the sky was coincidence. She hadn't heard the backstory.

She cleared her throat softly. "And has he ever traveled outside of Azgul, where there are stars in the dark sky?"

Trax slowly shook his head. *No.*

"Then he shouldn't come with us on any hunt beyond the Grey," she argued.

"No, he shouldn't. Yet, his master has bound him to you, paired with a tracking device so that you must be near him, and easily found, at all times, and you are bound to me, who will surely be sent beyond the Grey very soon."

Jessop couldn't argue any of those facts. "Falco wouldn't risk exposure just to see through on an old threat," she explained. Falco was tactful in his vengeance.

"No, probably not... but there are many who would see it through on his behalf. We know there is a bounty on the boy."

Jessop couldn't believe this. "Hanson Knell knows this and he has chosen him to be paired to me still. He sends his favored student out to face a very real threat of death."

"The Council knows that where the boy goes, potential links to Falco Bane will arise. If Bane comes for Kohl, you won't be needed any more."

"They would risk their own Hunter's life? And for what? There's not an Infinity Hunter alive who can take Bane in a fight."

"Many believe you would not let harm come to the boy."

Jessop stepped back, overwhelmed by this new information. "And do they not think he would do the same for me? That he would not throw himself between myself and Bane?"

She needed to think this through and prevent any excess of harm coming to Kohl. She hated Hanson Knell, and vowed he would one day pay for endangering his protégé's life in so many ways.

The Kuroi shrugged. "We all know you're the superior fighter. If Falco is lured out, the Council believes you would defend Kohl to the very end."

Jessop looked up to the Kuroi Hunter. "They think I love him too much to let him die."

Trax looked her over with a critical eye. "Don't you?"

She turned from him, knowing she needed to find Kohl. "Your Council doesn't know *anything* about me."

As she stepped out his door, she heard him speak. "Tell me something I don't know."

CHAPTER 9

Jessop met Kohl at his chambers, just as he had finished bathing. She sat at the foot of his bed as he dressed, waiting for him to speak to her. She had asked him, as soon as she had stepped foot in the room, if what Trax had said was true. Although, she knew in her heart it was, she needed to hear it from him.

"I missed you last night," he half-smiled to her, pulling his damp hair back with a tie.

She let her gaze drop. She had slept with him for many reasons... but things had changed. She knew more than she had before, their situation had changed when she had seen his reaction to her abilities, when he had once again forced her to erase memories she had no right erasing... forced her to hide parts of herself she did not wish to keep hidden from him.

"Did Falco threaten to kill you if you ever trespassed under the stars?" She asked again, ignoring his sentiment.

His large shoulders heaved with a slow breath. "He's threatened to kill lots of people."

"*Kohl.*"

He threw his hands out. "Yes, okay? Yeah, he did."

"And yet, Hanson sends you out to defy Falco Bane and risk your life."

Slowly, he sat beside her on the bed. "We all knew this day would come. What good is an Infinity Hunter if I can't travel beyond our city to protect and enforce the laws of Azgul? Falco has a bounty on my head, and most likely yours too; if the Council is set on finding him, sending us out into territory loyal to him is a surefire way of doing it."

Jessop couldn't tear her eyes away from the star-shaped scar, but all she saw were Falco's hands. "There are other ways. They are using us as bait, Kohl."

He chuckled at her words, an attempt to lighten the moment. "They send me, who trained alongside Falco, with Trax DeHawn, the youngest Council member and greatest Hunter in training *before* Falco, and you— the one none of us can best in the Hollow. Not to mention whoever else will accompany us... If any group can deal with Falco Bane, I think it's ours," he smiled.

She could feel his hand on her back, slowly rubbing the tight muscles around her spine. She stood up. She didn't have time for his optimism.

"You're not stupid enough to truly believe that, are you? No 'group' can deal with Falco Bane. There's a reason he still lives and breathes, Kohl. He's the best there ever was."

He stared at her with gritted teeth, frustrated. "What would you have us do, Jessop? It's our duty to find him, to fight him. I'm just being positive."

She ran her hands over her face, equally agitated. She didn't know what was wrong with her... everything was coming together, exactly as she had planned it. Yet, she was seemingly coming to pieces.

Why? Because you care for him? Because you've grown a conscience in his presence?

"Well, don't be. Be realistic. It's much more helpful."

Her voice was louder than she intended it to be, overpowering him and the voices in her head. She didn't want Kohl to die.

He looked at her with wide eyes, his mouth pulled in a hopeful, soft smile. "This is what I'm trained for," he reminded her.

"You're talking about Falco Bane. I don't mean it to be cruel, but you have *nothing* on him, no one does," she explained, shaking her head at him apologetically.

He took her hand in his, and brought it to his lips. "I have you, don't I?" He smiled, his breath warm against her fingertips.

She still needed him to get the tracking device installed... So she didn't voice what she was silently thinking, but she saw his face in her mind, the one filled with horror upon seeing her true abilities.

No, you don't.

* * * *

The tracking devices were approximately four inches long and two inches wide, made of lightweight steel. Central to the steel panel was a small screen, and a series of buttons. Around the periphery of the rectangular device there were small holes—where the screws would go.

"You're going to fix these to our forearms?" Jessop asked the medic, staring down at the devices on the silver tray beside the white sheet-covered bed her and Kohl sat on.

The medic, a man with a head of thick dark hair whose name she had already forgotten, continued to make notes on his glass clipboard. "Indeed," he mumbled, his eyes still fixed on his board.

She hadn't been back to the medics' floor since her first day in the Blade, when they had healed Kohl. This was the first time she had gone past their reception room, to one of the many brilliantly white, clinically clean examination rooms. While the rooms were not made of transparent materials, unlike the rest of the Blade, nearly all of the equipment inside them was. The bed they sat on would appear entirely see-through were it not for the sterile white sheet tucked into its corners, and the machines appeared as though they were forged from crystals and glass. Even the small stool on which the medic sat appeared entirely clear.

It gave Jessop a headache just to sit there.

"And the reason you can't anesthetize is… ?" Kohl pressed, staring at the tracking devices with the same displeased look that Jessop wore.

"Orders from above," the medic answered, his eyes still firmly locked on his clipboard.

Jessop sighed heavily, and looked to Kohl. She knew the procedure would hurt—and she needed him to undergo it. "Are you good?"

He offered her a small smile. "I've survived worse."

Jessop stared at the bare flesh on her left forearm. She wanted it on top of her arm, where the skin was rougher, as opposed to the softer underside. The medic finally lowered his clipboard and glanced over her and Kohl. A small smile finally crossed his face as he reached into a glass drawer and pulled out a fresh pair of gloves. "Who first?"

"Me," Jessop and Kohl both answered in unison.

The medic looked from Jessop to Kohl and back to her, his dark eyes darting over them with amusement. "Ladies first," he quipped, wheeling his stool towards Jessop.

Jessop took a deep breath and leaned forward, resting her arm on the side table, beside the tray that held the devices. The medic reached into a glass cabinet beside them and rummaged around until he finally pulled out an electric drill. He pressed on the drill's power button and it whirred readily. He smiled up to her, placing the drill on the table. "This will only hurt for a moment."

He grabbed a small canister off of the tray and sprayed the top of Jessop's forearm. "Antiseptic," he explained, ensuring the area was clean. She could feel Kohl's fingers curling around her free hand. The medic then picked up the silver-tracking device and slowly lowered it onto the top of her forearm. She saw, sitting on one side of the silver tray, a pile of tiny silver screws, and the tracking device had six holes along its perimeter. Which meant she would have six screws drilled into her bare flesh.

You can handle this.

As the medic reached for the first screw, Kohl began to question him. "Who ordered you to not use anesthesia? Because they must have been mistaken. This constitutes *torture*."

"There was no mistake, Hunter O'Hanlon, and you both have the option to not participate," the medic answered dully, lowering the screw into a corner hole of the silver device. Jessop could feel its dull tip pressing into her flesh. She took a slow, deep breath as the medic placed the drill bit into the groove of the screw.

She could sense Kohl's nerves overcoming him, his hand tightening around her as he pressed on. "This is ridiculous—there's no reason you can't do this painlessly."

At his words, the medic glanced up from his power tool to Kohl. He looked the Hunter over for a second, and nodded. "No, there's not."

And then he pressed the power button.

* * * *

Jessop couldn't stop shaking. It hadn't taken long, but it had been an excruciating torture. Her arm rattled against the table as the medic began to spray her with another round of antiseptic. He held out some gauze. "To wipe the blood away."

She couldn't reach for it. She couldn't move. Tears and blood had dried against her skin. She wanted to kill the man. Kohl grabbed the gauze from him and gingerly dabbed at her arm, softly touching the metal plate. Bruises were already formed around the perimeter of her bulging flesh, where the metal pressed unnaturally into her.

She couldn't let Kohl undergo this—not the way she had. She knew someone could have helped her with that pain and she was determined to help Kohl. He had held on to her, the whole time, telling her she would be fine. She would protect him, even if it meant giving too much of herself away again. Even if it meant wiping a few more memories… She couldn't let him suffer the torment.

The medic pulled the side table away from her, forcing her to retract her arm. She could kill him, with a simple slip into his mind—she could end his life. She glared at him as he wheeled himself and the side table to the space directly in front of Kohl. "You're up, Hunter."

Kohl shook his head at the medic as he placed his forearm onto the table. "I'll see you lose your job over this. You and whoever gave you these orders."

The medic nodded slowly. "If you say so," he mumbled, spraying the top of Kohl's arm. Jessop rested her injured arm in her lap, and with her free hand she grabbed onto Kohl's shoulder. The medic had placed the silver device onto his forearm. She took a deep breath and closed her eyes.

She was in. She was swimming amongst the sea of images, memories, thoughts, and dreams. She needed to find the moment they were living, she needed to disconnect Kohl from his experience, separate his brain from his body and block his pain receptors. She knew it was possible, as it had been done to her before, but she had never had much reason to do it for another.

She could feel his body shaking under her touch, and she could hear his muffled agony. She worked faster, until she found what appeared to be streams of red light, travelling around his mind, seemingly setting fire to his conscience. Those had to be the messages of pain, being created in real time, travelling to and from his bleeding forearm to his suffering mind.

She took a deep breath and concentrated on the red streams of light. She envisioned herself grabbing them, containing them, and squashing them under her mighty grasp. It was different from tearing at a memory—it was more abstract, as no memory was yet formed. But as she envisioned attacking the streaks of red light, Kohl grew quieter, his shaking subdued.

When she was certain she had the pain receptors isolated, she opened her eyes. The medic was drilling the last screw into Kohl's arm. She watched as the blood trailed down his forearm, staining his hands. She tilted her head, and found Kohl staring at her with his large hazel eyes, glossy from tears. He was no longer in pain—and he knew she was the reason for it.

* * * *

The medic stared up at her from his stool, his narrow eyes darkening with suspicion. He flicked his gaze from Kohl to her, to Kohl's bloodied arm, to her again. "What did *you* do?" His thin voice was tight between his pursed lips.

"What?" Kohl asked, looking down to the medic, who continued to stare at her.

"He stopped feeling it—*what* did you do, woman?" The medic yelled, leaping up from his seat and leaning into Jessop. She moved with a speed he could have never anticipated, kicking him in the chest so roughly that he practically flipped over his swiveling seat. She hurdled forward, sure to keep her freshly wounded arm close to her chest. She crouched on top of the man. Her feet on either side of his chest, her face right before his, her good hand resting on his sweaty cheek. He stared at her with a horrified gaze.

"Jessop!" Kohl yelled, but he didn't touch her.

She was in the medic's mind in an instant. "You will only remember installing the tracking devices, and that we were both in excruciating pain. Nothing else. When I get off of you, you will instruct us on how to use the devices. And you will never do anything like this again," she ordered him aloud as she worked through his mind, snipping at his memories and tweaking his sadistic desires.

When she was through making the necessary changes she stood, backing away from the man slowly before taking her seat once again beside Kohl. She could feel his stare boring into her, but she kept her gaze on the medic. He stood, seemingly confused but unbothered. He corrected his stool, sat, and began to clean Kohl's arm.

"If you press this command button, the screen will come on and you will be able to communicate to one another with visual feed. This button is simply audio and this one brings up the geo-location of the other on a map. The most important thing is that you're never more than one mile apart, otherwise, a small detonator will go off and it's bye-bye arm," he explained, his voice flat and dull.

He pressed one of the buttons, and the screens lit up on both her and Kohl's arms. He pressed it again, and the screen went black. He said nothing further and he did not look at her again as he limply stood, turned, and walked out the door.

As soon as they were alone, she leapt off the white-sheeted bed. "I don't want to hear it, Kohl. Yes, I can do more than you know, and I can get in people's heads, and I got in yours to make sure you weren't in pain—because I couldn't stand it!"

She took a step back, bumping into the swivel stool as he stood. He moved the stool, his hazel eyes locked on her.

"I couldn't let you suffer, not like that, not because of me, so if you want to be mad, be mad, but you either accept it or—"

Before she could say anything further, he had pulled her into a tight embrace. She felt his mouth against her neck, his strong arms firmly grasping her, his warm breath as he exhaled deeply. "Thank you, Jessop." And she relaxed in his arms.

She hugged him back. Had the circumstances made him more receptive to her abilities? Could he, possibly, handle the truth?

"This all makes more sense," he spoke, his lips moving against her skin. "Now, I can explain to the Council what they have been sensing. You can show them your abilities, and we can fix all of this," he offered. He was still holding her tight.

It was a sharp pang of realization, a tightening around her heart... He still couldn't keep the truth about her a secret from his mentors. Whether he learnt in anger or with gratitude, he was loyal first, and always, to the Council.

She continued to hold him as she raised her hand to the back of his neck. She continued to hold him as she worked through his mind, erasing, once again, the truth about her.

* * * *

Jessop held her arm against her chest as they walked the glass halls, leaving the medical wing behind them. She was in pain, but not simply because of her arm. She didn't know why she kept hoping he could know the truth about her and be able to keep it to himself. She didn't know if it was to assuage her own guilt for sleeping with him or for lying to him, or if it was because some part of her truly had cared for him, the option which made her feel guiltiest of all... She knew that in the time she had been in the Blade, Kohl O'Hanlon had gone from being her means to an end, to something *more*. She just didn't know what... or how.

"I can't believe I don't remember the pain," Kohl mused, shaking his head down at her.

"Yeah, shock can do weird things to a person," she shrugged, keeping her eyes forward.

"I'm going to find out who did this, Jessop, I promise. Whoever made us undergo that, with that psychopath, will have some serious explaining to do." Jessop couldn't believe the unwavering faith Kohl had in his mentor. It almost made it difficult for her to spell it out for him.

"Hanson did this, Kohl. Hydo is knocked out, Trax wouldn't, the other Council members had nothing to do with the tracking device idea—it was Hanson."

Kohl stopped abruptly and extended his good arm, touching her shoulder to yield her. "You can't just say things like that, Jessop. I know you two don't like one another, but you don't know he did this."

She shrugged his hand off, walking past him. "I'm not in the mood for this, Kohl."

He was in her way in an instant, blocking her path. "Well, I wasn't in the mood to have my arm scarred up for you, but hey, these are the things we do for one another."

"I didn't force you to do that, Kohl, and I didn't ask Hanson to pair us or to send you on any mission. Open your eyes, it was your damn mentor," she snapped back, raising her voice to match his.

He threw his good arm out in the air with frustration, his loud voice echoing off the glass and reverberating around them. "Hanson wouldn't have some medic try to torture me."

"Are you kidding me? He is using you as bait for Falco Bane, he nearly killed you in some sadistic Hunter ritual that no one talks about, and he's the one who forced you to get this damn device put in, in the first place!"

His dark eyes locked on her with anger. "Stop talking about the ritual—you think you know something about it because it messed up Falco, but you don't! You don't know anything about the ritual, about Hunters, or me, for that matter."

She was furious. She sidestepped him and he got in her way, again and again. She had never seen him so mad and she had never been so mad because of him. She didn't know if it was the pain, the torture they had undergone, or their histories of suffering that made them incapable of changing their loyalties and thoughts. She didn't know if it was their feelings for one another, which she could only deny for so much longer, or her hatred of Hanson Knell for what he had done to him… She felt as though she knew nothing save one singular fact. "I know your loyalty blinds you, Kohl O'Hanlon!"

He looked her over with ridicule and doubt. "What could someone like you ever know about loyalty?"

She resisted every urge she had to hurt him, every urge she had to once again show him the truth. "Just wait and see."

CHAPTER 10

Her forearm was the color of a plum, and quite possibly the worst bruise she had ever donned. She stared down at the metal contraption, screwed into her flesh, and grimaced. She was as upset about the idea of being linked to Kohl as she was about being disfigured in the first place. Gingerly, she dabbed the damp cloth against the marred flesh, touching at the freshly wounded skin with the soapy cloth until she felt as though she had sufficiently cleaned it.

The device was disgusting. She felt as though she were somehow part human, part machine, and fully deformed. It wasn't her vanity that plagued her, for she had a body covered with scars. It was feeling like her independence, and her privacy, had been permanently impaired. She had a part of herself bound to Kohl; he could reach her at any time, whenever he pleased, and see her and know her whereabouts. It was as though they had married her off to him.

She stared down at the small screen. It made her feel on edge, as though she were anticipating his face to appear on her arm at any given moment. She cursed the Council under her breath and forced her gaze away. She studied her reflection in the mirror, her face becoming clearer as the steam from the washing stall slowly dissipated. Her long dark mane was still damp, hanging in long vines around her small face. Her dark, wet lashes framed her large green eyes. Her nose seemed slightly bruised, and her full lips curled tightly around a curse she hissed in Hanson's name.

She couldn't quite put into words the extent to which she hated the old Hunter. He had done nothing but train and torment Kohl for all the younger man's life. She thought of her life in the Blade, and how vastly different it was compared to her years in Aranthol. She had her reasons for seeking out the Hunters of Infinity, but they did not know all that she knew, all that she was capable of, all that she thought of them. Women were not trained to be Hunters, women were not meant to know Sentio, and she didn't come so far only to be killed by the Council for disclosing her true self to them.

She would continue with the Council, and Hanson, as she had with Kohl and Trax. She would win over their trust, she would prove herself to them, and with time, they would become more receptive towards the possibility of her true nature. She wouldn't hide forever, but she knew, thanks to Kohl's reactions, that it was too soon still. She fixed her tunic, forcing her gaze away from the hideous tracking device. She knew she needed to go speak with him. Their relationship had, admittedly, gotten out of her hands. She hadn't remained in control with him, and while sleeping with him had secured her a position within his life, it had also opened doors she was not prepared to walk through. Doors she would *never* be prepared to walk through.

She knew the love that resided within her... And she knew how controlled she would always have to be around Kohl O'Hanlon because of it.

* * * *

Jessop stumbled back, quick to guard her forearm from further injury. She had collided with Kohl, both of them having turned the corner of the corridor too quickly. She held her arm to her chest protectively, watching as he hissed in pain, assessing his own forearm.

"Sorry, I was actually coming to find you," she said, glancing over the scarlet flesh surrounding his device.

He slowly lowered his arm. "Same."

She forced a small smile as they stood in silence. She knew she needed to repair their relationship... she just didn't know how to go about it. She had taken so much from him, and he had disappointed her so greatly, but worst of all—she had let herself *care*. She had made herself vulnerable to disappointment. She cared about his negative reaction to her true self; she cared about manipulating his mind again and again... She didn't know how to properly care for him, and she didn't know how to *stop* caring entirely.

"The Assembly Council has called a meeting, so I came to get you," he explained.

She nodded slowly. She had expected this. Their tracking devices had been fitted, it was time for her loyalties to be put to the test. They were going to be sent on a hunt. She looked Kohl over slowly, from his dark eyes, to his twisted scars, to his tied back mane of golden hair. And she felt fearful. She didn't want him to fall prey to Falco. There were many things she could do—but stopping Falco from killing his former friend was not one she was most certain of.

"They are going to send us on a hunt, they just need to tell us formally," he added, staring at her as he spoke.

She couldn't do anything right by Kohl O'Hanlon; she couldn't feel or proceed with him any differently. She could never give him what he wanted; the future he envisioned was not one where a warrior, such as herself, stood by his side. He yearned for a wife, a gracious, childbearing woman who lived to love him. He deserved such a life. He may have loved her strength, but he hadn't understood it was the same strength which she used to build walls up around her. She couldn't offer him a future, nor honesty... the least she could do was attempt to ensure his safety.

"Jessop, are you even listening to me?"

His voice pulled her back, and she found his hand resting on her shoulder. She looked over his scarred fingers, the way they curled around her skin with such tenderness. She followed a slender, silver scar down his hand, and over his wrist. Another, one that appeared to be from a burn, curled over his forearm before disappearing into the messy red skin that still smarted from his tracking device. She looked up into his hazel eyes and before he could say anything else, she kissed him.

She draped her unharmed arm against his chest, her fingers turning around his neck, and she kissed him deeply. He kissed her back with relief, wrapping a hand around her back and pulling her near. She could fall so easily into him again. She kissed him because she needed to, and because she knew she should never do it again.

Finally, she pulled away. "I'm sorry, Kohl," she whispered, stepping back from him.

He took her hand in his, creating a bridge of wounded flesh and metal between them. "It was just a fight. We both said things we didn't mean."

She smiled up at him, knowing that once again, he had failed to understand her.

* * * *

Jessop recognized the two young Hunters from training time in the Hollow. Daro Mesa had short dark hair and a small, strong body. He was an expert knife fighter and Jessop had fought him once before, when she had first begun training with Kohl. Teck Fay was tall, slender, and silent. He wore a robe, keeping his face constantly half-concealed, his mouth always shut. He had ink etched into his face, forming two sinewy trees, one under each eye. Jessop knew less about him, but had seen him fight once before. He was of the Oren, a north Azguli tribe, known for their mysticism. She had encountered one Oren before in her time, and it had not ended well.

They stood on the other side of Kohl, forming a line that ended with her, in front of the Assembly Council. Shrouded in darkness, she held Trax's stare, and he hers. The silence was dull to her, the darkness had no intended effect, and she had grown weary of the pomp and presumptiveness of the Council. Yet, she had to show respect, and if that meant standing, in darkness and silence, for unknown periods of time, then so be it.

She wondered briefly if the others knew who was standing beside them. She and Kohl had entered together, the other two already present. Had they known it was her and Kohl who joined them? Could they see her, as she saw them, secretly keen-sighted in darkness? She had questions... many of them. They came to her day by day, and winning over the trust of the Council ensured she was one step closer to receiving answers.

"You will go beyond the Grey."

The voice belonged to Hanson, which was unsurprising to Jessop. He had orchestrated the entire plan. She was simply thankful he had decided to speak finally.

"News has come to us that Okton Radon has been taken over by a band of raiders. You will go and relieve the weigh station with those who stand beside you, with Master DeHawn leading the way."

She held a tight smile as Trax dipped his head, acknowledging his role in the plan. They all knew of Okton Radon. The weigh station was one of thousands, a place for travelers, Hunters, and tradesmen to check in as they entered the city, to make their presence known to local government. Jessop also knew that many places with weigh stations, like Okton Radon, had no protection or security from raiders. Towns such as those relied on one or two sentries and traveler compliance. If any real danger ever presented itself, they called for their overarching authority, the Infinity Hunters, to help.

"You will leave at first light and meet Master DeHawn in the south docking bay. Pack light, provisions will be provided."

As Hanson finished speaking, the room began to brighten. Jessop closed her eyes to avoid the visual adjustment. Blinking, she was startled to find Trax standing right before her.

"Master DeHawn," she smiled, touching her chest softly and catching her breath.

"I've been briefed on recent... changes," he spoke, his eyes locked on her forearm.

"Yes, I will be travelling as an extra translator," she spoke, her voice tight through pursed lips.

He smiled at her, his glowing eyes looking her over. "You'll make waves—everyone will speak of the most dangerous translator in the world, the fluent Kuroi speaker who fights with Falco Bane's blade."

Her smile disappeared at his sentiment. "I wouldn't want that…"

"Then perhaps you should leave the recognizable blade here?" Kohl's voice startled her as greatly as Trax had. He took the place by her side, standing somewhat between her and Trax.

"Never." She shook her head at him.

"Why's that?"

She shrugged. "This blade cut down my enemies and cleared a path for a new life for me. I carry it with me as a daily reminder," she explained.

"Of your strength?"

"No, of Falco Bane's."

At her answer, Kohl narrowed his gaze at her. He didn't understand what she had meant.

"Yes, a token of your achievement—overcoming the greatest of fighters, Bane, to be here," Trax explained for her, looking from her to Kohl. Kohl nodded, trying to understand.

Kohl took her hand in his, staring at her with his usual thoughtfulness. "He's not the greatest *anything*, he's the worst." He squeezed her hand tightly and then let go, offering her a supportive smile before turning and leaving her with Trax.

Trax looked her over slowly, nodding. "We won't let anything happen to him, *Oray-Ha*."

She held his gaze, but remained silent. She had said too much already, had shared too much. She brought her sore arm to her chest and cradled it softly. She could do nothing more to prepare for their trip aside from wait.

"I'll see you tomorrow, *Oray-Ha*," Trax spoke, offering a small smile as he rested his hand on her shoulder.

"Tomorrow, *Hasen-Ha*."

* * * *

That night, Jessop couldn't sleep. She watched Kohl as he slumbered sweetly in her bed. He had come to her chambers late in the night, hoping for nothing more than to sleep beside her. He had fallen into his slumber with ease, and she sat beside him, tormented. His blond hair was loose, fanning out behind his large head. Even in the darkened room, she could make out his scars, painted across his broad and muscular chest, his stomach and arms.

She knew that somewhere, trapped in the confines of his pretty head, was the memory of the day he got the scars. She had seen glimpses of that day through Falco Bane, and it had been torturous to witness. She was quite certain that if she found Kohl's memories of the torture, Hanson Knell wouldn't live to see another red sky. She did not understand the practice... In her mind, what the Council did to their Hunters was nothing short of a betrayal. She thought of Falco Bane, and of his mentor, Hydo Jesuin. And then she crawled out of bed.

* * * *

She had entered the minds of the two sentries standing watch with swiftness and ease, convincing them they had never seen her trespass. That was all it had taken to stand before the unconscious body of the great Lord Hydo. She had kept all of the lights out, enjoying the darkness of the room, languishing in the blackened space where no red sky entered.

He looked older to her, in his incapacitated state. His eyelids fluttered, as though his internal self was fighting to escape the prison made of his own body. His hands seemed restful though, his wearied fingers interlocked over his chest, loosely holding onto his Hunter's blade. His skin was like Hanson's, weather-beaten, worn and leathery, but she could still make out the scars. He too had suffered their ritual once, long ago.

She readjusted her footing, inching slightly closer to the old Lord. He had been the one to welcome her into the Blade, had instructed her to assist in the hunt for Falco, and then had disappeared, first from the Blade, and then from reality. He, the original strongest, the longest standing Lord to have ever ruled, was trapped in his own mind. Slowly, silently, Jessop raised her hand. Her fingertips hovered above his face, in the darkness, for the longest moment. Finally, she rested her hand against his large cheek. The skin felt plump and waxy to her, like worn rubber. Without thinking, she manipulated his flesh with her fingertips, and found his face to be quite malleable.

She exhaled deeply, and closed her eyes. The supposed greatest of Lords lay vulnerable in her capable hands. She brought her other hand up and cupped the other side of his face, and the sensation of holding him, when he was in such a state, overcame her. She leaned over his large body and rested her forehead against his, slowly tilting his head back and forth, fighting the urge to enter his mind and see some of what Hanson and the other Council members had seen. Somewhere, trapped inside his thick skull, was everything anyone could ever want to know about the Blade of Light. She thought of Falco and how everyone feared his abilities, how all who had seen this unnatural sleep their Lord lay in were wrought with fear.

She stroked his temples softly and resisted entering his mind. She did not need to see anything more. It was of too great a risk this night. She simply needed to see him, and know that he would be here, just so, upon her return. She saw Kohl's scars and his unwavering obedience, and she thought of Falco, and how his greatest scars were the ones no one could see. She thought of Jeco, and his place in Daharia. She thought of Hanson and of Hydo, She took a deep breath and smiled, whispering, "I'm going to fix everything."

* * * *

"Where'd you go?" Kohl asked, his voice muffled by the gray pillow. Jessop pulled her tunic loose in the dark, quietly undressing.

She stepped out of her boots and pushed them silently against the wall. "Nowhere. Go back to sleep."

But he sat up instead, his messy hair standing on end. She kneeled on the bed and crawled past him, taking her place on his side.

"Have you ever fought him?"

Jessop blinked in the dull darkness, confused by Kohl's odd question. "Fought who?"

"*Him,*" he answered, lying back down beside her.

"Yes. I have fought Falco," she nodded, feeling him turn to face her.

"You're the best fighter I've ever seen, at least since him. Hanson thinks so too," he whispered, settling in beside her.

"I know." Her words were a whisper of honesty, not arrogance, in Kohl's presence; her abilities were not currently a point of pride.

"You really think he'll come after me on this hunt?"

"I don't know."

"I'm... not afraid of him," he whispered, his voice disappearing into a yawn.

"I know," Jessop nodded.

He was already snoring, once again passed out peacefully beside her. She turned over and studied his young face. She touched his cheek and marveled at how different his flesh felt under her fingertips. She traced the outline of the scar on his cheek, whispering quietly to him. "But you should be."

CHAPTER 11

The red sky seemed unusually still, almost dull, and the air thick. She tried hard to recall the last time she had breathed air outside of the Blade. The white-uniformed technicians were packing the Soar-Craft. As usual, all of them had ignored her upon her arrival. She had shown up early enough to walk out to the supernatural entrance of the docking zone, to look out onto the Red City. Were one approaching from the sky, they would see nothing but reflective glass, but her view from inside was quite different. The mystical barrier that concealed the entrance into the Blade showed a red city through what looked like thick, warped lenses. The few Soar-Craft that had passed, the Levi-Hubs, the handful of travelers—they looked blurry and abstract. But it was better than nothing. There was not much activity in the morning hours of the red city. Azguli were not early risers.

"*Hei, Oray-Ha*," the familiar voice greeted her. She listened to his footsteps, and soon he stood beside her.

"Good morning to you, too, Trax," she greeted him, keeping her eyes forward.

They stood in silence, each taking in the morning view, and the mission ahead of them. She felt at ease with the Kuroi Councilman, as she always had with his people before him. She felt as though she didn't need to hide quite the same way she typically did.

"We should be ready to leave soon," he spoke, breaking the still silence between them.

She nodded. Soon, they would be travelling back beyond the Grey, taking Kohl to a desert land of darkened sky and stars. She closed her eyes and saw his face, and felt afraid. It was a sickening feeling, one she had not truly experienced in years. She couldn't quite explain it, the tension in her stomach. It was as close to fear as she could remember the sensation feeling like—she truly didn't want him to get hurt.

"We will keep him safe, *Oray-Ha*," Trax repeated, knowing her mind. She turned to him. "He is in more danger than the rest of us."

At her words, Trax laughed. A broad smile cracked his face. His glowing yellow eyes squinted down at her as his bellowing chuckle echoed around them before disappearing down the dark docking zone.

"What?" she asked, defensively crossing her arms over her chest.

He fought his chortle, touching his chest as his smile faded. "You don't truly think that anyone here is in more danger than *you*, do you?"

Jessop turned away from him, looking down the dark bay, before suddenly whipping around to face Trax. "Relative to all of *our* abilities," she whispered, leaning closer into the tall, dark Hunter. "Relative to all of *our* secrets, I suppose I would say we are all in pretty equal positions."

* * * *

He softly tugged on her hand as he spoke. "You left early this morning."

She studied his hazel eyes, watching the way he watched her. She saw how he had begun to study her face for signs of deceit—he was losing his trust in her. She couldn't blame him—she would feel the same if she were losing key parts of her memory of their time together. She couldn't maintain the relationship with him that she had begun, but she couldn't push him away either. He needed to be near her at all times, for his own protection… and hers.

She squeezed his hand tightly with hers. "Nerves."

"Jessop… stop worrying about me," he smiled, his eyes softening.

She shook her head at him, silent. She couldn't simply stop. While she couldn't make sense of her feelings most days, she knew she felt responsible for him. Maybe more than that… She couldn't help but feel a deep desire to keep him alive for more reasons than just self-preservation and necessity. She knew she seemed a selfish woman, in every sense of the word, but she had to act for the greater good of them all.

She closed her eyes and saw the gray gaze she had long ago grown so accustomed to. If she seemed to be selfish then so be it—she had a mission. As she had told Hydo, she *would* fix everything.

"Please, just remain near me during this trip," she pleaded, looking up to him. He looked as though he was about to protest, but something in her stare convinced him otherwise.

"It's not like I have much of a choice," he smiled, waving his device-rigged arm about. She smiled at him, lowering his hand gently.

He leaned down to kiss her, but in the corner of her eye she caught Trax's stare—and she pulled away. Kohl said nothing though, his attention caught by the sudden appearance of Daro Mesa and Teck Fay, the two other Hunters accompanying them on the trip to Okton Radon. Jessop had little interest in Daro Mesa. He was a good fighter but he possessed no intrigue. Teck Fay was a different story. She leaned away from Kohl to get a better view of the tall Oren tribesman with the blue inked trees on his face.

She caught his stare, from under the dark hood of his cape, and it took everything she had to not enter his mind. The Oren people were a dangerous sort, comprised of mystics and mages. They could cast images and curse trespassers; they traveled in shadows and spoke in many rare and ancient languages. Everyone knew of them but few knew them personally, as their tribe kept to themselves. Jessop had never heard of one becoming a Hunter, but the opportunity to be near one of the Oren was a rare one indeed. She had only ever encountered one other desert mage, and he had left her badly scarred, but that was from a long time ago—before the refinement of her abilities.

She did not fear Teck, or his people. She was quite interested in seeing the extent of his abilities. As if on cue, she felt a small prodding against her mind. The sensation was as though her head were too full of thought, and she realized it was the Oren. She held his gaze as he attempted to enter her mind—and she closed it off to him. She was too interested in learning more about him to bother feigning ineptitude and granting him access to her private thoughts. She knew he would also say nothing; he wouldn't admit an attempt to invade her mind, not in front of Kohl. She felt him, pushing at her, straining against her fortified walls of Sentio—and she was almost disappointed when he surrendered.

She saw the perplexed look in his dark eyes; she watched the way his blue inked trees moved as he squinted at her. And she smiled. He was the first Oren she had encountered personally since the one who had marked her back, and she was glad to know where the tribe of mystics fell in the hierarchy of abilities after all this time. Like countless others, just below her.

"What is it?" Kohl's voice pulled her gaze back to him. He was watching her smile, a confused look on his face.

"Nothing." She shook her head, and kissed him on the cheek.

* * * *

Trax waited at the bottom of the metal ramp, herding them onto the Soar-Craft impatiently, distracted by a techie ranting at him about landing procedures. Jessop ducked her head as she entered the giant steel ship—one of the largest she had ever traveled in. The Soar-Craft was nothing like Hanson Knell's death trap, or any other small personal vehicle. It was an enormous iron ovoid, lined with standard canvassed passenger seats, air vents, and various switches and panel boards. Everywhere she looked, colorful loose wires stuck precariously out of the steel grates. She walked across the metal flooring and took a seat near the front of the ship, quickly buckling herself in. She did not like flying.

As she glanced up, she was amused to see the Oren hunter taking the seat opposite her, staring at her pensively. She smiled at him confidently, causing him to lean over from his seat towards her. "We need to talk, Lady Hunter."

His whispered voice was low and raspy, and from the closer proximity she could see that his eyes were entirely dark blue, with no shades in the iris or pupil to be seen. Dark blue, like the inked trees beneath them. She continued to smile, mesmerized by the Oren, pleased to know after so many years that her abilities surpassed the desert mages.

"All in good time, Teck Fay," she nodded.

"But we—"

The ink-eyed Hunter looked as though he might protest, but before he could, Kohl had sat down beside her. He looked from Teck, to her, and back to Teck. "Good of you to join us, Fay."

He leaned back in his seat, sighing heavily. "We all know why the Council is sending me beyond the Grey with you."

Trax brushed past them, making his way to the pilot's seat. "Not all of us Kuroi fear your Oren kind," he remarked, sitting heavily in his seat. Jessop knew the Kuroi shunned the mysticism of the Oren, believing them to be a dark and cursed people. The Kuroi drew their power from the lands; the Oren drew theirs from their own blood, which carried with it the power born from the dark deeds of their ancestors. She looked from Teck, whose hood covered his downturned face, to Trax, who stared at the younger Hunter with glowing eyes.

"*Sekha'nasey-do, Hasen-Ha?*" She asked Trax if he feared him, and watched his golden gaze turn from the Oren Hunter to her.

"*Nei. Huk'hana dore' sekhan'na Oren,* and for good reason, too, *Oray-Ha,*" he answered, telling her that while he did not fear the younger Hunter, others had good reason to.

She nodded slowly. Trax was chosen for this mission because he led all missions beyond the Grey, she was sent to have her loyalties tested, Kohl was sent to bait Falco Bane, and Teck Fay was sent because his kind were feared in the region. Slowly, she turned her gaze to Daro Mesa. He was sitting further back, reclined in his seat with his feet on the back of the chair in front of him. He had a knife in his hands that he cleaned his nails with, one of many on his person, Jessop imagined. She watched him closely, his relaxed demeanor and disinterest in the group now garnering her attention. Perhaps, she had been wrong to think nothing of him earlier. It seemed they had all been sent on this mission for a reason, handpicked by Hanson Knell. All of their purposes had been made clear, except for the knife expert's…

She crossed her arms and rested back in her seat. She recalled fighting him in the Hollow—she had won, but she remembered how his knife wielding skills had impressed her. She couldn't recall anything spectacular about him though; he wasn't of a tribe she knew of, nor did he have a mentor—

Bevda.

The realization struck her so suddenly she jolted upright in her seat. Daro Mesa's mentor had been Councilman Bevda—who everyone believed had died at her hands. Had it not been for Trax's sudden testimony to the contrary, who knew what would have become of her. She pictured the old man, wildly raving and desperately loyal to Hydo, yelling at her before he fell to the ground, grasping for life as death struck him suddenly.

When she looked up, Daro Mesa's eyes were on her. She felt confident that she knew why the knife-expert had been sent on the mission. Should she fail to prove her loyalty to the Blade, he would be the one ordered to kill her. Who better than the protégé of a man whose death was widely believed to be her fault? She felt on edge, staring back at the Hunter, watching him roll his knife in his hands with expert ease, holding his stare as he boldly smiled at her.

* * * *

Kohl was asleep. She watched his fluttering eyelashes and listened to the whistling breaths escaping his pursed lips, and found herself to be, once again, amazed by him. He was traveling further from his home than he had ever traveled before, to a region dominated by those loyal to Falco Bane, who would exact their leader's vengeance against Kohl in a heartbeat. And yet, he slept peacefully.

They had been flying for some several hours, Trax silently piloting the ship, Teck Fay seemingly meditating under his cloak, and Daro Mesa looking out a window, one blade permanently spinning around his fingers. Jessop unlatched her seatbelt and slowly sat up, careful to not disturb Kohl. She stepped past Teck Fay, who remained motionless, and carefully sidled around Trax's seat, before lowering herself into the co-pilot chair.

Trax kept his eyes trained on the sky, but he entered her mind quickly, and she his.

This morning before we left, you knew I was in more danger than usual, didn't you?

Trax glanced over to her, flicking his golden gaze over her. *You have realized Daro Mesa's purpose, then, Oray-Ha?*

"I won't be intimidated," she spoke, accidentally voicing her thought. He looked between her and the sky.

"Then don't be, Oray-Ha," he said, looking ahead. "Don't be."

* * * *

Jessop crouched down, perched on her haunches, and struck quickly. Just like that, his blade was in her hands, and she twirled it around her fingers in the same impressive manner he did. He jolted, surprised by her. His wide eyes watched his blade spiraling around her fingers, clearly wanting his weapon back.

She smiled up at him, keeping the knife spinning, as she rocked on the balls of her feet. "I didn't kill your mentor."

His lip twitched, his dark eyes following her hand as she rolled his blade. "If that's your story."

She rotated the knife, spinning it in the opposite direction. He wasn't the only one who could wield a small blade. "That's the truth."

He leaned forward, resting his arm on his knee. "You know we have all been told not to trust you."

She nodded slowly, unsurprised by his words, but somewhat taken aback by his candor. "Well, how many of you have been instructed to kill me should I fail to prove myself to Hanson?"

His mouth tightened, his dark eyes trained on her. He didn't seem as bothered by the fact that she had guessed his true purpose as she had anticipated him to be. He exhaled a loud breath. "Can I have my knife back?"

Jessop flipped the blade in her hand, and offered him the hilt. She didn't fear Daro Mesa, she didn't fear Teck Fay or Hanson Knell, or the raiders in

Okton Radon. Her greatest fears were currently surrounding the sleeping blond Hunter behind her. Slowly, Daro took the knife from her.

"Why are you even here?" he asked, turning the blade over in his hand, like a comforting habit.

She took a deep breath and rested her elbows on her knees. "I am here, Daro Mesa, because I love someone very much. I had metal bolts drilled into my flesh because I love someone very much, and I am contending with veiled threats and contingency plans for my demise because I love someone very much."

She watched as his eyes glanced over her forearm—they all knew about the tracking device. Her words seemed to have some impact on him, his dark eyes softening. He stopped twirling his blade and looked at her with an earnest expression.

"He is our brother—we love him too," he spoke, his voice low and certain.

Jessop half-smiled at his words, rising up slowly. "No, Daro Mesa, I don't think you do." She took a step back and shot him one last look, extending her finger at him in warning. "And keep your knives to yourself."

* * * *

They hadn't passed another Soar-Craft in hours, and as the sky began to darken Jessop couldn't help but feel as excited as she was concerned. She would be beyond the Grey, in Kuroi territory, and even if the mission was intended to be short, and she was supposed to simply translate and protect Kohl, it would still be better than sitting in the Blade amongst Councilmen who plotted against her.

"We've been together for some time now." Kohl's tired voice startled Jessop and she looked down to see his hazel eyes watching her from beneath long, fluttering eyelashes.

"I thought you were asleep," she answered, studying the star-shaped scar on his cheek. He offered her a tired smile. She felt his fingers running over her hand, past her wrist, and abruptly halting at her tracking device.

"You've undergone such pain for me," he spoke, his voice so quiet she almost couldn't hear it over the droning of the Soar-Craft engine.

She turned her arm, feeling the pang of guilt. "I'm fairly certain you underwent that pain for me."

"You didn't have to stay... at the Blade, I mean. You could have left. You stayed despite what they did to you, to hunt Falco and find a way into Aranthol with us... You didn't have to be with me, or let me love you, or deal with Hanson and all of *this*," he continued, rolling his hand around to gesture to the world around them.

Jessop shifted uncomfortably in her seat. "Please stop, Kohl."

"I had a dream about you... You saved me, just like the first time we met," he spoke, stretching out slowly.

She watched his large body twist into comfort, trying hard to not think of the first day they met, and the bloody wound he had suffered. She wouldn't let him get hurt like that again. She held his hand tightly. "I would always save you."

He relaxed his body and breathed heavily, his easy, sleepy smile playing on his face as he rested his head back in his seat. He looked at her with his warm eyes and she wished he were still sleeping.

"I would save you, too, you know? If you ever needed it, if it ever comes to that, I would save you, too."

She didn't know why, but she could feel tears building up inside her, and she fought them back with all her might. She nodded at him, ignoring the stinging pain in her eyes and the tightening of her throat. "I know you would."

She leaned over and kissed his forehead. It was part of what she feared most... that he would die trying to save her. When the truth was, Jessop had never truly needed saving in all her adult life.

CHAPTER 12

She watched Kohl, sitting beside Trax in the cockpit, staring into the dark sky. She felt at ease in the dark, knowing that she could see better than all of the men she traveled with, barring perhaps Trax. The Kuroi were built for the darkness; they had evolved to live under the stars, and under the stars they still lived, either in the towns beyond the Grey, or in the Shadow City of Aranthol. She could hear the slight clipping sound of metal as it hooked around calloused flesh—Daro Mesa's spinning knife. She could hear the low, nearly silent breathing of the meditating Teck Fay. And she could feel the way Kohl's heart raced in his chest.

But nothing from Trax.

He made no noises; his breaths were silent, his mind calm. He was like her in all of these ways—all of the tricks of the Kuroi that she had learnt. They disappeared in the shadows, and she knew that if Okton Radon had fallen to foreign raiders, she and Trax could deal with them easily. Kohl, the mystic, and the knife-expert would all be unnecessary distractions. She wished she could order them to stay in the Soar-Craft, to simply let her and Trax go on without them—but she knew that they would never allow it. This wasn't a mission team assembled for efficiency—they were all sent to serve a purpose. And Jessop knew that if she left, she wouldn't be by Kohl's side, where she needed to be in order to keep him safe. Not to mention, the devices that bound them to one another prevented any rogue missioning.

She sighed, running her hand over her long braid, staring into the dark sky between Kohl and Trax. She wondered if the Council was right, if Kohl's presence would bait Falco. It wouldn't be like him to show up in the middle of Okton Radon just for Kohl.

She turned in her seat, eyeing the mystic, Teck Fay. She wasn't sure if he had slept at all during the trip; he had been still and silent since speaking to her briefly upon boarding. She looked him over, a perfectly motionless robed figure. "I've only ever met one Oren before," she spoke, leaning forward in her seat.

Slowly, the robed head turned in her direction. "This surprises me. My kind does not know of one of your kind."

She smiled at his words. He was a smart Hunter. "The one of your kind I met did not live very long. And I'm just human, Hunter Fay."

He inclined his robed head at her. "Not quite.

"The infamous female fighter, only person to ever escape Falco Bane," Daro Mesa spoke up, his voice filled with false amazement as he joined their conversation from his spot behind Teck.

"I'm not the only one," she denied, turning to him and watching his spiraling blade.

He stopped spinning his blade as he fixed his gaze on her. "Yes, you are. Falco has killed hundreds upon thousands. He has destroyed entire cities. He has enlisted an army of the most dangerous kind in Daharia, and everywhere he goes he leaves nothing but shadows in his wake."

She forced herself to remain calm. "You think you know more about what Falco Bane has done than I do?"

He leaned forward in his seat. "I think if you were as impressive as everyone thought you were, you would have found a way to kill Bane in all those years."

She contained her rage. She would not be provoked by him so easily, not when he was looking for any excuse to slice her open. "You know nothing of Falco Bane or what it would take to kill him. And you know nothing of me."

She realized the rest of the Hunters had silenced, tuned in to her and Daro. Her heart had sped up, her hands tightening around the canvas of her seat. She held his dark stare as he began to roll his blade over his fingers again.

"I know you have a large scar between those plump breasts that would be perfect for me to slip my blade into."

Kohl was on his feet in an instant, having leapt back from the cockpit to stand between her and Daro. "That's enough."

Jessop forced her breathing to slow and concentrated on loosening her grip on the canvas. She did not know how he knew of her scar, but she imagined Bevda had shared an account of her first night in the pool with his mentee. She looked past Kohl to Daro. "You're not a good enough fighter to threaten me, Daro Mesa."

"We'll see about that," he scoffed, turning his gaze away from her.

Yes, Jessop thought, *we will.*

* * * *

The usual ashen sky appeared, the day just breaking as they landed on the outskirts of Okton Radon. The dark sky was beautiful to her. Jessop hadn't slept for the entirety of the trip, and neither had Trax. She looked at his weary face, noting the slight dullness of his usual glowing eyes, and knew they would not be hunting any raiders any time soon.

"We will make camp by our vessel, remain on the outskirts for the day—Daro will take first watch. When the gray sky darkens, we will go to the weigh station and find the raiders."

As he spoke, the group nodded along, happy with his plan. Except for Jessop. She wouldn't sleep as long as Daro Mesa was on lookout. She shot an irritated look at Trax, who raised his eyebrows at her, before realizing her issue.

"Kohl—you'll take first watch with Daro," he spoke, finding a solution for her problem.

She didn't want Kohl to take watch while she slept either... but it was better than trusting Daro to watch her back, or to forgo sleep any longer.

"I can take watch," Teck volunteered, his voice low as it emanated from the darkness of his pulled up hood.

Trax shook his head. "No. In fact, I don't want you to be seen. I don't need a Kuroi war party hearing about a nearby Oren."

They nodded, Kohl squeezing her shoulder softly. "And if anyone recognizes *me* and plans to exact vengeance on behalf of Bane?"

Trax looked Kohl over slowly, one eyebrow arched. "Then kill them, Hunter."

They remained silent. Trax had an authoritative tone befitting his superior position in the Blade. She admired it, and the manner in which the Hunters respected him. He was a natural leader, but he had also lived many years as a follower...

Jessop couldn't understand the way they all kowtowed blindly to their superiors. Or maybe she did. She just didn't understand the way they could forgive those who had most betrayed them. More than forgive, but follow. This, she supposed, and not her gender or abilities, was the true reason she would never be considered a Hunter.

* * * *

Daro and Kohl walked the perimeter around the Soar-Craft as she and Trax set up tents. The ground beneath her feet was hard sand and rocks. They had landed in a gorge surrounded by giant boulders, to take advantage of the natural shield the terrain offered from prying eyes of any nearby tribesmen, villagers, or raiders. The city of Okton Radon was some miles down an escarpment, Trax had explained to her. She enjoyed the sound of sand grinding beneath her boots, of canvas beneath her fingers as she smoothed her hands over the tent wall. She welcomed the gray sky and blanket of encroaching darkness.

She enjoyed the air and the breeze, the smell of heat and dry land, the sheen of fading light as it reflected across the boulders. Her eyes fell onto Kohl, who stood strong as the wind attempted to move his formidable frame. He spoke with Daro, seeming so trusting of his brother. She looked at his eyes, narrow against the sandy winds, as he stood beside a boulder. She studied Kohl's face for any anger that he might show against the other Hunter, but found nothing.

"That love in your heart still lives?"

Trax's question caught her off guard. She turned her attention, and gaze, to him. "Of course it does."

He nodded slowly. "Just checking."

She fastened a tent flap, studying his pensive gaze. "You don't need to check. I have proven my loyalty."

"Of course," he answered quickly, his voice soft, his tired eyes still on her. She knew he held his tongue though, and it irked her to wonder his thoughts. She wouldn't enter his mind just to discern them.

"What is it that you think but don't voice, Trax?"

He shrugged, his large shoulders heaving slowly. "It doesn't matter." He stepped around the tent, preparing to duck inside. She grabbed his elbow, stilling him gently.

"It matters to me."

He sighed heavily, holding her stare. "I thought the whole reason you were sent on this mission was so that your loyalty could be tested."

She ran her lip against her teeth, astounded that he would speak to her in such a way. But she had pressed him. She looked over her shoulder, feeling Kohl's hazel stare on her. She smiled at him softly before turning back to Trax. "My loyalty is intact and without question, with the ones who matter most."

* * * *

Jessop had experienced no issues falling right asleep. She didn't know how many hours had passed, although she knew true darkness had not yet fallen. She could hear Trax snoring in the adjacent tent, as the wind from the early day had clearly settled. She turned over, readjusting her position on her bedroll, bringing her knees up to her chest.

She blinked slowly, staring at the pale green canvas as the gray sky seeped through its worn fibers. She thought of Trax's words earlier, questioning her loyalty. He was tired, and he held high affections for her, so she anticipated comments of an inappropriate nature from time to time... but not questions of her loyalty. She thought that he, of all people, would know her better than to question that. She would speak to him later, when they had a spare minute.

"You truly trust her?"

Her ears perked up at the sound of Daro's voice, carrying on the remaining light breeze.

"Of course. She saved my life, she's... she's magnificent," Kohl answered, his deep voice travelling from where he stood outside her tent with Daro.

"Sure... but that doesn't make her trustworthy. You've never wondered about the timing of it all? Her, Bevda, Hydo..."

"Daro, we all know you suffered a great loss, but it's not Jessop's fault and Trax confirmed that then and there. You were wrong to speak to her as you did."

Jessop sat upright. She needed Daro to change his line of questioning. She didn't want to deal with him, but she didn't need him putting any more thoughts in Kohl's mind.

"They are just friends," Kohl spoke, his voice tight. She imagined the look Daro had given him to warrant a reminder of the nature of her relationship with Trax.

"I'm sure they are. But he looks at her the same way you look at her."

Jessop knew this had to stop. She crawled towards her tent flap, pulling it open and crouching through the exit. To her surprise, as she stood, she saw it was not just Daro and Kohl, but Trax had also just emerged from his own tent, and stared at his subordinates with a dark gaze.

"And how, exactly, *do* I look at her, Daro Mesa?" Trax asked, his voice deep and filled with anger

Daro looked from Kohl to Trax to her. She glared at him, watching him stand awkwardly beside Kohl, a knife spinning in his hand.

"Answer me, Hunter," Trax pressed, taking a step forward. Jessop moved quickly, touching his arm to calm him.

"Leave him to play with his knives, Trax, he knows nothing about this," she advised.

"About what, Jessop?" Kohl snapped his gaze back to her, crossing his arms over his chest.

"I didn't mean it like that," she answered quickly, pulling her hand back.

Before she could say anything further, Daro spoke. "You look at her the same way O'Hanlon does—like you're in love with her."

They stood in silence, forming an awkward, angry square in the sand. She narrowed her eyes on Daro, certain she could kill him for pointing out the last thing that needed to be pointed out. She could see Trax's heaving chest in her periphery, his fists clenched so tightly she could hear the air attempting to escape between his fingers.

"So what if I do?"

His name escaped her mouth without any thought. "*Trax!*"

Kohl took a step forward, his hands dropped down, one landing on the blade on his hip. "What did you just say?"

Trax took a step towards him.

"Bevda was right, you're all blinded by her…"

"*Enough*," Jessop hissed.

Kohl held Trax's stare, his voice shaking with anger. "She doesn't love you."

Trax flung his arm out, gesturing to her. "You don't know anything about—"

"TRAX!"

Slowly, the three men shifted their gazes to her. Daro shook his head with clear disgust, but remained silent. She looked from Trax to Kohl, and held her hands out to motion peace between them. "Enough of this. We didn't come to Okton Radon to discuss *me*. We came to hunt. And last I checked—you all were Hunters."

Kohl slowly crossed and uncrossed his arms; Trax dropped his gaze to the sand beneath their feet. Daro flipped his dagger in hand, pointing the hilt at her menacingly. "You'll be the end of a brotherhood, woman."

He continued to point the end of his blade at her, looking up at her from under his furrowed brow. She stared at him, holding his dark gaze without concern, and with a great deal of self-restraint. "Watch yourself, *boy*." She issued the stern warning, and in her mind she imagined how quickly she could best him.

He flipped his blade and caught the hilt, staring at her darkly as he began to walk off. "Yeah, I'll do that," he sneered, the words slick over his tight lips.

He gave her a wide berth as he passed by, quickly disappearing into the ship, and leaving her in the middle of Trax and Kohl.

* * * *

She had lain with Kohl until he fell asleep, but she couldn't stay in the tent. She couldn't relax. She had walked the perimeter of their camp, always keeping one eye on the doorway of the ship, lest Daro made his exit. Trax had gone to speak to him, to reassure him of the solidarity and unity of the Hunters' brotherhood, to assure him that he needn't worry about him, their Councilman.

She stopped pacing, a small cloud of dust forming about her boots, as the ship door opened. Trax emerged, rubbing the back of his neck as he closed the door behind himself and walked down the ramp. He approached her slowly, as if looking to see if anyone else was near her.

She looked as the last of the gray light began to fade into true night, and immediately felt more at ease, knowing that soon, it would be completely dark. "How did the talk with Daro go?"

Trax nodded slowly. "Could have gone better."

"What am I supposed to do here, Trax? What *was* that with Kohl and you? You know how I feel."

He shook his head, lost for words. "I don't know."

"Well, rein it in. Whatever is going on with you and Kohl, we will deal with it in Azgul. We have too much to worry about tonight."

He looked at her as though he would protest, but he remained silent. Whatever he and Kohl felt, they knew that they had come to Okton Radon for a reason, and it wasn't to fight it out over her. The last thing Jessop wanted to worry about was the two of them, not when they were in a territory loyal to Falco Bane, with a potential threat looming against Kohl, and Daro Mesa waiting for any good excuse to go for her neck.

"Night is falling. As soon as Kohl wakes, we will begin the descent into the city and make our way to the weigh station," he spoke. It amazed Jessop how quickly he could rid himself of the emotional tones and glances, and return to his prominent position of objective Councilman. He amazed her—but not enough to change anything.

"I'll go wake him."

Before she could turn from him, he had grabbed her hand. His glowing eyes held on to her for the longest moment before he spoke. "I am sorry, *Oray-Ha*."

She squeezed his large hand softly before pulling away. "So am I, *Hasen-Ha*. I truly wish things could be different."

* * * *

When Jessop entered the tent she was surprised to see Kohl sitting upright, his arms wrapped around his bent knees, his brow furrowed. She crawled over the rough ground and sat beside him. He looked at her, his amber eyes trailing over her face slowly, as if searching for something; perhaps for whatever it was that had made him fall in love with her in the first place. Jessop didn't know what he looked for, but she did know he was unhappy.

He exhaled loudly before speaking. "I don't know how to deal with this, Jessop. One brother has fallen in love with you, whilst another threatens your life. What am I supposed to do here?"

She shrugged softly. "Nothing. You do nothing and let me handle it."

He shook his head. "No, I must speak to them both. Daro needs to understand that you—and the way I feel about you—won't bring about the end of the Infinity Hunters. I mean that's nonsense. And Trax needs to know how you feel."

She studied his frustrated eyes and felt a pang in her chest. Loyal first and foremost to the Hunters, to his brothers, he was still the same boy she had met that day fighting in a tavern, no matter how many times she had tried to tell herself otherwise. "Trax knows exactly how I feel. But this mission has been too concentrated on me and not enough on the raiders. We have to go deal with them, Kohl." She tugged his hand, urging him to get up.

"We should speak with Daro first," he began, pulling her towards him.

She tugged her hand free from him with anger. "No. We shouldn't. You just keep Daro away from me, and I will make sure the raiders don't get the best of you or your *beloved* brothers."

He stared at her with reproach, confusion pulling at the corners of his lips. "You have always known I was an Infinity Hunter, first and foremost. You know my loyalty must be to my kin first, and *they* are my kin, however misguided some of them may be," he spoke, his voice low and soft.

She took a deep breath, calming herself. She needed to stop *this*, she needed to control her emotions, and to get rid of that nag in her voice, the one that made it seem like maybe *she* was the one who had lost sight of the mission. She was beginning to believe her own lies, and she knew that doing that was to walk a path much more treacherous than any she already roamed. She studied Kohl's golden brown eyes and took a low breath. "You would do anything for them, right? Absolutely anything for the ones you're most loyal to?"

He reached out to her slowly, and softly ran his hand down her arm. "Yes. I truly would—and they for me. You have to understand that, Jessop. It's not that I love my brothers in the same way that I love you, because I obviously don't, and it's not that I love them more, because I have now begun to realize that that is not true either. It's simply that I loved them *first*. I swore fealty—and that means something to me. Do you understand?"

She blinked and saw a body of scars, a shared history of pain. She cupped his hand with hers, and offered him a small smile. It was the first time she had felt as though they did understand one another. "I really, truly do."

CHAPTER 13

Jessop restrained her swift steps, as she knew Trax did, during their trek down the desert escarpment, towards the small town of Okton Radon. The dark was too easy for them, but it was not just herself and Trax navigating the space with ease, she noticed. The Oren mystic, Teck, with his hood pulled low over his face, even in the cover of night, seemed to glide over the jagged rocks and across the deep dunes, as if his feet, concealed by his long robes, never touched the ground.

Kohl remained at Daro's side, keeping him from her, as Jessop had requested. She kept an eye on the two of them as they trailed adjacent to herself and Trax. She wasn't nervous for herself—she was nervous for Kohl. She knew, better than most, how many would jump at the opportunity to please Falco Bane through an act of violence. She knew that lurking behind the next boulder, or perhaps outside the weigh station, there would be someone who recognized the star scar and remembered the threat made by Bane years ago. His followers were everywhere, hiding in plain sight, ready and willing to fight and die for their Arantholi Lord.

He is safe with us, he is safe with you, Trax pushed the thought across her mind softly.

Any who anger Bane forsake their sense of safety in doing so, including him.

Trax turned his golden gaze on her as they descended down a steep dune. *You have the power to keep him safe.*

Jessop shook her head, digging her heels into the fine sand as she slowly slid down the slope. *He knows nothing of my power.*

But Bane does, Trax added quickly.

She shot him a knowing glance. *And we both know he does not fear it. He does not fear me.*

Before Trax could push any further thoughts, the Oren Hunter came to a halt, silently yielding before them, raising one cloaked arm out to the side to indicate they stop behind him. They stood in silence, and only then did Jessop realize how loud the screams of the winds were as they shrieked through the dunes, circling their small Hunter pack. The Oren's cloak billowed around him, but he remained steady, his arm still outstretched.

Jessop used her keen eyesight to look out ahead of the mage, to scan the desert around them, but she saw nothing. She glanced back to Kohl, knowing he could not see what she could, or in this case, *couldn't*, and took a slow breath. She feared for his safety so much it pained her, she could feel the fear and the caring she had for him, like a glob of thick grease, in her chest. It traveled around her cavities, it seeped over her heart, it dripped thick into her lungs, and spread, everywhere it rolled, a sense of concern, of anxiety. She needed Kohl O'Hanlon to be safe; she owed him his life, as she had been the one to endanger it.

"We are not alone here," Teck spoke, his clear voice cutting through the wind with a mystical ease.

And although neither Jessop nor Trax could see what the mage Hunter foresaw, they could both sense it. She could feel the tingling of her skin, the fine current of electricity travelling from her fingertips, through her hilt, into Falco Bane's Hunter blade. The mystic knew what he spoke of—they were not alone, but who accompanied them, they did not know.

"We carry on, with vigilance," Trax ordered, and she saw the way his own hand had curled around the hilt of his blade. She could hear Daro's spinning knife, but she would not concern herself with him, not when whoever neared them could be after Kohl. She knew Daro would take any opportunity he had to strike at her, but not at the cost of a brother. He would be fierce in his defense of Kohl, this she knew.

"Kohl should stay in the center of us, for greatest protection," she suggested. He kicked up sand as he walked over to her, quickly wrapping a hand around her arm, his thumb gently rubbing her skin.

"No, you should, we will protect you first," he explained, and she could, even in pitch-blackness, see the love in his eyes.

She shook her head. "We are in territory where the threat is directed at you."

"An equal threat lays against you—you have been the one to anger Bane most recently," he reminded her.

"There is no death threat against me amongst his followers though," she rebutted.

Kohl shook his head, confused. "How could you possibly know that?"

Jessop glanced to Trax, and back to Kohl, chewing the inside of her cheek. "Because..." she began.

"Because the Council would have heard if there was a credible threat, and we haven't yet," Trax explained, answering for her.

Kohl nodded slowly, his grip on her tightening. "Okay, well, just because it hasn't been confirmed, doesn't mean there isn't one. We will both stay in the middle," his voice lightened with his soft smile.

"Fine," she conceded. They repositioned themselves, and began their trek once more.

Teck waited for her and Kohl to pass him. *I'll take the back, with Daro,* he explained in silence.

She nodded to him approvingly. She trusted the mage far more than his knife-wielding brother. They both saw too much, she knew that to be true, but the way they interpreted what they saw was what determined her opinion of them, and the extent to which she valued their lives. She had learnt a long time ago that life was easier when you could identify threats and opportunities quickly. Daro did not trust her place in the Blade, he resented her position beside Kohl and her effect on Trax, and he both feared and underestimated her abilities.

Teck, on the other hand, was smart enough to know that she was different from anyone he had ever encountered, and *she* was smart enough to know that, despite whatever protests she made, she truly *was.* His thirst for knowledge, the driving force behind Oren mysticism, was what set him aside. He wanted to know what she was, and for that, he wouldn't just let her die. Daro was a threat; the mystic, an opportunity.

They continued on, in silence, on alert, until the dunes panned out and the sand began to turn to hardened rock, flattened by footsteps of those who traveled through Okton Radon. They knew Teck had been right, they had *not* been alone, but whoever would cross their path had kept a safe distance, watchful from afar. It could have been someone interested in Hunters, or specifically Kohl, or it could have been Kuroi, keeping an eye on an Oren in their lands. It could have had nothing to do with them, or it could have been someone plotting an attack. Jessop did not know, but what she did know was that, despite her fears for Kohl's safety, being in Kuroi territory allowed her to feel more at home than she had in the longest time.

They could see the lights from the weigh station, not far ahead, but her eyes made out more than the building. Coming up in the road, there was a small group of people, maybe four or five. She concentrated on them, until her keen eyes could make out the telltale glow of a Kuroi tribal person.

"*Seksu'da Kuroi.*" She pointed them out to Trax. He nodded slowly, seeming much less comforted by the sight of his people than she was.

"We are coming up on Kuroi tribesmen, Teck, you stay in the back," Trax ordered, his voice low and strong in the darkness. She took a step forward, leaving Kohl behind her, to stand beside Trax. *This* was her role, after all, to be a translator and assist in relations with the Kuroi. They were a people she truly loved, having been cared for by them for many years, but she knew how they felt about Oren, and she knew how they felt about Falco Bane—Teck and Kohl needed to stay behind them.

There were four of them, three men and an older woman. Jessop thought that perhaps she was their mother or a tribal elder, possibly both. She had green eyes that shone like gemstones on fire in the night. All the men had glowing golden eyes, like Trax. Jessop suppressed a smile at their beauty, and their familiarity. Women were revered in Kuroi culture, and it was not uncommon to see many sons travelling with women from the tribe, to ensure their safety at all times.

As they all came closer to one another, the three young men circled the woman, forming a small shield for her. When they were not more than ten paces away in the road, Trax halted and bowed low, Jessop following suit. He had recognized her as an elder, and elders were greeted with low bows and kind words. They rose slowly, and Jessop could feel the eyes of the male travelers on her, wondering what she was doing with a pack of Infinity Hunters, led by none other than the Kuroi Councilman renowned in these parts, Trax DeHawn.

"*Dorei Dorei, Mesahna,*" Trax spoke; a formal greeting, using the Kuroi word for elder.

The woman reached up and slowly drew the hood of her cloak back, nodding at Trax with approval. "*Dorei Dorei,* Hunter DeHawn."

Her recognition of him did not surprise Jessop or Trax—he was the emissary in Kuroi regions because he was *the* Kuroi Councilman.

"*Sed'awey ha,*" Trax began, but the woman cut him off with a wave of her hand.

"We can speak in the native tongue of your fellow Hunters," she advised.

Jessop inclined her head, offering respect, "*Dan'ahei Kuroi, Mesahna.*"

The older woman tilted her head to the side, eyeing Jessop with a small smile and narrow eyes. "You speak our tongue, child. *Huk'ana hey oray-ha, lo vei nor-emsuk.*"

Jessop followed the woman's tongue with ease as she marveled over her, realizing they all shared the same eyes. She was thankful that the elder had enough tact to remark this realization in Kuroi, for Jessop hadn't the time or want to explain it to the others.

"She was cared for by Kuroi in her upbringing," Trax explained quickly.

"And where was this upbringing?"

Jessop pressed her lips tightly together as she thought of a polite answer. "That is a question that requires a long and tragic answer, *Mesahna*, one not best explained in the night, with raiders afoot."

The older woman nodded slowly, understanding. "Raiders indeed. My sons and I had been travelling for some time, when we came by the weigh station and saw it had been overrun by the scum," she explained, her accented voice soft and clear. "They know better than to upset a Kuroi elder, so they let us on our way, but if the Hunters do not remove them, we will."

Her voice, however aged and soft-spoken, exuded more menace than any man Jessop had encountered. The Kuroi were a powerful tribe, and their elders hailed from great conquerors and fierce warriors. For Jessop, there were few she respected more.

"We will remove them, *Mesahna*," she spoke, making a clear promise to the older woman.

One of the young yellow-eyed men shot her a sharp look. "You are not a Hunter, lady traveler."

Before she could answer the man, the older woman spoke, once again raising her hand to command silence and attention. "No, *Desda*, my son, she is not a Hunter. Can you not sense it?"

Her words ignited inside Jessop. The Kuroi people enthralled her and yet she feared how much this elder sensed, and how much she could divulge.

"She is more than Hunter, much more than the silent Oren mage she travels with, more than..." The older woman let her voice trail off, but Jessop could see the knowledge, like a fire, residing in her eyes. She knew what Jessop was.

Abruptly, the older woman took a loud, deep breath. "We must be on our way. Rid this place of the raiders, and one day soon—for I am old, girl—return to tell me that tragic and long tale."

Jessop felt the relief spread through her and she smiled, bowing her head to the elder. "I will do that."

The older woman looked to Trax, *"Had'away ha, Trax DeHawn."*

Watch over her, Trax DeHawn, she had advised. At her words, Trax nodded, and then bowed low. Kohl, Daro, and Teck followed suit, and as Jessop began to lower herself, allowing the elder to pass with respect, she felt the woman's hand clutch her shoulder. The fingers dug into her skin, strong and sure. Jessop stayed low, but looked up into the glowing green eyes of the elder, just in time for the woman's voice to fill her mind, echoing through her, reverberating down her spine, and filling her every cell with adrenaline.

He wants you back, young one.

Just as quickly, the elder released her. Jessop pivoted on her knee, watching carefully as the woman and her three sons passed by Kohl, who unknowingly kept his head bowed low to the ground. The Kuroi family stared at him, eyeing the back of his pale neck with slow contemplation as they passed. Only once they had carried on several paces did Jessop dare to breathe, dare to remove her hand from her hilt, her blade already several inches unsheathed. She loved the Kuroi—but she would cut down any who came near Kohl. And she sensed, as the elder and her sons disappeared down the sandy road, into the darkness, that they knew just that.

Jessop rose sharply, darting her gaze between Trax and the road behind the men, where the elder and her sons had disappeared. *"Han'havay'ha, han'havay Bane,"* she spoke, telling Trax she knew that the elder and her sons were aligned with Falco Bane.

"I know, I sensed it," he answered quickly, his gaze travelling down the road after them. Teck, taking his cue from Trax, turned and watched the road as well.

Kohl took a step towards Jessop. "What? Sensed what?" She said nothing as he grabbed her hand. "Jessop, you're shaking."

She squeezed his hand tightly, then dropped it, not knowing which eyes watched them in the night. "They were Kuroi aligned with Falco Bane," she answered.

Kohl nodded, but he didn't seem surprised. "Many Kuroi are aligned with him, Jessop, we all know that."

She didn't add what she wanted to add. That the elder had been in communications with Falco, that she had looked at Kohl's neck and seen it as something to break, that she had looked into Jessop and seen who she was.

"I… I know. It just surprised me—it's been a long time since I encountered one of his followers," she offered, knowing it was all she could say.

"Well, she clearly didn't recognize you from your—*er*—time in Aranthol, or me, so we are fine," he explained, still, somehow smiling softly down at her.

She stared up into his golden brown eyes and bit her tongue, refusing to tell him that he was wrong, that the woman and her sons had definitely recognized them, and that it was only because the elder had an understanding of what Jessop was capable of did they walk on...

She had imagined every possible scenario as they neared the weigh station. She could run ahead, remaining within the mile tether to Kohl, and deal with the raiders herself. She could go in and erase Kohl's memory of whatever she did, whatever happened. Or, she could continue to walk in dreaded silence towards the small, deteriorating building, and force the raiders out, with the Hunters, as planned.

She was capable of nearly anything, and yet, she could do nothing. She kept Kohl in her periphery, her heart racing every time his face blurred from her vision, every time he was more than an arm's reach from her. She wondered if she should circle back, get rid of the Kuroi who had seen them. That would anger Trax, though, even if she did it begrudgingly. She couldn't risk angering Trax. She also couldn't admit that some part of her hesitated greatly at the thought of harming Kuroi. Trax was the only person she could rely on—and she wouldn't betray him, or the tribe they shared, with any ease. It angered her to realize that she hesitated to betray Trax, when she had deceived Kohl's mind so many times already.

Kohl couldn't accept who Jessop was. She couldn't do anything for him; she couldn't fix what had already been done, what had been set into motion so long ago. All she could do was keep him alive, and that was all she could think about as they approached the weigh station's large steel doors.

The station looked like it was about to crumble before them, and Jessop wondered how old it actually was, having been in Okton Radon for at least her entire life. It was a large, square building that Jessop imagined to be an eyesore in the daytime, completely contrary to its desert surroundings, with its wooden frame and metal entrance.

From fifteen paces away, she could hear the rowdy group inside. She could also sense them, and she knew how quickly she could disband them and drive them out from Okton Radon. She wondered if any of the raiders would recognize her, or Kohl, or if any of them were even Falco's loyalists—they could have just been raiders from a far-off place, who had mistakenly thought Okton Radon was an unprotected source of drink and shelter.

As she eyed the long line of shabby scrap-metal Soar-Craft parked beside the building, she knew that any ideas of this being a mistakenly chosen location seemed unlikely. "There are seven Soar-Craft, which means there could be upwards of fourteen, maybe more, inside."

"Raiders tend to stick to their own kind, travel in groups of ten or so," Daro spoke up, reminding Jessop that the raiders, the Kuroi, and other potential loyalists weren't the only dangers around.

She glanced over her shoulder, sizing him up. "How do you know about raiders?"

He cocked his head to the side and briefly stopped spinning his blade. "There were three sons born in the house of Mesa—one of them has lived his life as a raider."

His confession surprised her. She knew he spoke of a *true* brother, a blood sibling whom he had known before his life in the Blade began. She hadn't thought of him as the sort to have ties outside of the Blade, but if the man was a raider, Daro probably *didn't* have ties with him, outside of blood. Hunters made the very laws that raiders mocked and defied.

"We have had no reports of injuries or deaths caused by them yet, so we offer them the opportunity to leave immediately," Trax ordered, turning their attention to him.

"Their resistance will mean their death. I want this over with by tonight so we can return to Azgul as soon as possible. This place is not safe for too many travelling with us," he continued.

They all nodded, obedient in their agreement. Trax took the first step towards the building, and she followed, keeping Kohl between them. She pushed the thought into their leader's mind quickly.

Compliant or otherwise, if any of them recognizes Kohl, or myself, I'll kill them.

He looked at her from the corner of his eyes, and with acknowledgment of her words, he nodded.

CHAPTER 14

Trax held his hand out in front of him and slowly dragged it horizontally through the air, and as his hand moved, the giant steel door dragged to the side and rolled open. With one hand still extended out, he took a slow step into the weigh station, Jessop and Kohl beside him, Daro and Teck following. Kohl unsheathed his blade immediately, standing beside Trax at the ready, but Jessop waited, her hand resting on her hilt.

The large room was in complete disarray, filled with barrels of drink and food—some tipped over, some broken open—chairs overturned, tables shattered, a wall that had been stuck like a pin cushion with throwing knives and a sword, and, center stage, a makeshift bar compiled of pushed-together tables and scrap metal. There were eleven raiders, and one was even sitting, with his legs up, in a Soar-Craft. Jessop couldn't fathom how they had gotten it into the building. The majority of them were human, one was Hakta—a species found several regions away—and another was unknown to Jessop, but possessed a face made up entirely of metal and wires and glass.

The raiders looked at them with little surprise, seeming more disgruntled than afraid. The one lounging in the Soar-Craft slowly sat up, a wild mane of red hair sticking out in all directions. He had only one good eye—the other clouded and dark—and a mouth of sharpened teeth that he ran over his lower lip as he stared at the group of Hunters.

Trax slowly lowered his hand to his blade. "Okton Radon is a weigh station under the protection of the Hunters of Infinity. You trespass on Hunter territory," he warned them.

A few in the small group laughed, but they all also turned their bodies and lowered their drinks, directing their full attention to Trax.

The one-eyed man—their makeshift leader, it seemed—propped himself up onto the back bonnet of his Soar-Craft, and swiftly grabbed a blade from his boot. Each of the Hunters moved for their swords, but quickly halted as the redheaded man began to simply clean his long fingernails with the tip of his knife. "This here is not Hunter territory. This here is Falco Bane territory. We know that. The Kuroi know that—which means *you* should know that," he spoke with a thick accent that Jessop could not place.

Her heart flipped as she began to slowly withdraw her blade from its sheath. They were loyalists, which made them more of a threat than their simple raider status. Trax flicked his hand at her, gesturing for her to wait. She conceded, respecting his wishes.

"Call it what you will, you will disband on this night and be on your way, or this will be your *last* night," Trax warned.

At his threat, two of the raiders stood, and Jessop couldn't help but hold one of their stares. He had a head of long black hair and half a mouth of teeth. His leathers were old, but his boots new, and he had a cloak of dark red color, bound haphazardly around his neck. He seemed familiar to her, as she apparently did to him from the way he stared, and while she couldn't place him, she felt certain she would have to kill him.

"Trax," she warned, pulling on her hilt.

The raider leader stood and stepped out of his Soar-Craft, which he slowly walked around, his red locks bouncing about, navigating a half-sober path around his crew until he stood before Trax. "I think it's *you* who should be on *your* way, Hunter," he threatened back.

Jessop could feel the dark eyes of the red-cloaked man studying her, and she stepped slightly back to conceal her face.

"We will not warn you again," Trax hissed, staring down at the drunken raider.

"Marsda, look at the girl," the red-cloaked man spoke, and Jessop immediately turned her face to avoid any stares.

Marsda, their leader, didn't listen to his comrade though, instead trading barbs with Trax.

"Trax," she whispered, knowing she would need to end this.

"Marsda," the red-cloaked man called again.

"*Trax*," Jessop hissed.

"Marsda!"

Their leader pivoted on his heel, flinging his hand out to the side, his knife coming precariously close to Trax, as he turned to face his follower. "WHAT?"

"That's her! She's Falco's woman," he spoke, pointing a short, pudgy finger out into the air, pinning Jessop.

She took a slow breath, turning her face to be seen by them all. It was too late. She felt Kohl tense at her side, bringing his blade slightly up, ready to protect her. The old raider turned back slowly, his one good eye focusing on her face, his brow furrowing as he searched her appearance for some telltale sign that his companion was right.

He took a step towards her, but Kohl and Trax both blocked him from nearing her. His one clear eye still studied her though, through the gap between Kohl and Trax's shoulders. She stared right back at him.

"Is it true? Are you the woman who belongs to Falco Bane?"

Jessop cocked her head to the side, pulling her lips between her teeth sharply. "I belong to no one, raider."

"It is, Marsda, it's her. I recognize her from Aranthol, when I took that package to Bane for you, she was there," the red-cloaked raider rambled on.

Marsda narrowed his good eye at her, and then nodded, taking a step back from Trax and Kohl. "It's time we get on our way then, boys," he announced to his pack of raiders.

There were some grumbles, but no true dispute. Marsda turned back to the Hunters. "We are under strict instructions—no harm shall come to the girl." As he spoke, though, Jessop could see him eyeing up Kohl. She took a step forward, standing protectively at Kohl's side and kept her gaze on the raider.

The raiders began to ready themselves, grabbing up their weapons and drinks. Jessop watched Marsda, but he was no longer watching her. His good eye was fixed on Kohl. She pushed at his inebriated mind and immediately knew his plan—to circle back for the boy with the star scar.

As Jessop pulled her blade free, it rung out, a metallic cry of liberation, and drew the attention of every man in the room.

Kohl rested a hand on her shoulder, yielding her. "What are you doing? They're leaving."

She shook her head, keeping her eyes on Marsda. "He recognizes you," she explained.

Kohl looked from her to Marsda, remaining silent.

Marsda laughed, a sharp smile pulling across his face. "Girl, we have no fight with you. Give us the boy and we will be on our way."

"Not going to happen," she growled.

Trax took a step towards the raider. "Leave. While it is still permitted."

"There's quite a bounty on you," Marsda's raspy voice grew louder as he addressed Kohl. Several of his raiders neared, looking over the shoulder of their leader, eyeing Kohl. As Marsda inched forward, Jessop whipped her blade up, the black tip of her weapon pointing directly into the raider's one good eye.

"This is not a fight you can win, raider—now be on your way," Trax warned, taking a slow step towards the raiders.

"Why would they care for O'Hanlon but not you?" The question, so calmly voiced and out of place, came from Daro. Everyone adjusted their positions, looking back at the knife expert. He took a step forward, his brow twisted in confusion, his dark eyes watching her. He extended his arm, pointing his knife at Jessop.

"These enemies of the Council, loyal to Bane, who would surely want your head, are ordered to not harm you? To retreat from you?"

"Likely so that Bane could deal with me himself," Jessop snapped at Daro, flicking her gaze between him and Marsda, who remained motionless at the end of her blade.

Daro took a step closer to her. "Then why wouldn't they be ordered to capture you?"

"I don't know—" Jessop began, but he cut her off angrily.

"You may have blinded my brothers, but I know better! I know you're nothing more than a wh—"

The crackling snap silenced the room, and with a heavy *thud*, Daro's body hit the ground. His knife skittered across the floor, landing at Jessop's boot. She stared at the weapon, her gaze travelling over the filthy ground, over the lifeless hand of Daro Mesa, to the man standing behind him, whose hands were still poised from the snap.

Falco Bane.

Falco smiled as he brushed his hands together, as if dusting them off. "That's no way to speak to a lady, now, is it?"

His dark hair was shorter than before, clipped nearer to his ears, and his gray eyes were somewhat brighter, as if the mere sight of her in Okton Radon brought an unknown amount of joy to his life. Her eyes trailed over him, over the long, silver scar that went through his brow, over his eyelid, and down his cheek. She had seen the scar for so long, she had almost forgotten that it was the result of a wound that nearly cost Falco his eye. He wore all black, dressed like a Hunter, as he always had. What was most different about him was his lack of a blade—for it was now resting in her hand.

He smiled at her, *just* at her, and her heart felt as though it had caught fire, as though the flames sucked at her oxygen, her ability to move, to think, to feel anything other than his presence.

And then Kohl moved—and it spurred her into action. She grabbed at his shoulder, pulling him back from his bold step towards Falco, and forcing him behind her. She stood in front of him so that no one was between her and Bane.

She watched as his broad shoulders heaved, a large sigh escaping his lips. "Jessop, you look so well," he spoke softly.

She cleared her throat as discreetly as possible, concerned that she wouldn't be able to speak. To her surprise, her voice was clear and convincing. "I *am* well."

He took a step towards her, and she felt Kohl and Trax come up closer behind her. He noticed their protective nature, and smirked. His gray eyes traveled past her, over her shoulder. "Kohl O'Hanlon, it has been a lifetime."

"Not quite," Kohl spoke, his voice deep and filled with anger so hot it emanated from his body.

Falco turned his gaze past her, and Jessop knew he was studying Trax, looking him over as if he compared the man before him with the man he remembered from many years ago. "*Hada'na nei hey'wa, DeHawn?*"

"*Dand'e dore dona, Falco Bane,*" Trax answered, sure to keep his voice as low and menacing as possible. Jessop was the only one in the room capable of understanding what they said to one another, and it did not need to be translated.

And then his eyes were back on her, and she felt her whole body tremble.

He ran his hand through his dark hair, and slowly knelt to the ground. Reaching out near her boot, he wrapped his fingers around Daro's blade and began to twirl it, as expert as its former owner, as he looked up at her. "Ready to come home yet, darling?"

"She's not going anywhere with you," Kohl hissed, and she struggled to keep him behind her.

Falco nodded, and then laughed softly, rising up. "He speaks... for *my* woman," he murmured softly under his breath. He moved so quickly that it stunned her—she had almost forgotten the skills that he had, the ones that had left a mark on nearly every person in that room. He had flung the blade directly at Teck Fay's face, and not even the expert mage possessed the skill or foresight to shield himself. But somehow, in the way that set her apart from all others, in the way that she knew Falco Bane better than anyone else, Jessop *did*. Her arm flung out before her, her fingers curled as if holding the very blade. She froze the weapon in mid-air, its point just grazing the Oren Hunter's cheek before stopping.

"Very good, Jessop, I see they haven't slowed you down," Falco beamed, clapping his hands together.

"Not *him*, Falco," she spoke, ordering him to leave Teck alone. She could hear Kohl's voice dying in his throat, inaudible, behind her. Was the quick maneuver too much to show him? Would it be just one more instance that she would have to wipe from his mind, because the extent to which she had a grasp on Sentio was too sensitive a subject to him? It mattered not. Not with Falco in the room, not with so much at risk.

Falco gauged her seriousness, and nodded. With a wave of his hand, he cut through her intangible, supernatural grasp on the blade, and forced the weapon to the ground, where it fell with a chiming *clink* at Teck Fay's feet. The young man exhaled loudly.

"You should leave, Falco," she advised, her voice tense and her heart racing. Emotion ran through her like a fire, trailing from the dark knots of her heart and zipping through her tight veins. He was truly there, right before her, dangerous as ever, with a temper unlike any other. And behind her was Kohl. And Trax. And to her side, poor stunned Teck. And at their feet rested dead Daro.

So many lives he could take, bodies to add to the pile.

"Falco, *please*," she urged, lowering her hand slowly.

A playful smile crossed his face, his eyes alight with dark intention. "If you're not ready to come home yet, darling, I understand. It hurts, but I can be patient. You'll come back... But you know I have a bone to pick with your little friend."

At his words Kohl brushed past her, standing squarely before Falco. "I'm here, Falco. I wasn't afraid of you then—"

Jessop grabbed his arm, trying to pull him back. "Kohl!"

"—and I'm not afraid of you now."

"Kohl!"

He was in Falco's face, fist clenched around blade. "So, have at it, Bane, do your worst."

Jessop wrenched the young Hunter back with all her might, forcing herself, once again, between him and Falco. Falco's eyes fell to her, his smile still there, but somewhat tighter. He did not fear Kohl O'Hanlon. He did not fear anyone. "He taunts me, Jessop."

"Falco, please," she begged, raising her hand slowly, knowing all the ways she could calm his temper.

She took a low, deep breath. Then, very slowly, she touched the back of his hand, trailing her fingers over his skin. His eyes dropped to watch her touch him, and he breathed deeply, seemingly calmed. "Just *go*, Falco," she urged, his blade still tightly clenched in her spare hand.

"Okay," he sighed, dropping his shoulders, convinced. He nodded, slowly looking back into her green eyes. "Okay, I'll go, and we will do this another time, you and I," he offered, grabbing her hand tightly in his.

She stared at him intently—she heard his words, but she *knew* him, and the words did not match the man. She could feel the watchful eyes of his loyal raiders, of the Hunters, on them both. She studied his dark face, his piercing gray eyes, his scar, and his shadow of a beard and knitted dark brow, the small curve of amusement pulling at the corner of his lip. They both knew what was going to happen.

Suddenly, his grip on her hand became wicked, wrenching her closer to him with force. She knocked into his large body, air catching in her lungs, as he turned his attention to his raiders. "Kill the Hunter party."

"NO!" Her voice bounced around the large, decrepit place, surprising even herself. Falco looked at her, perplexed, but still he pulled her closer. In her periphery, chaos had broken out.

Falco's strong arms locked around her, forcing her against his broad chest, her neck craning back as she looked up into his gray eyes. He studied her face thoughtfully, his brow twisting as he spoke. "Are you ready for this, darling?"

She could feel his hand travel over her arm; she could feel his adrenaline as if it were her own. They were born to fight—to feel more in violence than they ever could in affection. "Yes."

She spat the word out, angry and defiant. Without further warning, he shoved her back, lashing out quickly and smacking her across the face with the back of his hand. She fell to one knee, nearly colliding with Trax and Marsda as they fought. She tightened her fingers around her sword as she looked up to him. She could feel the bruise already forming, but she knew it could have been worse.

His arm was outstretched, and she darted her gaze in the direction his hand pointed, and watched as the sword, stuck in the wall by the errant raiders, flew across the room to him. He caught it with ease, spiraling it about his body with an artful flair, testing its mobility as a weapon. Satisfied, he took his stance, and pointed his blade directly at her. She rose to her feet, prepared to fight him. She couldn't pay attention to Trax, as he skewered Marsda through. She couldn't watch Teck Fay, using powers unknown to them all to disappear and reappear in different spots around the room, like a shadow. And she definitely couldn't pay any attention to Kohl, who fought several raiders at once, blood trailing down his face.

She could only watch Falco.

CHAPTER 15

They circled one another, blades extended. They held one another's stares, unblinking, each as fixated as the other. He inclined his head slightly to her, "We both knew this day would come, darling."

She said nothing, taking one measured step after the next.

"You can put a stop to all of this, whenever you want—you can ensure their survival for now," he reminded her.

"They can ensure their own survival," she snapped back, readjusting her grip on her hilt.

He smiled, staring at her with skepticism. "Against my raiders, maybe, but against me?"

"Leave them be, Falco," she ordered, turning in their circle once more.

"I know what he means to you."

"Falco…"

"It's fine. Just mark my words—I *will* kill him. Perhaps not tonight, but in the future, he will die at my blade."

"Falco, just—"

He shook his head at her, warning her off the topic. "Let's just get this over with, I have plans with Jeco to attend to."

Jeco.

Her knees faltered, her step clumsy. She had fought so hard; she had tried, every day to ignore the name pulling at her mind. She did all of *this* for something greater than herself. She was the way she was—so secretive—for a reason. Jeco. She stared at Falco's gray eyes, and fought back a tear.

"Fine, let's do this," she answered, her voice cracking. She forced the tears back, and she could see Falco falter in his movement. He was surprised by how much the words had hurt her. Before he could say anything more, she made her move.

She turned in and pivoted on her left foot, bringing her right leg out high above her, and kicked him in the jaw. She regained her footing and, using his momentary incapacitation against him, stepped into a forward kick, connecting with his solid chest, sending him flying back several feet.

She flicked her blade about her, closing the gap between them, but he was ready for her. He sliced the air between them with a far-reaching semi-circle, grazing her tunic with his blade. He lunged and she parried. Their swords clashed, an echoing orchestra of sharp violence around them. She ducked under his arm and wove about his strong body, avoiding connecting with him as much as possible.

Their fight was a spectacle; as the raiders died all around them, as the Hunters prevailed over their enemy, Jessop and Falco fought. She was faster, he was stronger, and she knew that to all who saw, they were seemingly matched in skill. She knew they also saw wrong—Falco was still the superior fighter. They had simply fought so many times, they could telegraph one another's next moves with ease.

"We are running out of time, love," he smiled softly, regarding his fallen comrades.

"You mean *you're* running out of time," she snapped, ducking under his blade. She could see Trax, freeing his blade from the gut of a raider, his eyes already on her. She could see Teck, perched atop the bar, the blood of his enemies dripping from his bare hands like raindrops onto the wood beneath his feet. He watched Jessop duel the greatest fighter of all time with a dark interest. And then she heard the dying gasp of air, puffing through the cracked lips of Kohl's opponent. She saw all of this, and so did Falco.

"Just one last thing then," he hissed, dropping his blade abruptly. She curved her arm up and brought her sword down, aiming at his collarbone. He caught her wrist with his strong, quick hand, and sharply turned it outward. Her blade fell to the ground beside his boot, but she couldn't move for it. He turned until her shoulder cracked and her back twisted, and she fell to her knee before him. The strong, scarred fingers ran over her forearm. She stared up to him, trapped and immobile, and watched as his fingers grabbed at the corner of the tracking device.

"NO!"

The thunderous shout came from Kohl, and it nearly concealed her own cry as Falco ripped the metal device off of her flesh.

The metal clinked at her side as he held her arm up high. Falco extended his bloody fingertips, using Sentio to stop Kohl and the others from being able to move, from being able to help her. She bit into her lip, cursing silently. She was immediately light-headed as the blood rushed down her arm, over her tunic, around her neck. There was only one person who could have taken the pain away, like she had done for Kohl the day the devices had been fixed to their arms, and he was the one responsible for the agony. He freed her wrist, staring down at her with pained eyes.

She rose, weakly, to her feet, and watched as he turned to the Hunters, fixed in their positions by his overwhelmingly powerful abilities. He stared at Kohl.

Bloodied and beaten, she stepped in front of him, blocking the path between him and her comrades. "You won't touch them, Falco," she ordered, holding her wounded arm tight against her chest.

Anger flashed across his eyes. "You would die for them?"

She knew the truth though, and so did he. He wouldn't kill her to get to them.

She looked from his gray eyes, to her bloody arm, to Daro's body, to her sword beside Falco's feet, and she knew this had gone exactly as he had intended it to go. He knelt slowly and picked up his sword. He took slow steps towards her, but she remained still, ready for whatever else he had planned. When he was not an inch away from her, he locked his hand at the base of her neck, pulled her near, and kissed her forehead.

As he kissed her, the pain in her body dissipated; she felt his strength travelling over her skin, absorbing the bruises and cuts and grazes, healing her. She let her arm fall between their bodies, and felt tears in her eyes as the pain completely disappeared.

He pulled softly away from her. "I'll be seeing you soon, my darling." His words swelled through her, and she felt paralyzed with fear, terrified at the thought of what would come next for them. He stepped away from her, and before she could do anything to deflect, he froze her with his abilities, rendering her as motionless as her Hunter comrades. She followed him with her eyes, and felt horror consuming her every thought, as he slowly approached defenseless, paralyzed Kohl.

She watched as Falco studied the star scar. She knew what he thought, she knew what he could do, and she felt terror trembling throughout her body. With fierce aggression, and no hesitation, he grabbed Kohl's arm, and ripped the tracking device off of him.

Kohl's forcibly shut lips muffled his scream, but his eyes were on fire. Falco dropped the metal device to the ground and grabbed Kohl by the neck. "If you touch her again, if you fix any other torture devices to her,

I will rip your arm off before I kill you." His voice was deep and loud, louder than the muffled agony of Kohl O'Hanlon.

He squeezed tightly around Kohl's neck, as though he contemplated killing him right then and there. And then he dropped his hand, stepping away from his former friend, his former brother, his enemy. He glanced over the fallen raiders and surviving Hunters, over the blood and mayhem. He turned his gaze back to her, and spoke to her with his eyes, as he had always done. With a slow nod, he voiced one word.

"Soon."

And just like that, Falco Bane turned and walked out of the weigh station, disappearing into the night.

* * * *

Several minutes passed before Jessop felt the sensation of mobility return to her. Her legs flailed underneath her, and she fell. Catching herself, she was reminded of her healed wounds. She studied her forearm, searching the skin for a wound that was no longer present. He had healed her, like no other could do. It was part of what made him Falco Bane. He had a grasp on his abilities that no Hunter or tribe could conceive. He could reanimate the flesh... and you didn't need to be a medic to know what possibilities that opened up.

She could hear the men behind her, regaining control of their bodies. But she didn't turn to them. Even though she knew she should—she knew she should run to Kohl's side, she knew she should embrace Trax, and check on Teck. She knew what she *should* do; she knew what she was *supposed* to do. But she was as immobile as she had been minutes before. She could see only those gray eyes, think only of Jeco and all that had happened since she left him behind in Aranthol, feel only the numbness that came when Falco had removed the pain he caused.

"Jessop. *Jessop*," Kohl's pained voice fell over her. He knelt at her side, covered in blood, and pulled her into his chest with his one good arm. She rested her head against him, feeling the slick of blood—his blood. Falco had let him live... but not because he had spared his life, or forgiven past trespasses. He let him live so he could hurt him more, later. So that he could truly wound him before killing him.

Because of her.

He knew. Falco knew everything that had transpired, and there would be no reasoning with him. He would kill Kohl O'Hanlon because she had cared about him. It would be her fault.

"Jessop, are you okay?"

But she wasn't in the room anymore. She wasn't in the weigh station, surrounded by blood she was responsible for, surrounded by men who would die for loving her. She was home again, in her mind. She was safe, and warm, and loved, and she was with Jeco.

And then everything went dark.

* * * *

When she woke, they were in the Soar-Craft. She was lying down, wrapped in warm blankets. Kohl was looking down on her. His eyes brightened when he saw her wake, but his happiness seemed grotesque under so much dried blood. "You're up," he smiled.

She didn't speak. Her throat was dry, but other than that, she was physically fine. He seemed so pleased. In his mind, he had escaped Falco Bane and a horde of raiders. In her mind, they had postponed the inevitable, worsened it even. She had nothing to say to him. She forced herself to roll over, turning away from his bright eyes, squeezing her own shut, until she found comfort in the darkness once more.

* * * *

They had thanked her repeatedly. They had commended her bravery and retold the ways in which she had stood between them and certain death. And as they spoke, she knew she had succeeded in her mission. Even though Daro lay dead, everything else had gone as well as any could have imagined—her actions would win over the trust of the Council. Just as she had hoped. She knew what she risked, and, as she looked up to Kohl, hearing nothing of what he said to her, she knew it wasn't *her* life that had been imperiled.

He hugged her before disappearing down the corridor with a medic. She waited, aimlessly, in the brilliant, white reception area. She thought back to that day, her first in the Blade. She thought of Hanson grabbing her by the throat, recognizing the Hunter blade, threatening her and telling her to leave while she still could. It had been so long ago, and she wondered how different things may have been if she *had* listened to him. If she had just walked out the door, taken a Soar-Craft, and escaped the Blade. Her life would be something different, something she struggled to conceive... but so would Kohl's, and Hanson's, and Falco Bane's, and Jeco's, and Hydo

Jesuin's, and Trax's. She saw the faces of so many men, and wondered if saving lives made up for endangering them in the first place?

She imagined Daro Mesa wouldn't think so.

* * * *

Jessop stood alone in the bathing room of her chambers, before the large mirror. It was the first time she had felt truly alone since arriving at the Blade. She would never admit it aloud, but she was thankful to no longer have the tracking device bound to her flesh. She studied her green eyes, her full lips and long dark mane. She had traces of dried blood under one eye and matted in the roots of her hair. He had fixed her bruises and healed her wounds, but he hadn't removed all traces of the pain. She looked horrendous.

She undid her tunic and pulled it over her head, dropping it to the floor. She continued to strip until she stood naked and exposed to her own critical eye. She studied her body, the twisted muscle and taut skin.

The scars.

There, between her breasts, was the most intricate of them all. The one Daro had threatened. The lines, as intentionally woven as the Hunter's mark on the back of her neck, were still so clear to her. She rested her hand above them, and she could feel her heart pumping forcefully beneath her flesh. The longest line in the scar drew down low, and then turned up, like a fishhook. Out of its side came several small semi circles, one with a line through it, that all melded into the long body of the hook. She knew the mark looked bizarre to the untrained eye, but it was something they had designed together—it was the only thing she had thought belonged so near her heart.

* * * *

She had no Hunter's blade now. He had taken it back from her. She rolled over on her side, pulling the blanket up to her neck. She couldn't train, couldn't spar with anyone. She supposed there were blades she could borrow... but they wouldn't be the same. It was early, and she knew she should check on Kohl. She would make another stop first, though.

She dressed quickly, quietly, and felt the pang of loss once more, as she reached for an empty sheath. She was sick of her own feelings, and of the days, of the life she led. She had done her duty, she had fought, she had killed, and she had saved. She wanted to be home again, once more. She closed her eyes, and saw his, and her heart ached.

She tossed the empty sheath down with anger, pivoting on her heel and exiting the room. She knew it wouldn't be long. Falco had been truly angered and everything she had worked so hard to hide would soon become very apparent. She had told herself, time and again, to care *less*, to keep distance between herself and Kohl. She had ignored her own instincts and better judgment. She had saved his life, she knew that, but for what? A more painful death, it seemed.

There was much she could say about Falco Bane, much more than many could say about him. She knew many truths about him and many lies, but of all of these things she knew, the one that was most true was that his word was his bond. If he wanted someone dead, they would die. He had built an entire Shadow City, fostered an entire movement, and taken on followers so loyal they would kill for him, die for him. He had decided to kill Kohl long ago, and because of her actions, he would be sure to see it through.

She hooked sharply around the corner, deep in thought. Kohl would be beyond convincing—he didn't fear Falco, or for his own life. She would never be able to *stop* Falco. She had turned his mind from killing before, but everything he did for her he did out of his incomprehensible, unwavering love. He would spare some lives for that love—and he would end others for it. She would not be able to use his feelings for her to Kohl's advantage. She hissed with anger and frustration, certain about the fate of the young Hunter.

She would protect him, as best she could. She would help keep him alive for as long as possible, because she owed it to him. Because he deserved it… Because she didn't think she could live in a world where he didn't, no matter if she could reciprocate his feelings or not. Her heart may have belonged to another, but that did not mean she didn't also, in some way, love Kohl O'Hanlon. She was quite certain their lives would not be carried on *together*, but she would do all she could to ensure that they would be carried on. She had guaranteed his death, and now, she would find a way to guarantee his life.

The automated voice announced her presence, and the door slowly slid to the side. She needed assistance, advice—a plan of some sort. She needed things to be moving both faster and slower. She needed to check on Kohl, and she knew it was likely that he would only be safe for a few more days at most. As the door fully opened, she looked up to Trax and sighed heavily, "We need to talk. Now."

CHAPTER 16

"You're going to become an Infinity Hunter."

She had told him everything, all of her concerns and everything she had planned, and that was his answer.

She stared at him. "What?"

"Hanson is going to hold a Council meeting, but it's already been decided. You risked your life against Falco Bane to save the lives of three Hunters. You did it, Jessop. The first female Infinity Hunter to ever exist."

He sounded more enthused than she felt. Perhaps this was everything she had worked so hard for, perhaps it wasn't. Perhaps she was just too drained to have the reaction she should have been having. It was seeing Falco again… hearing him talk of Jeco. Losing her blade. Knowing the threat to Kohl in her name… This was, indeed, all she had wanted and all she had worked for. She just couldn't feel the excitement she once thought she would have.

She quickly found herself once again thinking about actions versus intentions, and wondering if she deserved this honor. She had done what they claimed, she had set out to achieve what she had, she had saved them, but what risk was there really, when she knew Falco wouldn't have killed her to get to them?

"This is a good thing, *Oray-Ha*." He smiled. She looked up to him from her seat and watched him cross the room to her.

He squeezed her shoulder thoughtfully. "The plan is finally in motion."

She nodded, staring at her palm, envisioning the inverted *F* scar. "You know what will happen if they do this, if they make me the first female Infinity Hunter."

"I do."

"And still you are pleased?"

Trax knelt down before her, looking her over with his glowing eyes. "I know too much of the truth to let things carry on the way they have been. I know what is right and what is wrong, *Oray-Ha*. There is nothing wrong with you becoming an Infinity Hunter, or what it will mean for Daharia and the Blade of Light's true protectors."

She closed her eyes and saw Jeco's face, and she hoped beyond hope that her loyal friend was right.

* * * *

"Are you alright?" Kohl's voice trailed through her hair as he hugged her tightly. She pulled away from him slowly, careful not to bump into his healing arm. He had stitches across his brow and in his forearm, and several dark bruises trailing down the side of his face, but he seemed, for the most part, alright.

She smiled softly down at him. His wounds had not warranted laser treatments, which meant the slower, more traditional recovery. "You're lying in bed in the medic ward, asking me if I'm alright?"

"I know. I can't believe I spent a night in this place," he laughed. "Veritable torture chamber," he added.

She laughed, with an earnest sincerity. She wondered if she felt affection for him because she knew how she had endangered his life just by being a part of it, or if she had always felt it, but was simply more aware of it knowing he might now truly die.

"Honestly, are you alright? I can't imagine what seeing him, let alone fighting him, must have been like for you."

She stood from the bed, running her hands over her arms. "It was fine. Really."

It wasn't the truth. But it wasn't a lie, either.

"Jessop…"

"I don't want to talk about it, Kohl."

They stared at one another in drawn-out silence, equally stubborn in their pursuits.

"Hanson has been to see me."

She held his expectant stare, silent.

"He seems truly upset. As though, despite treating us like bait, he realized he could have really let me die. He's very grateful to you."

She hesitated, unsure of what to say to him. Hanson hadn't cared about Kohl's life until he nearly lost it. That wasn't profound, or moving. It was pitiful.

"Trax also came to see me," he added, catching her attention. Trax hadn't said anything to her.

"What did he say?"

He studied her face, annoyed by the way he had piqued her interest. "Nothing much. That I was lucky."

She rested her hand softly on his knee, before remembering herself and removing it. "We all were."

He shook his head, slowly disagreeing. "It wasn't luck that saved us. It was you."

"You fought off all the raiders," she reminded him, hating how dumb the sentiment sounded aloud.

"We saw you fight him… It's true, none of us can move like that. The speed and agility you both have. He is a legend for it, and one day, you will be too."

She studied his face, finding his words curious. Falco wasn't a legend for his fighting style—he was a legend for what he could do with his abilities; his attempted coup and his following, for being the purported next Hydo Jesuin before that, for becoming the Arantholi Lord. Did Kohl think she was going to do something legendary as well?

"Because Hanson told me…" he pressed on, arching one brow at her.

She stared at him blankly.

"Oh, come on, Jessop! I know you're going to be made a Hunter!" He exclaimed, his animated face smiling up at her.

She finally relaxed. Of course Hanson had told him. She smiled, knowing she needed to appear more excited about this news for Kohl than she had with Trax. "I may have heard a rumor or two this morning."

"This is incredible! Now this, *this* is legendary. The first female Infinity Hunter. You know what this means right?"

She smiled, silent, waiting for him to answer his own question.

"It means they trust you, Jessop! Hanson, the others on the Council, they truly trust you. You saved their Hunters and a Councilman, *again*. You fought Falco Bane… You truly are more deserving of this than most."

He beamed at her, his brilliant smile clashing with his badly bruised face. She felt awful, but she couldn't show it. She reached for his hand and squeezed it tightly. "I would never have gotten here without you."

She regretted the words as soon as she heard them, knowing how they meant something quite different than what she intended.

"Of course you would have. You have saved me twice. You're the most incredible person I have ever met. I owe my life to you."

His words cut into her as cleanly as a blade. He owed his life to her. She knew that he had that all wrong. She owed *him* his life.

"Swear something to me, Kohl," she pressed, holding his hand tightly.

"Anything."

"Swear to me you'll always be safe. You won't do anything—*er*—stupid or brave. You'll never try to fight Falco or anything like that."

She knew she sounded like an idiot, but she wanted to hear him make some sort of promise, something that would let her know he wasn't about to rush off to his doom.

His brow turned up at her and his smile softened. "I love you too much to go get myself killed."

"I love you too much to let you die," she whispered, fighting back tears of shame. It was the truth. And if Jessop had learnt one thing in her life, it was that the truth was deadly.

* * * *

She sat at the foot of Kohl's bed in his quarters, watching him dry off. His body was nearly as bruised as it was scarred. And she didn't have a mark on her from their ordeal in Okton Radon. He had asked her about Falco's ability to heal, and she had answered the only way she knew how. His capacity to heal, like all of his abilities, was just exponentially more advanced than anyone else's. He had also asked her about how she had saved Teck from the blade, and that had led to a less pleasant conversation.

"You know, if you want to keep secrets from me on a personal level, it hurts. Truly, it does. But I could understand it, given your past. The same way I understood when you stopped sleeping with me."

He crouched down before her, allowing a clear view of her crimson blush. She couldn't explain anything to him anymore. Not without lying, and she didn't wish to lie. "Kohl... I stopped sleeping with you *because* I felt like I couldn't be myself in front of you, because you'd never accept me."

He stared at her, stunned. "How could you think that?"

But the question was too frustrating for her. She thought it because it was the truth. She had tried time and again to reveal herself to him, and he could not keep her secrets in confidence. He always wanted to share them with the Council. And whether she was becoming a Hunter or not, she was not prepared to share her biggest secrets. The Council may have trusted her, but she did not trust them. She had to lie—always. Lives depended on her ability to keep others out of her mind.

"I told you from the beginning. I can hear a thought, open a door, push a little."

"What you did, stopping that knife like that, controlled by someone with abilities like Falco, that's more than 'push a little'," he rebutted.

She sighed, resting her elbows on her knees and leaning down to him. "I don't know what to tell you, Kohl."

He rose, angry. "How about the truth?"

She mirrored him, standing and crossing her arms. "You like the truth so much, but you never share anything, do you? What's with all the scars, Kohl? What's the ritual that happens?"

He shook his head at her, stuck between concealing his own past and prying further at hers.

"See? Not so easy when it's your history on the table," she snapped, stepping past him. But before she could leave the room, the automated voice announced Hanson's presence.

The door slid open and revealed the old Hunter, holding a parcel in his hands. It was the first time Jessop had seen him since Okton Radon, and she couldn't pretend to think he looked well. He looked *old*. He looked grayer than before, and weary, perhaps even sick. But his appearance did not seem to surprise Kohl, who had said his mentor was struggling with his own recent decisions. Jessop couldn't help but wonder if she wore her shame just as badly.

"Jessop, good to see you in one piece," he greeted her, his voice soft and somewhat tentative, less gruff. He spoke to her with more kindness than usual, but he struggled to hold her gaze.

She had recently found herself to be much more forgiving than she had once been. Perhaps because she had never felt as though she had been the one to need the forgiveness until now. She offered him a slow nod, a faint smile. "And you, Hanson Knell."

"I—*err*—I brought you both these. Funerary gowns for... for Daro Mesa," he explained, handing the parcel to her. She took it from him softly and passed it to Kohl.

"Umm... Thank you," she spoke, unsure of what else she could say. Hanson had been in control of the Blade for such a short time, and during his brief tenure he had nearly gotten his protégé killed, a young Hunter had died, and Falco Bane had nearly killed their entire mission party. Hanson had failed in his leadership, and he wore his failure with great shame.

"Yes, thank you," Kohl added, holding the parcel tight against his chest.

She hadn't really had a spare moment to think about Daro's funeral. She had been too busy thinking about everything that had led to his death.

"His family will be arriving in the morning. The ceremony will take place in the North Tower," Hanson explained, running a hand over Kohl's dresser softly. "I will bring them to the Blade... but I would like you to escort them to the tower, Kohl."

Kohl nodded, "Of course."

Jessop hadn't thought of the family. She knew that Hunters had them, of course, but they were just an abstract idea to her, an afterthought. She thought of what Daro had said, of there being three sons within his house. She couldn't guess how many people she had directly been responsible for the death of, let alone fathom how many family members' lives she had ruined. She didn't want to meet Daro's family, not when she would have been willing to kill their son herself. She didn't want to meet a mother who had lost a son; she didn't want to know what that agony looked like.

"Jessop, you'll help Kohl with Daro's family?"

She nodded slowly, "Of course." She had no choice but to do whatever was necessary to ensure Hanson didn't change his mind about her becoming a Hunter. She did wonder, briefly, how he and the others could make such a decision without Hydo. Perhaps they thought he would never wake, and that they had to carry on without him.

"Good, thank you. And sometime this week, after the service for Daro Mesa, we will be having a Council meeting. You'll both be expected to attend," he explained, flicking his gaze from her to Kohl. Kohl nudged her side, a knowing look in his eyes.

"Of course," they answered in unison.

* * * *

Kohl gently placed the parcel down on the dresser behind her, a pensive thought shadowing his eyes. "You know, if they are making such monumental decisions without Hydo, they must think he's never going to return to us."

She turned her head up at him. "I was just thinking the same thing."

He ran his fingers slowly down her arm. "You know what that means, then, don't you?"

She shrugged, not wanting to say the wrong thing.

"It means they will be looking for the next Protector of the Blade of Light. They will be searching for an active replacement for Hydo."

She nodded, silent, thinking of their search. As far as all of Daharia was aware, there had only ever been one person who could have bested Hydo Jesuin—and he was the sworn enemy of the Blade.

"If you could leave this place and live anywhere in Daharia, would you?" she asked, grabbing his hand as she abruptly changed the subject.

"What?"

"If you could live a different life, would you?"

He chuckled softly. "No. Of course not, I'm a Hunter."

She held the back of his hand against her chest, pressing further. "But if you had to choose to live somewhere else where would you choose?"

"I would want to live wherever you were," he smiled, his voice soft and low.

"But if you couldn't—"

"Jessop…"

An image of a blonde woman with hazel eyes flashed in Jessop's mind—a piece of his memory she had trespassed. "Please, Kohl. I know your whole life has been here, but do you truly remember nothing of your family, your home before you were brought to the Blade?"

He sighed heavily, regarding her with frustration. "Not really. Somewhere in Gold Breen, I think. I suppose I would like to go find my parents maybe, if I had no place in the Blade."

She kissed the back of his hand. "Thank you."

"Any other weird questions?"

She kept his hand pressed against her lips softly. "Just one…"

He nodded, feigning exasperation.

She smiled, brushing her cheek against the warm skin of his fingers. "Who took you from your parents all those years ago… Hydo or Hanson?"

CHAPTER 17

They waited, in silence, down on the docking bay. Jessop ran her fingers over her grazed knuckles, her green eyes studying the darkness, waiting for any sign of Hanson. He was escorting Daro's family into the Blade, and he had told them to be waiting in the docking bay early. She and Kohl had been there for some forty minutes already.

"Hanson's never late," Kohl repeated for the third time, turning on his heel in his black funerary robe. The robes were long and formal, similar to the one Teck lived in, except the ones for the funeral rites had the Hunter's sigil emblazoned on the back.

"Dealing with a grieving family can be a long process, Kohl," she reminded him—for the third time.

He stopped in front of her, taking her hand in his. "I should have gone to meet Daro's family. He died on my mission."

"He died on the Blade's mission, and Trax was the senior member of that team—you were all his responsibility."

He raised a dark brow at her, his blond hair falling into his eyes. "Are you suggesting this is somehow Trax's responsibility then?"

She pulled her hand free, crossing her arms over her chest. "Of course not. It's mine."

A heavy sigh fell from him. They had already had this discussion. The issue was that when they spoke about it, they were actually talking about very different things.

He ran his hand up her arm. "What Falco does has nothing to do with you."

She scoffed, nearly turning from him to conceal her eager rebuke. "We may both keep secrets, Kohl, but let's not pretend that we live in a different world than this one. We both know that's not true—what he does has *everything* to do with me."

He took her hand, holding it tight against his chest. "You're not yourself today."

She closed the space between them with a step, resting her head against his broad chest. "I don't like funerals," she spoke, as if that could explain everything away.

His breath was warm against her. "Yes, I imagine you've been to too many."

"I've been to none. I'm typically the killer, not the mourner," she answered. Her candid words were hot between them, her eyes widening at her own disclosure. She pulled back, tilting her face up to him to measure the extent of her damage.

But he immediately had his hands around her jaw, his lips on her forehead. "Never say that. You're not a killer. You've done everything to simply survive."

She closed her eyes and saw Jeco. She didn't do all of this for her own survival; perhaps before, much of it she had done for that very reason. But not since Jeco.

"Survival isn't an excuse for what I am," she whispered.

He kissed her cheek, soothing her without knowing the true cause of her pain. "What you are is amazing."

"It's very likely that you won't always think that," she admitted.

She pulled away slowly, stepping back, putting the distance between them that she never should have removed.

He looked at her with narrowed eyes. "Why would you say that?"

The whirring engine of a Soar-Craft pulled her attention away, and the bright lights of the vehicle stung her eyes as it came into the dock. Hanson lowered the Soar-Craft gently to the ground and cut the lights of the giant machine.

Jessop watched as the grated ramp descended from the door, the metal contraption fixing a bridge between the Soar-Craft and the floor beneath. She took slow, shallow breaths. Would these people sense that their son was dead because of her? Would they know how he had hated her?

The heavy metal door of the Soar-Craft lifted slowly, curving over the body of the vehicle until it tucked neatly away on top of the machine. Kohl stepped forward, standing beside the ramp, adopting a solemn expression that seemed to come quite easily to him. She had never attended a funeral, but it seemed as though he had attended one too many.

The woman who appeared in the doorway was striking—and pained. Tears reddened her large dark eyes and her full lips twitched as they held back sobs. She fought for composure, clearly a woman of great pride. She walked down the ramp with her chin parallel to the floor, her eyes high, and her shoulders, pointed under her dark robes, tightly back. She had a mane of black hair, streaked with gray, that she wore in a severe bun. She seemed uncomfortable in every sense of the word.

Her husband was a handsome man, and he too had the visible signs of suffering. His white hair was brushed back into a near perfect coiffure, barring the few strands that his fingers loosened when he cried into his worn hands. He, like his wife, wore all black.

Jessop felt true pain for them. Whatever she had thought of Daro, his parents seemed to have more than loved him, and they appeared haunted by his loss. It made perfect sense to Jessop. She too had a history of such loss and sadness—she knew these people's pain, simply from a different angle.

Kohl bowed to them. The gesture was nothing grandiose or awkward, but mournful and respectful. She followed suit, lowering herself just slightly, dropping her eyes from those of the woman whose own held such a pain it scared Jessop.

When he rose, she rose. Suddenly, standing beside Daro's parents was Hanson. She caught his gaze briefly, before they both looked away. She watched Kohl study his mentor's face, eyeing up the black bruise on the old Hunter's cheek. Kohl looked confused, but knew better than to inquire.

He took the father's hand in his, shaking it warmly, regarding them both with soft eyes and speaking in a low voice. "Master Mesa, Madam, on behalf of the entire body of the Hunters of Infinity, I offer my deepest condolences for your loss. I had worked with your son for some time, he was a most impressive man, and a true brother."

The tone of his practiced words made it clear to Jessop that he had done this many times before. She wondered if Kohl, with his scarred face and forgiving eyes, was paraded out to each set of parents of the men who fell within the Blade. He was so young and boyish, the perfect proxy son whom parents could feel attached to during the service. Did his presence keep them comforted, or sedated, while they were at the Blade?

As he took the mother's hand in his, Jessop regretted the thoughts. Which wasn't to say the theory was wrong. She didn't like that she was the sort of person who would always assume the worst. She knew that wasn't a quality one could change in one's self. But even if it were, she didn't know if she would... Her cynicism and realistic outlook hadn't protected her from harm, but it had prepared her for it. She dealt with pain better than most because the hurt was never a surprise. She actually wished Kohl were more like her in that sense—so that the pain, without the surprise, wouldn't smart quite as greatly.

"Jessop?" The way he said her name made her realize it wasn't for the first time—she had gotten lost in her thoughts. It was her time in the Blade; with every passing day she was struggling more and more with the decisions she had made.

"Sorry?"

"I was just saying you joined the Blade not too long ago, and that you too had fought beside Daro," he explained, his voice tense, his eyes filled with agitation.

"Indeed, yes." She regarded the parents with solemnity, tilting her head with each word. "Your son was a gifted fighter with a keen acumen. A true master of blades," she complimented.

She spoke the truth. Daro had been a masterful wielder of knives, a capable fighter, and he had been astute, to a fault. Jessop had learnt that neither a magnificent mind nor an expert blade hand proved enough when faced against Falco Bane. Against him, everyone somehow seemed untrained, ill-educated, and unprepared. He had a way with pain that was truly singular. Yet, Daro had been spouting vitriol at her when he died, and here she stood, at the behest of *his* brethren, representing him to his family. Perhaps the brotherhood of Hunters had their own singular sick notion of pain too.

"I do not understand. How do you fight here, girl?" Master Mesa asked, his voice thick with an Eastern tribe accent that Daro had not had.

Hanson took a step forward, "Jessop's story is a complicated one, but she does fight for the Blade, and is quite adept, at that." She bowed her head with humility, knowing the words were probably the nicest he had ever spoken about her.

"Good. In the Eastern Sands, we see no issue with women using the blade either. Good for you, young girl," Madam Mesa spoke, her voice thick with accent.

"Yes. We have always thought it odd that Azgul has halved its army by refusing the entry of their women folk," Madam Mesa's husband agreed. Jessop wondered if they knew their son had felt differently towards the matter. Perhaps she was wrong, perhaps Daro's issue with her hadn't been that she was female, but with simply who his brothers became when she was around them. She thought of her own irritation with Kohl and Trax on their mission. Daro hadn't been wrong about the effect she had on them—but his hatred had blinded him when danger had been so near.

"Well, Azgul has always had the Hunters," Kohl reminded them, smiling softly with his gentle words.

"And now the Hunters have the girl," Madam Mesa answered back, her tone pleased. It was as though she were proud of Jessop. The sensation was one of warmth, welling in Jessop's chest, different entirely from the fire of rage and retribution that permanently burnt inside her. This was a feeling of acknowledgment, and, unlike with her rage, she felt entirely unworthy of it.

"Please, enough about me. Let us move to a more comfortable location," she insisted, quickly stepping to the side and gesturing for Daro's parents to pass her. Her words were a reminder of the occasion, and any lightness their brief conversation had brought them quickly disappeared.

* * * *

They sat in silence. A silver tea tray rested on the small glass table between them, untouched. Kohl had led them to a small room high up in the Blade. It was quiet and quite peaceful, but the air had an uncomfortable thickness to it, perhaps due to the knowledge that this was a waiting room for mourners. The seats were a dark gray, and plush in material. The floor was covered in soft rugs, woven by desert tribes, and the walls were covered with heavy curtains. One wall was still made entirely of glass, and the red sky shone softly through paper blinds fixed over it. There were small potted plants in the corner of the room, which were so distinctly out of place that Jessop couldn't help but stare. She had never seen any sign of foliage, no greenery from the outside world, inside the Blade.

Jessop was coming to understand the structured process for those who arrived at the Blade to grieve their kin. Young fighters who would act as their guides greeted them, then they would be taken to a room that was entirely different from any other room in the Blade, for it was a room of comfort and solitude—not brutality and order. There, they would wait together.

Jessop knew that the architecture of the Blade, built for transparency, was the complete antithesis of the Infinity Hunters' modus operandi, for there was no true openness between the brotherhood and the outside world.

"How long will we be here?" Madam Mesa spoke, running her hands over her robed knees, her eyes fixed on the silver tray.

Kohl cleared his throat and leaned forward, resting his elbows on his legs. "Not much longer, Madam Mesa. Are you sure I can't make you some tea?"

The older woman shook her head, her eyes staying low. Her husband took her hand in his, squeezing it tightly. Jessop watched the two as they held one another, the way the mother swayed slightly and the father's legs tensed, his feet pushing hard into the floor beneath. It was as though they were bracing themselves for what was yet to come.

Jessop watched the mother fighting back tears, her stubborn lip shaking wildly.

She leaned away from them, and then cleared her throat. "When I was young, I watched my family perish in a fire."

She felt them all move, Kohl and the parents, turning in their seats at her admission.

"It was intentionally lit by the enemy, this much I know, and I was left there to burn with them, but somehow, I was saved…"

Kohl reached over and grabbed her hand, his eyes wide as he stared at her. She had always maintained that she had no recollection of her childhood, and for the most part, that was true. She didn't remember many things, but the fire—*that* she remembered. The fire was, regrettably, unforgettable.

"Jessop," he spoke, pulling her hand towards him softly.

"I know… I said I didn't remember, but it's simply too awful a tale to volunteer out to people," she explained. Madam Mesa leant forward in her seat, her fingers interlocked with her husband's as they waited for her to carry on.

"I was left to burn, but I was saved… I was saved, Madam, by an Infinity Hunter."

She could feel Kohl's surprise, his stare burning into her. She saw the sadness in the mother's eyes, the sympathy in the father's tight lips.

"That is what Infinity Hunters are meant to do. They save people. Your son saved people. He was a hero, and if it weren't for men like him, there wouldn't be women like me," she explained.

A large tear clung to Madam Mesa's smooth cheek, resisting gravity's pull. She nodded, and then rocked forward, knocking the tea tray as she took Jessop's spare hand into hers and held it tightly.

"Thank you. Thank you, child."

CHAPTER 18

Hanson sent word for them shortly after Jessop finished telling her story. A boy appeared wearing funerary robes. He offered a sheathed blade to Kohl and explained he would lead them to the North Tower for the service to begin. Whatever comfort Jessop had provided Madam Mesa and her husband was fading. They supported one another physically through each slow, shaking step down the glass corridor, moving like one in their black cloaks, a shadow of their former selves.

Jessop walked slowly behind them, beside Kohl. "This is for you," he whispered, handing her the blade. She took it from him, noting its dusty sheath and aged hilt. "It's just for the service," he added quietly, noting her look.

"Jessop… what you said about the fire…" he began, but she shook her head, taking his hand in hers.

"Not now, Kohl. Later." She squeezed his hand tightly, knowing she owed him more of an explanation.

Knowing she owed him much more than just an explanation.

* * * *

Their flight up the glass chute of the North Tower was painfully long, thick silence cut only by Madam Mesa's soft cries. When they finally emerged from the glass bullet, the young robed boy led them down a short corridor, until he reached two large silver doors. He raised his hand to the scanner pad beside the doorway, and as it recognized his print, the doors slowly pulled to the sides, opening up and revealing a grand outdoor terrace.

The terrace was formed in the shape of a large circle, with floors of polished gray stone; each slab had the Hunter's sigil engraved into it, and walls of crystalline glass separated the attendants from the thousand-foot drop. In the center of the large circular terrace, there was a smaller circle, in which a large glass chute stood.

The terrace was filled with Infinity Hunters, many of whom Jessop had already met or sparred with in the Blade, and all of the Council, barring, of course, Hydo Jesuin. She found Trax quickly, his yellow eyes glowing from under the dark hood of his funerary robe, leaning against the glass wall of the terrace, alone. He nodded to her, acknowledging her presence. She readjusted her grip on the worn blade in her hand, and turned to Kohl. "I'll be back."

She turned on her heel and made her way through the sea of black robes, until she stood at Trax's side, eyeing the treacherous drop down. "I told them about the fire."

Trax seemed unsurprised by her admission. "That must have been hard for you."

She shook her head slowly. "Harder for Kohl. I keep springing these bits and pieces of information on him."

He turned his head to her, slowly twisting his body around to face her. "Suffering a crisis of conscience? So close to achieving everything you have worked so hard for. So close to becoming the first female Infinity Hunter."

"Don't lecture me, Trax. My plan remains set, I simply wish things could be different."

"Why? Everything you have done, all you have kept from him, it's been for the right reasons. You could never truly be yourself with him, never really confide in him."

Jessop raised her hand, silencing him. "I know. You know this is not about that. You know how I feel. It's just having Daro's parent here. I simply wish that I weren't the one responsible for causing so much pain."

He nodded down to her. "We have all caused pain, Jessop. It is why we must take assurance in the fact that we do it for a true cause, for the greater good of all."

Jeco's face flashed to the forefront of her mind, and she did not voice what she thought—she was not doing this for the good of all, she was doing it for the good of one.

"Do you want to meet Daro's parents?" she suggested, changing the subject.

He shook his head. "I've met them before."

Jessop couldn't imagine why Trax had met them before; he would have been too young to go recruit Daro, and parents were not openly welcome to visit the Blade.

Noting her perplexed look, he answered. "I met them when their first son, Hayo, died. He too was a Hunter."

She couldn't conceal her surprise, her eyes automatically darting back to Daro's mother. Of three sons, one was a raider, and two had been lost to the Blade.

"They said nothing… *Hayo*—that name sounds so familiar," she mused, turning her attention back to Trax.

"You've probably heard of him. Several years ago, he died trying to breach the walls of Aranthol."

Immediately she could see his face, and knew his name and the way he died. It felt surreal and eerily interconnected, the way this family had suffered such loss surrounding her. Her stomach tightened as she forced the image of the two dead Mesa boys out of her mind.

"What a small world," she whispered. The words felt like acid on her tongue, still seeing the dark eyes of Daro's fallen brother.

"Indeed. Worlds are small when everyone is involved in the same war."

* * * *

There were two chairs, for Daro's parents, facing the glass chamber in the center of the terrace. Jessop followed Kohl's lead as they all began to form a circle around the glass chamber, encircling Daro's seated parents. They stood quietly, the wind whipping about the glass barricade, their hoods low over their faces, a wall of black robes.

After a long silence, one Hunter stepped forward, his face concealed by his hood. By his long silver braid, which rested down on his chest, Jessop knew it to be Hanson. He cleared his throat softly, his hands held behind his back. "We are here to honor a brother, Daro Mesa, who has been with us for nigh two decades. The enemy has taken him from us, but he does not move into the next world alone. We all know that his brother, *our* brother, waits to be his guide."

Daro's mother rocked forward in her seat, hideous gasps of air expelling from her throat as she fought back the tears.

"This family has given their blood to the cause, and we honor them. Let us come together, as Hunters, protectors of Daharia and the Blade of Light, to say farewell to one of our own."

As he spoke, Jessop noticed a movement in the middle of the circular glass fixture. Something was rising up from an unseen chamber below. A table, or a platform, with something atop it... *It was Daro.* A metal platform ascended in the center of the glass circle, and on it, Daro Mesa's lifeless body, wrapped in tight black cloth. Jessop finally understood what the glass chute was—a funerary pyre.

Hanson took several slow steps, until he was standing before Daro's parents, a dark figure between parents and child. From behind his back, he drew a long sword, which Jessop quickly recognized as Daro's Infinity Blade.

He knelt down, bowing his head as he presented it to the parents. Daro's father, silent tears freely cascading down his face, took the blade from Hanson. Hanson bowed as he backed away from them.

"Hunters, your swords," he called out, an authoritative, deep-voiced order. At his command, the circle of robed figures unsheathed their blades in unison, holding them vertically, their tightly clenched hands in front of their hearts, the blades parallel to their noses. Jessop had quickly followed suit, fast enough to be just in time with the men. The crimson sky darkened around them, and they formed a circle of reflective star glass blades.

"Take a knee," Hanson called out, and with perfect synchronicity, they all knelt down, swords still held up before them, forming a circle of protection around Daro and his family.

"Repeat after me," he instructed. Jessop could hear the hushed whistling of gas, filling the glass chamber.

"This, our Hunter's Prayer. We ask our gods, take this soldier into the bosom of your vast sky, and shape from him a star of brilliance, to shine as his valor shone in life."

The group repeated the words, slow and measured, with such rhythm and earnestness that Jessop felt their wishes and hopes in her own heart.

"Guide our brother, as he joins the ranks of those who have come to pass before him."

As the words were repeated, Jessop heard the keen sound of a fire igniting.

"He will come to you on the winds of your making, cloaked in smoke and wearing the Hunter's sigil. He was a protector of the Blade of Light, a protector of Daharia, a brother to many, and a hero to all. This is our Hunter's prayer."

Jessop kept her head bowed low as she finished repeating the words. Daro's mother wept freely and the glass chute was filled with bright flames, the smoke travelling up into the sky above. Jessop could not bring herself to watch the burning. She kept her head down as they remained kneeling.

They stayed on bended knee as the fire burned, as Daro's mother's cries turned from sobs to soft tears, as the red sky grew darker, scarlet and angry, around them. They remained kneeling through the last of the unkind smoke, until there was nothing left in the pyre but the ashes of someone who had crossed Falco Bane.

* * * *

Jessop removed the funeral robe and handed it to Kohl. "That was a moving ceremony," she remarked, running her hands over her tunic.

"One too many for that family," he answered, leaning against the wall.

"You never told me about Daro's brother."

"I didn't want to remind you of Falco any more than you already constantly are."

She took a deep breath, crossing her arms over her chest. "What I said earlier, to his parents, about the fire. I should have told you that sooner," she admitted, but she didn't mean it. What she meant was, she never should have gotten so close to him that keeping secrets from him riddled her with guilt.

He nodded slowly. He didn't seem mad at her or even upset. He seemed composed, and, as always, empathetic. "I understand that we both keep certain things close to our chest, the secrets we have… I just wish we weren't the sort of the people who felt we had to keep them."

She wanted to say something optimistic, she wanted to say something like maybe in the future things would be different… but she was sick of lying to him.

When she said nothing, he spoke. "You remember your family then?"

She shook her head. "I remember the fire, the circumstances, bits and pieces…"

He nodded, watching her with sad, dark eyes. "You remember you were saved by an Infinity Hunter though. Do you know who?"

She sighed heavily, not wanting to lie, she opted to omit and avoid. "I simply knew he was an Infinity Hunter by his sword and the sigil on his chest."

"And ever since then, you've fought to join us in the Blade," he spoke, assuming the rest of the story. He regarded her carefully, as though he finally understood what dark history forced her onto this path.

"Something like that," she answered.

He pushed off the wall and took a step towards her. Leaning over, he kissed her forehead gently. She reached up and touched his jaw, letting her thumb run over the soft skin of his star scar.

He cupped her hand with his, and smiled softly. "I truly believe in my heart that, one day, things are going to be very different between us."

His words made her want to cry, but instead, she forced a smile. "I'm certain you're right."

* * * *

That night, Jessop found herself once again standing in the dark, looking down at Hydo Jesuin's weary and resting face. She had gotten past the guards with her usual ease, and had been standing in the welcome darkness for nearly an hour, simply watching him.

His hands, beaten by years of battle and age, rested on his sternum, still loosely holding his blade. His lips seemed cracked, his skin worn. He did not look well and she wondered whether his loyal brethren had somehow begun to forget about his needs. They were making large institutional changes without him, they were leading funerary services, instructing missions that ended in death, and allowing her permanent, *real* access to the Blade.

"And it's all because of you," she whispered, lowering her hand gently onto his cheek.

Slowly, she bent over, folding at the waist, until she could rest her ear against his chest. She listened carefully for his heartbeat, wondering, for a brief moment, if she would be able to hear one. Sure enough, the low, rhythmic beat became audible. She sighed heavily, and crouched over him, her elbows propping her up so that she was just inches away from him.

"You seem dehydrated… and you need to be bathed," she told him, referencing his stale smell. "I can speak to Hanson about your treatment… although, he has been leading quite the busy life as the Blade's acting leader. It's as though they have forgotten you. How awful… forsaking their leader, believing you to be in a sleep that will take your life. How disloyal it seems," she spoke, running a finger down his jaw line.

"Things are about to truly change around here, Hydo, and I do so want you to be awake to witness it all," she added, her whispers trailing over his papery skin.

"I'm growing more open with Kohl—in fact, I told him about the fire today… He was so understanding of the whole thing. He asked me if I knew the Hunter who saved me that day. I couldn't tell him, though, could I? I couldn't put all of our secrets out there in the open, not just yet."

She ran her hand up his face, her fingers grazing his temple, and she entered the dark confines of his mind, where they both could remember the heat of the flames from that day long ago.

CHAPTER 19

When Jessop woke, Kohl was sitting at the foot of her bed. His pale blond hair was loose, hanging around his tanned jawline. He wore garments for training, his sword on his hip. She rubbed her eyes, sitting up to face him. "When did you come in?"

"Ten minutes ago. I have word from Hanson," he answered, his hand resting on her blanketed foot.

She ran her hands over the knotted mess of her dark hair, waiting for him to continue. She wasn't sure what hour it was, but it felt very early. She had been out late the night before and was more tired than usual. She imagined it was the funeral service; it had been a very draining day, both physically and emotionally.

"The Council wants to meet with you. Today." His deep voice was filled with excitement, and he squeezed her foot tightly.

She forced down a yawn. "You think it's about making me a Hunter?"

He nodded, his eyes wide. "I know it is." He smiled down at her and she lurched forward into his arms, embracing.

He hugged her tightly; running his hands over her back, and then released her. "Go bathe. We can get in a sparring session before we go to meet with them."

She pulled away from him. "No. I don't want to fight you."

He arched his dark brow at her. "What?"

She thought of how badly she needed him to be fit and healthy, and how much of a danger she was to him, and she knew she didn't want him in the Hollow. "I just don't feel like sparring," she corrected.

He nodded, patting her on the leg. "Okay. We probably wouldn't have had time for it anyway. Just go bathe."

She gauged his disappointed expression, and once again felt bad for how she treated him. "Kohl, I just don't want to see you get hurt."

It was the truth, and she so rarely had the opportunity to share it with him.

"Were you planning on hurting me?"

He waited for an answer, but she couldn't give one.

"Jessop, you act like I'm some childhood friend who spent the past twenty years as a tailor or rug maker. I was raised in the Blade, I have been fighting all my life. I have been badly hurt, and survived. I have killed and nearly died, mourned and carried on. The hurt is intrinsic to my way of life, and you need to understand that. I'm not fragile."

She nodded slowly. He was right, and she knew it, but it didn't change how she felt. He did live an inherently dangerous life; he had nearly died the day they met. That didn't change the fact that she didn't want to be the cause of his pain, not any more so than she already was.

He didn't wait for her to say anything. He stood, and pulled her out of bed. "Now go. I'll wait for you."

She smiled up at him softly. "You don't have to."

He stared at her with such resoluteness, entirely in love with her; he had a way of showing his whole heart in a single glance. "I'll always wait for you, Jessop."

She forced a smile as she turned from him, knowing that would always be the problem.

* * * *

She was standing in the same sole beam of light, in the same room, in front of nearly the same Council, as she had on her very first night in the Glass Blade. But this time, she stood there with an ease and sense of achievement. She could still so easily remember the sense of wariness and indignation in the room from so long ago.

She could remember how suspicious they were, how Hydo had chosen to allow her to stay. She remembered how they had tortured her in the pool, searching her mind, certain she wasn't who she claimed to be… and here she was, joining them as the very first female Hunter of Infinity.

"Jessop, not long ago I made a decision that endangered the lives of several Infinity Hunters, and claimed the life of one. I could have lost my mentee, whom I view as a son," Hanson spoke, his voice travelling softly around the dark room. She kept her gaze cast downward, listening keenly.

"If it weren't for your actions, which I had so greatly doubted the intention and scope of, I could have lost Kohl twice, I could have been responsible for the deaths of Teck Fay and Trax DeHawn, and I, myself, could have died that night in the tavern.

"Too many Hunters owe their lives to you, now, for us to pretend any longer that what keeps you from entering the brotherhood is little more than arrogance and semantics. The Hunters of Infinity no longer need be simply a brotherhood, but an inclusive family of Hunters, dedicated to protecting one another, the Blade of Light, and all of Daharia."

The room fell silent and she took it as an opportunity to speak. "Thank you, Hanson Knell. I am moved by your words."

"I should have been moved by yours long ago, Jessop. You saved Kohl's life, and my own, on our first meeting. You came here willing to help, and we wounded you. I wounded you, again and again. All I ask now is that you do not begrudge the Hunters for my trespasses against you. Join us."

Jessop took a deep breath and resisted the urge to smile too broadly. The day had finally come. Everything she had worked so hard to achieve, all of the pains she had endured and the hurdles she had overcome, it had all been for this moment—to become a Hunter of Infinity. She nodded, incapable of hiding her smile. "It would be an honor."

They clapped, and it startled her, catching her off guard; she laughed. Kohl stepped forward from the shadows and took her hand in his, as excited as she was. Even though they had heard it rumored since their return from Okton Radon, the joy of it being actualized had not been dulled. Finally, Hanson cleared his throat, and they all quieted down to hear him.

"We will begin the service tomorrow afternoon. It requires five Hunters of Infinity, four of whom must be Councilmen. We have selected Trax DeHawn, Urdo Rendo, Balk Tawn, myself, and, of course, Kohl O'Hanlon."

Kohl tightened his hold on her hand and she could see Trax's golden eyes in the darkness, watching her keenly. She knew that the process needed multiple Hunters, as the Blade of Light, which was required for the ceremony, was kept in such confines that five approved hand scans were required to get through five barricades of steel and stone.

Everything felt surreal to her. So much planning had gone into this very moment that now that it was upon her, she felt somehow surprised by it. She steadied herself with Kohl's hand, turning her gaze out of the bright light and taking a slow breath.

"Do you have any questions, Jessop?" Hanson asked, and slowly the room began to light up.

She blinked, letting her vision adjust as the Councilmen came back into view. Some of the men, those who had been closest to Bevda, remained silent, perhaps unsure of their decision. Others, like Trax and Urdo, smiled down at her.

"No, not that I can think of," she answered.

Hanson nodded, a half-smile pulling at his mouth. "Good. We will see you tomorrow morning then… *sister*."

* * * *

Jessop woke late the next morning. Kohl had stayed the night with her, just to sleep by her side. She rolled over gently, avoiding knocking him with her elbow, and took a deep breath as she stared up at the ceiling. The day had finally arrived. She rolled out of bed silently and crossed the room to her bathing chambers. She undressed quickly and turned the showers on, stepping under the hot water.

She remembered the night Kohl entered the room and she had rendered him unconscious. She remembered every moment with him, especially the ones he no longer had memories of. She knew how greatly things were going to change, that from here on out, nothing would ever be the same for either of them.

As if on cue, he appeared in the doorway of the bathing room. He wore just trousers, his mane of golden locks tucked messily behind his ears, as he smiled to her. "Morning."

She looked over his muscular form, across all of his scars, and she turned her back to him, so that nearly all of her scars were visible too. "Morning." She remembered the day she had been lashed within an inch of her life. She remembered that when the whipping stopped, she couldn't tell; the mere air against her wounds had been so painful it had felt as though it were still ongoing. She had only been certain it was over when the blood that pooled on the ground was no longer just hers.

"Nervous?" he asked, and she looked back to see him tying his hair back into a tight knot.

She looked over his body of scars once more. "Should I be?"

He ran a hand over his chest. "This," he spoke, running a finger over a long scar across his torso. "This doesn't happen during the Initiation you'll undergo today. This happens long before that."

It was the most he had ever said on the subject. He eyed her scars. "And yours? Falco?"

He was referring to her back, the lashing scars "No, actually, not Falco. I was fifteen, there was a man who wanted to hurt Falco, and so he hurt me to get at him. Falco killed him."

She stepped out of the water and Kohl handed her a robe. "He saved you?"

She wrapped it around her body, hiding all the scars. "Yes. I suppose he did."

* * * *

There were no special robes, no pomp or display. Though when she met Hanson, he gave her a leather vest, with the Hunter's sigil on the breast. She immediately put it on. They walked in silence. She stayed between Kohl and Trax, as they followed Hanson, Balk, and Urdo down the long corridor on a floor so low in the Blade she believed they were actually *under* the Hollow. It surprised her that Balk Tawn and Urdo Rendo had agreed to take part in her initiation ceremony, but Kohl had explained to her that they had been open towards the notion of women joining the Blade long before she had ever arrived.

The corridors were dark, which worked well for her, and they traveled in near silence. She couldn't help but feel a sense of triumph, knowing that she would be the one to shape this momentous change within the thousand-year-old institution. She bore new scars, and new memories, and had made new allegiances, and it had all been for this.

They turned the corner and Jessop nearly walked into the back of Urdo Rendo, as they had stopped so abruptly. It was the first wall, made of thick, old stone, with a small steel door. "This is me," Urdo smiled, glancing at her over his shoulder before stepping up to the wall. Jessop propped up on her toes to see him touch the scanner pad in the door.

The whirring sound of electricity cut through the air as the device read his print, and then, with a *click*, Urdo pushed the door open, stepping through the thick wall, and allowing them access through the first barricade.

* * * *

As they got through the next barrier, and the ones after that, they explained to Jessop that it needed to be the hand of a different Hunter each time, to ensure that the decision to access the Blade of Light was not being made by any one individual alone. It was only once they had passed through the fifth wall, that Jessop felt surprised. They stood in an empty, dirty, room. The walls were made of stone, allowing no natural light, but a small electric bulb hung from the middle of the ceiling. The ground was covered in loose dirt and sand. There was a thick smell in the room, for the walls and soil were aged. There was nothing grand or remarkable about the space.

"Not quite what I was expecting," she admitted, walking around. When no one answered her, she turned to find all of them kneeling down in a circle, in the middle of the room. They each had one hand on the ground, and were concentrating very hard—using Sentio, it seemed. Hanson used his spare hand to brush dust away on the floor, revealing the Hunter's sigil carved into the stone they circled. She watched in silence as the ground beneath her feet began to shake.

She braced herself, securing her footing as she held on to the mossy stone of the wall beside her. Soon, the entire room was quaking violently, and the light from the one bulb began to flicker. Then the ground in the circle of their hands began to crumble and crack. With violent tremors, rock and dirt began to bounce around, and a large stone slab began to rise up from the ground. Underneath the stone slab was a cylinder, being wrenched up by the combined powers of the five Hunters. As the dirt fell away from it, Jessop saw it was a cylinder of thick glass, and that inside it, emitting a soft, golden glow, was the Daharian Prince's Blade of Light.

The blade seemed quite similar to their Hunter weapons, but the hilt was made entirely of glistening white stone and the glass was a pale gold, unlike any Jessop had ever laid eyes on. Slowly, the five of them stood, and the cylinder reached its apex height. Together, they moved their hands in a horizontal motion and, using their abilities, twisted free the stone slab from the glass cylinder like a bottle top. Hanson pulled the sleeve of his tunic back and reached into the large glass container, his hand just near enough to touch the hilt. He looked over to her, and warned, "You may want to cover your eyes."

As soon as his old fingers touched the hilt, the Blade lit up the entire room with a bright golden light. It was blinding, and Jessop quickly squeezed her eyes shut and turned away. When she dared open them, she found that she could see the very depths of the mortar and dirt between each slab of rock in the wall. The entire room was alight. It took her a minute for her eyes to adjust, but slowly, she turned around to face them, and found them all watching her, smiling.

"Worthy of its name," she said, taking a step towards the men.

"As you are worthy of being in its presence. The Blade of Light, as you know, is the one true weapon of Daharia, once wielded by the last Prince of the realm; whoever remains in possession of it is the rightful Lord Protector of Daharia, and leader of the Hunters of Infinity," Hanson explained.

She knew the story, and she knew the significance of the blade. She knew that Hydo Jesuin was currently the Lord Protector, but things had changed greatly in her time with them. And she knew they would just keep changing.

"There is only one way to gain access to the Glass Blade, only one way to gain access to any of the barricades we just passed through, and that is to bear the mark we wear on our hands, the *F*. Created during a time all too painful for each of us, for reasons too dark to detail, the *F* is marked into our palms as the Hunter's mark is to our necks.

"You, for the same dire reasons behind the creation of the second mark, already bear the Hunter's sigil. Now, it is time for you to join our ranks, and wear them both."

She took a step closer to them, and Kohl offered his hand out to her. She understood that this ceremony would have typically involved engraving the Hunter's sigil on her neck, as they each had undergone—but thanks to Falco, that step was not required. She gently placed her hand in his and acquiesced as he turned it over, exposing her palm to the others.

"Jessop, do you vow your life to serving the true Lord Protector of the Blade of Light, the Hunters of Infinity, and the lands of Daharia?"

She smiled, and answered with complete honesty. "Yes. I swear it."

Hanson nodded, also smiling. "Hunters," he spoke, and all of them raised one hand, Kohl using his spare, and turned them on the blade. After a moment, Hanson released his grip on it, and the weapon levitated precariously in the air. Once still, with the fixed concentration of all five Hunters, it slowly began to turn over, rolling over and hovering right above her fleshy palm. She took a deep breath, and watched Kohl and the others as they concentrated with all their might to perform the meticulous task.

As the blade began to cut into her skin, she couldn't help but smile. She felt no pain as they carved the letter into her hand, the *F*, which they all knew stood for Falco. This entire ordeal was because of him. It had been his coup that had led to these measures.

And then it was done, and Hanson once again took hold of the Blade of Light, and they all looked to her. She smiled down at the bloody *F* in her hand, and then smiled to all of them, beaming. "I have waited for this for a very, *very* long time."

"Welcome to the Blade, sister," Trax smiled, and they each took turns giving her warm hugs and congratulations, all while she pushed the same thought through her mind again and again and again.

It's done.

CHAPTER 20

The five of them stood around her, forming a semi-circle. For the briefest moment, Jessop almost wished things could stay this way. She had never intended to win Hanson's pride or support, Kohl's love, or the faith of great Hunters such as Urdo Rendo. She had always known she would get to this stage, where she would be trusted to fight alongside the Hunters, but never did she imagine it would be in quite this way.

"Clean your hand up and then meet us all on the first terrace of the North Tower so we can celebrate with the others," Hanson advised. She held her bloodied hand against her chest and looked from him to Trax, to Kohl. The cut was deep enough to form the necessary scar, but she was still too stuck in the moment to feel any pain.

"That's one floor below the funerary terrace," Trax explained, noting her expression.

She smiled to him. "I'll be there as quick as I can." They nodded at her, patting her shoulder and offering supportive grins as they began their trek back down the corridor. Except for Kohl.

He took a step closer to her and reached for her hand. "I'll wait with you," he offered. She stepped back from him, guarding her hand from his touch. Before she had to explain though, Trax reappeared and clapped Kohl heavily on the shoulder.

"Actually, O'Hanlon, I need your help, with the *thing*," he explained vaguely, giving Kohl a knowing look. Kohl looked at him blankly, so Trax made a sword-fighting motion with his hands. It took Kohl a moment, but then he nodded, understanding.

He turned to her quickly, an apologetic look in his eyes. He ran his hand over her shoulder as he spoke. "Of course! Jessop, I'm sorry, do you mind?"

She took another step back, nearing her door. "No, I'll see you shortly," she smiled.

Trax led him away and as soon as they had disappeared down the hall, she ducked into her room. She leaned against the wall, bloody hand close to racing heart, and took a deep breath. It was all happening, and she needed to remain calm and composed long enough to see it through.

She ran into the bathing room and quickly thrust her bloodied palm under the tap, cleaning off most of the dry blood. Her hand was still dyed a pale red, but she didn't have time to be meticulous about it. She grabbed a roll of cloth and wrapped it around the wound, just needing it to dry.

She couldn't waste any more time. She looked around her room, and realized how few things she actually kept there. A few sets of tunics and breeches were all, really. She sighed, realizing she had done a pretty good job of never making a life for herself in the small space. Without hesitation, she pivoted on her heel and ran from the room, the room that had seen so much, and so little, of her. She left it all behind, taking off full speed ahead, for the docking bay.

* * * *

She closed the door to the room behind her silently, once again having slipped past the same guards she had eluded time and again before. She pressed her hand against her heart, and she could feel it beating violently into her bloody palm. This was truly it, the moment everything would change. She didn't want to take too long, for Kohl's sake. Trax knew what to do, but she needed to be quick nonetheless.

Hydo was unchanged, resting on his platter, motionless and decrepit. She crossed the room to him quickly, and looked down upon him with a sense of excitement and anxiety that she hadn't felt in the longest time. "There's a party going on upstairs, Hydo," she smiled, lowering her hand to his forehead, running her fingers into his hairline and taking hold of his skull.

She closed her eyes, taking a deep breath, and pushed inside his mind. She traveled through the memories, through the thoughts and fears, the secrets, lies, and dreams. It was like sifting through a pool of colored water, like being enveloped in a silent tornado of violet, teasing images. She traveled deeper and deeper, and then, like every time before, found the one memory they most greatly shared together. It was a memory just for the two of them; no one else was alive to recall it any more. It was so vividly crafted, in both of their minds, that she could simply step into it and, all at once, be in the world of the past that Hydo had been living for all these long days.

There, right before her, was a small wooden home. It was nothing grand or impressive. It wasn't imposing—quite the opposite, actually, with the way it had been built into the woods, tucked into the crevice of the mountain behind it. There was a pile of freshly cut lumber outside the front door; it was a little damp, with some mossy corners, and the grass underfoot was lush, all due to the recent rainfall, so rare in the surrounding desert terrain. She stepped forward, and she could see movement inside the small house, just through the window.

It was the most beautiful place in the world to Jessop, the green forest of the Grey Mountain, so different from the surrounding territories. It was also the place that housed all her nightmares. For though the place had been a silent and serene one, Jessop knew as she stepped closer to the cabin, it would very abruptly become a dwelling of mayhem and death. As if on cue, the screaming began.

A woman, struck, fell to the ground. Then the sound of a brawl followed by a guttural cry, and a child screaming with such clarity that it formed a truly terrifying knell. Jessop crossed her arms over her chest, unable to keep her eyes open at the horrendous sound.

The door to the cottage then flung open, and there he stood before her. His hair was darker and his skin younger, the scars fresher and the wrinkles much less prominent, but it was him, nonetheless. He slammed the door shut behind him and stumbled away from the scene, falling back and tripping over the woodpile. Jessop took another step forward, watching closely as he crawled back. She studied his face as he watched the house. She had seen every angle of this memory, and watching his eyes as he took in his doing was the view she most often found herself taking in. The smoke had begun to escape the window. The roof crumbled in, disappearing in flames, and all the while, there was still a girl screaming.

She watched as he got to his feet, not seeing her, not as she was *now*. He could see only the child, who was making a desperate escape through the small window. He lunged right at the girl, and grabbed her small shoulders. Without hesitation, he shoved her violently back into the burning house and forced the window shut.

He stepped back so quickly, he nearly bumped into memory-travelling Jessop. Though she was certain there would be no tangible connection between herself and the memory, she sidestepped nonetheless. She watched as he raised his hands out before him, concentrating hard, using his abilities to keep the doors and windows shut, forcing the fire to rage on. A fire that, despite all of the moisture in the ground, continued to burn, thanks to his great power... and all Jessop could do was watch him and listen to the small girl trapped inside.

She took a deep breath, knowing what would happen next, what always happened next when she revisited this place.

"Hello, Hydo," she spoke, but the younger version of the Lord didn't hear her, of course. No matter the extent of her abilities, she couldn't interact with the memories, she couldn't change anything, she could just watch. At her words, the modern-day Hydo Jesuin, older and wearied, appeared at her side.

Tears were running down his cheeks and he watched the scene unfold beside her. "Why do you make me relive this day? It was the worst of my life."

She regarded him speculatively, before turning her attention back to the fire, watching a younger Hydo burn down a younger Jessop's home. "The worst of both of ours then. Are those tears for me?"

He turned to her, his eyes wide. "I don't know how to apologize any further. I don't know what else I can do, Jessop, to show you how sorry I am."

She smiled to him. "You can come to a party with me."

His graying brow knitted with confusion. "What?"

"It's time to wake up now, Hydo."

* * * *

She led him down the corridor, a corridor that had always felt long but somehow never quite so long as it did with him by her side. "You've been asleep for quite some time now," she told him, walking beside him as though they were old friends, instead of the truest of enemies. He had a bloodied *F* in his forehead, from where she had touched him. It seemed fitting.

He knew better than to try anything, still too weak and confused. "Hanson and the others—they thought Falco did this to me?"

She smiled, gesturing for him to step into the bullet first. He did and she followed. "Of course. The only person capable of besting the great Hydo Jesuin... No woman in Daharia could possibly have done it." She mocked their naïve sentiment.

He stared at her hand. "And they made you a Hunter..."

She nodded, turning her hand over to reveal the fresh cut. "Indeed, they did. Not one hour ago."

His knees seemed to go weak, and he fell against the glass wall, clinging to it for support. "I disappear and things just go to the dogs."

She grabbed his arm and forced him upright. "I'll kill you where you stand, old man. Don't test me."

He looked her over, guilt and disgust in his eyes. "I made you into this beastly woman, I know that. I recognized you, you know... those unmistakable green eyes... like your mother's..." he began, but the look in Jessop's eyes, the strength behind her grip, warned him off the topic.

He stammered on, staring at her with fear. "But I had to be sure, I had to find someone from the Grey, from all those years ago... I took your family from you, and you have now taken my legacy from me."

She cocked her head to the side, releasing him from her steel hold. She'd had many conversations with him during her time in the Blade, but none with him conscious, barring their very first meeting. "Do you think we are even? Do you think that somehow, you'll make it through this alive?"

He steadied his balance, staring up at her as he held the wall. "No. No, I don't."

"Good. Evil but not stupid."

She turned from him and watched the passing floors as they rose higher and higher through the Blade.

Suddenly, he grabbed her wrist, his grayed, worn hand pulling at her supple skin. "I suppose I know why you put me in that dark sleep, to relive the memory of what I did to you, every day, all day... But why wake me? Why not just kill me?"

She wrapped her fingers around his hand and twisted it off of her. She continued to twist, further and further, until it was on the verge of breaking, forcing him to cower before her. She leaned down to keep her face near his, to enjoy the fear building in his eyes. He had been the greatest of them all, but months of slow starvation and immobility, combined with fear and the trauma of his sleep, left him weak in her strong hands.

She squeezed him just a little tighter, tempted to push him to the breaking point. "Because someone wanted to say hello to you first, of course."

* * * *

The doors slid open and she stepped out onto the terrace, Hydo stumbling beside her, weak and cowering. Before her, every young Hunter and aged Councilman stood in a tight circle, half of them with their backs to her. She saw how many of them were armed, with their long Hunter blades trained on the epicenter of the ring they formed. She closed her eyes for a quick moment, letting the late afternoon breeze wash over her, letting the adrenaline, and the exhilaration, envelop her.

She took a deep breath, aware of the smile playing on her face. "We aren't late to the party, are we?"

At her voice, half of them turned to face her, making a small gap in the wall of bodies, a gap just large enough for her to see the target of their blades. She first saw Trax, holding Kohl back. She was confused; Trax had clearly failed in their plan. But as Kohl struggled to the side, she saw another...

Very slowly, he turned to her and smiled.

"Hello, beautiful."

Surrounded by Hunters, an unknown number of swords pointed at him, he smiled with easy confidence. He had always had such a carefree smile, a perfect row of beautiful teeth, and the whole thing was really rather lopsided, a bit tilted, as his lips pulled more to one side than the other, always giving him a younger, somewhat cheekier, appearance. The long scar and the dark hair remained the same; it was the gray eyes that had changed, filled with more emotion than ever before, it seemed.

It was only then that she realized the surrounding Councilmen were physically frozen by Falco's use of Sentio, while the young Hunters were simply paralyzed by their own fear. There were too many for Falco to render immobile at once, but his reputation preceded him, and no one had dared be the first to strike against him.

"Jessop, get out of here!" Kohl screamed to her, his deep voice nearly disappearing on the wind, but not before stinging her heart.

She couldn't look at him, not as Trax held him back. She took an apprehensive step forward and stopped. With ease she tossed her hand back, and immediately Hydo fell to the ground, writhing in silent agony, paralyzed by her. The gasps from the surrounding Hunters fell on deaf ears, though. She didn't have time to regard their shock as they laid eyes on just one small fraction of her true self. All she could pay attention to was Falco.

He was finally in the Glass Blade, standing before her.

She took another slow step forward, and then another. He did the same, closing the space between them, holding her green eyes with his gray, letting the air grow thicker and thicker around them, until the entire world was a red blur in her periphery. He reached out to her and she leapt into his arms.

She ran her hands through his dark hair, over his neck and across his back. She stared into his gray eyes, eyes she had seen every day and night that they had been apart, eyes she could see whenever she closed her own, eyes she had longed for as they had lived these lies, and she kissed him.

He moved his lips against hers with ease and familiarity, and she finally felt as though she were home. His hands cupped her face and held her near him, and when she needed to breathe, they rested their foreheads against one another.

"That was the welcome I was expecting down in the docking bay, darling," he teased, kissing her again softly.

"I was in a hurry to bring you Hydo," she explained, pressing her small frame against his strong body.

He hummed softly, looking her over with love and longing. She kissed him once more, and he took her hands in his. "Business to attend to, my love."

She knew they had much to see to, in their moment of great culmination, but she needed to know one thing first. "Wait—how is Jeco?"

He smiled at her warmly, running his thumbs over the backs of her hands. "He misses his mother."

The words could have destroyed her if she hadn't known she would be seeing him so soon.

"*No,* no, no, are you kidding me? Jessop. Is this a joke?" She turned from Falco slowly, and forced herself to look into the heartbroken eyes of Kohl O'Hanlon. Eyes that were as dark and wide as the sky of Okton Radon, glistening, hopeful that some part of what he had just seen had been somehow wrong. He stared at her and longed for an explanation.

It was as though flames were licking her throat, forcing tears to her eyes, broiling her dark heart in the thick oil of rage that it had always resided in. Kohl finally looked at her as she had always known he one day would, and if she hadn't had Falco holding her, she may have fallen to her knees begging for forgiveness.

Before she could say anything to him, Falco spoke. "Yes, darling, Trax here tells me that he is under your strict instructions to protect Kohl O'Hanlon from me. He was in fact trying to remove him from the Blade. Is this true?"

She looked from Falco to Trax, swallowing her tears, and nodded. "It's true."

Kohl shook his head at her wildly, his mane of blond hair falling loose around his shattering face, tears welling over, slicking his star scar. "You're traitors   You and Trax..."

She stepped past Falco, gesturing for Trax to stand aside. He immediately acquiesced, and although every young Hunter jittered at his movement, they did not strike. They all knew that it would take more than one of them to stop Trax DeHawn, let alone the renowned Falco Bane, and they had learnt during her time with them that they couldn't take her. She looked over their scared faces. They were confused, lost without their mentors—and then her eyes fell on an immobile Hanson Knell. He was frozen, but his eyes darted between her and Kohl, and tears were streaking down his face. She was shocked to learn his tears pained her.

She forced herself to look away, to look to Kohl. "We aren't traitors, Kohl. We *are* loyal to the one *true* Infinity Lord and Protector. That's Falco."

He shook his head at her, his eyes filled with tears. "You're insane. He's held you captive and tortured you for so many years, he's brainwashed you, Jessop. Can't you see?"

Her chest ached to see him this way. And she hated herself for being the cause of his pain. "He never hurt me, Kohl. Not once. The man who set fire to my home, who killed my parents, was none other than *your* Lord Jesuin. He was drunk and had an eye for my mother; he had completely forgotten his mentee was with him that day, beyond the Grey. He killed them, and threw me back into the fire to burn alongside their corpses."

Kohl shook his head at her, refusing to hear it. "No... none of this makes any sense. You said an Infinity Hunter saved you. We made you one of us!"

"*Falco* saved me. He left me with a Kuroi family I knew and trusted, and then he told us of his plans to overthrow his mentor, and restore the Blade's integrity.

"He failed to gain access to Hydo, who hid behind his young Hunters, behind you, and refusing to kill his brothers, Falco fled, with nothing more than his blade and a Soar-Craft. He came for me, and with the help of those loyal, he began to build our Shadow City. He built it for me, so that I might never have to see the red color of fire ever again."

The tears fell silently between them, but still she spoke, needing Kohl to know the story.

"Many came for him, many came for me. None were successful. There are none with greater abilities than Falco, and we all know that to be true."

At her words, Falco stepped close behind her, running his hand over her arm slowly. "Thank you, pretty girl, but you and I have been neck-and-neck for quite some time now for that mantle."

She kept her eyes trained on Kohl. "It wasn't until I was much older that we realized we had completely fallen in love. Which was also right around the time we realized there were no true contenders for us any longer, barring one another. None could best me, or him, not with the sword or with Sentio."

Kohl shook his head, wildly betrayed, tears flowing freely down his face as he fell to his knees before her.

"When I had our son, we knew we needed to make a plan for a different life. A child born of our abilities would be the greatest Hunter to ever live; he would be the true Lord Protector—after his father's tenure, of course. We knew that the Hunters, under the leadership of the corrupt Hydo, would always believe us to be the enemy... they would continue to try to breach Aranthol, continue to try to corrupt our people into mutiny, and would never allow Jeco the opportunity to live, let alone rule. So, we began to formulate a plan.

"We arranged for the Aren to find a Hunter, and to plan an attack in the very tavern where I met you and Hanson. Of course, they didn't know I would be there to save you... Nonetheless, we knew that was how I would gain access to the Blade. We knew that Hydo would leap at an opportunity to get Falco, even if it meant keeping me here. Falco warned me of the pool, of the tricks and tortures I would undergo. We practiced for years, until we were certain that all anyone could see in my mind was what I wanted them to be seeing."

Falco crossed his arms, eyeing the blade of one of the frozen Hunters. "It's true—even I cannot explore the depths of her thoughts without her permitting it."

Jessop took a deep breath. She knew with every word she was breaking Kohl's heart further and further. She knew this was her fault, and that if she were a better person she would simply say nothing and continue on with her and Falco's plans. She wasn't a better person though. She had lived beside Kohl, had slept next to him, had trained with him and been allowed access into their sacred 'brotherhood' because of him. She needed him to hear her explanation—to hear the truth.

"I needed Hydo to see just enough of me, and my past, to grow curious about who I once was. Then I put him into a sleep that would last as long as I needed it to... Hydo had a nice time, reliving his murder of my family, again and again. Didn't you, Hydo?" she called over her shoulder, but he was still frozen in silent torment behind her.

"Of course, everyone would grow suspicious of me, so I needed someone who would champion my position in the Blade. Someone who owed his life to me... Someone who wanted me... And that's where you came in." Her voice was barely a whisper, her throat so tight it was as though she were being choked.

"I'm so sorry, Kohl. I never wanted to have *that* kind of relationship with you. I never meant to put you at such risk," she admitted, knowing she would anger Falco, who immediately took an intimidating step towards Kohl.

"Falco, don't!" She warned, holding her shaking hand up to him. He knew her well enough to yield.

"Kohl, I care for you, truly, I do. I know you hate me now, and I understand, but I needed you to know that the reason I couldn't love you back wasn't because of you, it was because of—"

But Falco finished the sentence for her. "It was because of *me*."

She couldn't fight the tears back, not as she looked into his dark, deceived eyes.

He continued to stare up at her. "You... You've been communicating with him the whole time?"

She nodded, wiping her tears on the back of her hand. "Yes... That's how he appeared in Okton Radon. I used Sentio to tell him that Daro Mesa had grown too suspicious of me, that I needed him to die in a fight, to solidify my place in the Blade," she admitted, watching Kohl's shoulders jerk with each heavy cry. She had done this to him. She cupped a hand over her mouth and took deep breaths.

He shook his head at her. "Daro was right—you killed Bevda?"

Trax readjusted his footing at her side. "No, that was me."

"*Trax*, how?" Kohl looked up at his Councilman with tearing eyes. Trax said nothing.

Falco moved to her side. "She's not 'just Jessop,' and she's definitely not 'Jessop O'Hanlon'. She's Jessop Bane, my wife. And I know what she had to do to get you on her side, and believe me, the only reason you aren't dead yet, *brother*, is because I love her more than life itself and I would die before I hurt her... and apparently, right now, hurting you would mean hurting her," he smiled with clear irritation.

Kohl simply shook his head, tears dripping from his jaw to the terrace stones beneath his knees. "I loved her."

Falco clapped him on the shoulder loudly, causing Jessop to take a nervous step closer, but he did not harm him. "Of course you did. You do still, and you always will. She's singular."

He shook his head, his wide eyes seeming confused. "And... um... and Trax?" His voice was more fragile than Jessop had ever heard it.

Trax said nothing, struggling to face his brother. Falco answered in his stead. "The Kuroi had been tortured by Hydo long enough to know who the true Lord Protector is. They knew I could have bested him then, they know I could now. The DeHawns go way back with Jessop and me."

Kohl wiped his tears away on the back of his hand; he looked past her, to Hanson, and then back to her. "Jessop... even if everything Hydo did is true, there were other ways to do this. Ways that didn't involve betraying everyone... betraying me," he choked on each word, completely devastated by her.

Falco scoffed loudly. "You mean to not betray everyone who betrayed us first? Hydo swore to protect the people beyond the Grey, and instead he killed a family because a man wouldn't let his wife be assaulted. And all of you—you were my brothers, and you bet your lives against me. I left you all alive that day, including you, *brother*, who I was once so close to. You swore to always have my back, and on the first chance, you sliced my face open... Talk to me or my wife about betrayal, how dare you?"

Jessop grabbed Falco's hand, knowing his temper, and pulled him back to her. Kohl simply stared up at them, absolutely stunned, entirely broken.

"Now, the only reason you aren't dead, *brother*, is because Jessop and Trax assure me there is somewhere else you can live out your life, away from the Blade."

He looked past Falco, to her, and she saw his shoulders drop, realizing why she had asked so many questions before this day.

She nodded to him, choking on the first few words, "I found out the details from Hanson—that's how he had that bruise on the day of the funeral... an accident I had to erase. I know where your family is, only me. I took the memory from Hanson. You can go and be with them now."

He narrowed his eyes at her. "You were supposed to be my family."

She ignored his sad reminder. "No one knows where they are but me, not even Falco, and I will tell you everything. They're perfectly safe, Kohl," she offered, hoping the enthusiasm in her sentiment might be shared by him.

He stared at her with reproach, his one eyebrow cocked high. "How could they ever be safe when a monster like you knows where they are?"

The words were a slap, but she deserved worse and she knew it. Still, she did not stop Falco from striking Kohl, a swift backhand. As he swayed on his knees, she saw another tear trailing down his face. He appeared defeated, and she couldn't help but think back to that first spar they had shared, when he had told her she was the first to ever best him. Little had he known, the battle was one much greater than their Hollow scrap. She shook her head, not knowing what else could be said. He needed to leave, or Falco would kill him.

Very slowly, Kohl got to his feet. He held her stare the entire time, letting her watch him rise up. He held his shoulders back and tightened his jaw. "Just tell me one thing. What's your master plan then, now that you're both in the Blade, surrounded by the greatest Hunters to ever live?"

Jessop looked at him with surprise, and respect. He faced Falco and her, along with Trax, with such confidence. She found it endearing that he would be so bold in the face of such failure. She slowly crossed her arms over her chest, uncertain if she should say the words until she was already saying them. "Kohl, we aren't the ones surrounded. It is all of you who are in the presence of the greatest Hunters there ever were."

He looked at her with unadulterated hatred.

Falco sighed heavily, running a finger over her shoulders. "Our master plan, if you must know, is to kill Hydo, get the Blade of Light, take over the Council, and allow everyone here the opportunity they deserve... to accept the new rule, and continue their lives as Infinity Hunters, unchanged. Even you, brother. Swear fealty, and you can take your place at my side, as I long ago hoped you would."

Jessop turned at her husband's words, as completely stunned by the offer as Kohl was. But Kohl was more than stunned. She knew his expressions well. He was intrigued.

He took a small step towards Falco. "You... you would let me assume a place by your side? Like we were true brothers again? Even after everything that has happened between me and Jes—your wife? You have it in your heart?"

Falco nodded slowly, his somber eyes fixed on his former brother. "She loves you as kin. As I once did. I have it in my heart."

"Brother, then let me advise you once again, like when we were young. You cannot simply kill Hydo. If he needs to go to trial before the Council, he will, and there will be justice for Jessop's family. But you cannot just kill him, Falco."

If Falco had been lulled into the pleasing words of his former best friend for a moment, it was shattered by any sentiment that resembled an instruction.

Falco arched his dark brow at him. "Can't I?" He unsheathed his sword and pivoted quickly on his heel, moving for Hydo.

"NO!" Kohl yelled, and his voice was filled with all of the authority and command of a seasoned Hunter, a man who had fought battles across Daharia and won wars of slim odds against fierce enemies. His voice, so imperious, startled Jessop, and it set off the young Hunters. As if they had received orders, and had regained the courage trained into them from youth, they leapt at Falco, a great horde of them, ready to kill.

Jessop didn't have time to think, or to truly concentrate, or even wonder if she, or anyone, for that matter, was capable of the maneuver she intended. But somehow, in an instant, every single man on the terrace, barring Falco Bane, was thrashing in pain on the floor.

They cried out, they rolled on the ground, buckling over and dropping weapons, their swords clanking against the stone floor, staring at her like she was some kind of demon. She had struck down the dozens of Hunters present. Slowly, stunned, Falco turned around, glacially pivoting, to face her. His big, gray eyes looked from the tormented men, to her, and his lips parted.

She could feel the blood trailing from her nose. She could feel the tension building in her mind, her muscles tensing so tightly it felt as though she were on fire.

"Jessop," Falco whispered, taking a step towards her. She could barely hear him. She could barely even see him, not when she could feel all of *them*. She could hear their silent screams; she could feel the muscles tearing and the blood pumping in each and every man. She held them down, forcing them to feel the pain she had felt for so many years.

She could see only red. The red of fire and blood, and Azgul. She could hear nothing but that child's faint scream, echoing in the depths of her mind. And in the blur of blood and pain and screaming, she could hone in on Hydo Jesuin, and she forced his mind into a pool of blood, and she held him under, beating him until his bones began to break and she could hear him truly screaming.

"Come back to me, Jessop. Come back to me."

Falco's voice cut through all of it, a blade of his own, sharper than all of the pain and chaos and supernatural ability. She heard his voice, and she needed to be with him again.

Just as suddenly as she had taken hold of the Hunters, she released them. She instantly felt weak, dizzied by the overexertion. Falco held her up, his arm locking around her waist. It took her a moment to refocus her vision, but when she had, he was smiling at her.

"I believe that just answered the question of who has greater abilities," his words whispered over her face. He held her near him and she could feel his powers washing over her, healing her. He wiped the blood from her face and kissed her softly. "You amaze me."

She was unsure of what she had done, or how she had done it. She knew that the amount of men who lay broken at her feet would have been too great for Falco to hold down with his abilities... too great for any. Yet, when his life seemed at risk, she had simply acted. She closed her eyes, holding him tightly as he shared his strength with her.

When she felt restored, she stood up straight, nodding to him that she was fine. He let her stand freely and together they walked to the front of the group, near the bullet, beside where Hydo lay on the floor. Falco took a deep breath, and smiled. Jessop saw Kohl, getting up to his feet slowly, blood trailing from his nose and ear, staring at her as if it were for the first time.

Falco smiled to her before turning to the surrounding men. "Brothers, do not resist. You have seen what we are capable of, and we all want the same thing. Help us restore the rightful leader in the Blade. You know who that is. You know we can lead Daharia into an era of invincibility, into an eternity of greatness."

The pause and stillness after he spoke, the time for them to deliberate on his offer, felt like an eternity to Jessop. The young men looked between one another, pushing thoughts wildly amongst themselves. Jessop didn't need to be a master of Sentio to know what they thought. They were afraid, and they were untrusting, but they were also intrigued. They had heard her tell her story, and had seen her powers. They had listened to Falco, and had seen his abilities, which many of them had only ever heard of before. There were those who had once been brother to him who looked between him and Hydo and nodded, as if they could see a world in which their Lord had disgraced the Blade—for they had been around during that time of ill repute.

And slowly, several of them got to their feet. They were the young ones, the newest Hunters. They left behind their frozen Council and knelt before Falco. A few of them looked back, before taking the knee, but one by one, the numbers grew, until many of those who had been so quick to defend Hydo were ready to swear fealty to Falco. Falco welcomed many of them with a firm arm shake, even a few with a strong embrace, former brethren, prepared to restore their flawed system. Jessop knew some of them acted out of fear; certain that whoever was telling the truth about their history didn't matter, but that if it came down to a battle, Falco and Jessop would prevail. It was only when so many knelt before him that finally, Kohl, with his dark eyes and red face, took a small step towards them.

He bowed his head low, dejected, deep in thought as his shoulders heaved with a low breath. He then raised his head high, his cheeks still soft from tears, his blond mane falling around his strong, proud jaw, and, with proud strides, he crossed the terrace, joining his brothers in their new reign.

Jessop nodded him along encouragingly. She knew that with Falco's offer, perhaps having heard the truth, understanding their histories, things could slowly be repaired between the two men. He knew that she had done all of this for the right reasons. Falco knew she had done all of this for him, and for their son... He had spoken of Kohl for years, of his lost brother, blinded by the ways of the corrupt Council. She had always known the way he missed him, and that the hatred he espoused was simply his reaction to betrayal. Falco had also had his heart broken, the day his brother turned on him. Perhaps, all that she had done, for all of the reasons she had done it, could restore a bond that she knew these men lived for.

They stood before one another, eyes narrowed, minds racing. Falco eyed Kohl over warily; Kohl studied Falco for any sign of danger or deceit. And then, without word or warning, they embraced.

Jessop shook her head with wonderment. She had never thought that this moment would have been possible for them. She had pictured every scenario. She had imagined Kohl's hurt and Falco's anger and her shame. She had thought of the shock amongst the Hunters, the anger and betrayal, and eventual acceptance. She had imagined watching Hydo die, again and again, but she had never been able to envision such reconciliation between the two men she cared so deeply for. For the first time, she felt a sense of relief. And as Falco released his brother, she opened her arms to him.

He inclined his head towards her, the soft smile she had grown so accustomed to appearing on his face. They held one another's gazes, as they had time and time before. They had come to know one another so well, she loved Kohl, for all that he was and all that he stood for, and she knew that the love he held for her would transform into something more like friendship, but equally important, something that resembled her own feelings. He outstretched his arm, reaching for her, like family, and she couldn't help but smile.

He moved so quickly she had no chance of defending herself. In fact, she was so amazed by his quickness, that she hadn't actually felt the sword's blade as it plunged into her stomach. She looked down, confused at the sudden pain. A hilt, made of black gems, was protruding from her abdomen, Kohl's fingers tucked tightly around it.

"We had this made for you, for your initiation," he hissed, shoving the blade deeper into her, before releasing. She buckled, falling to her knees. He had stabbed her... with the Hunter Blade they had made for her.

She could hear Falco screaming her name as she fell to the ground. She felt faint. Her skin was numb but she was aware of the blood, the blood seeping through her clothes, travelling down her chest as she lay back, her body tilted in an unnatural angle having collapsed on her own legs. Blood trickled from the wound to her throat, pooling around her collarbone. She felt cold… and confused. Kohl had stabbed her. He had loved her and he had tried to kill her. She could hear only Falco… she could see only red… and then there was chaos.

She felt pressure all around her. Someone was holding her… She forced her eyes open. Falco had her in his arms, and she knew that his distraction freed the Councilmen from their paralysis. He was trying to heal her, and he could not hold them immobile whilst doing that. She blinked; the sky was so red it hurt her eyes. The young, newly aligned Hunters turned against their mentors, who fought them back, surrounding Falco and Jessop as her blood pooled around them, forming a makeshift barrier.

Falco grabbed hold of the hilt and looked at her with great concern and apology. She felt confused, not knowing why he looked so sad… and then he ripped the blade free from her gut. She heard a scream, and knew that it had somehow come from her. Her face felt wet—was she crying? It felt as though her back had been pulled through her stomach. Her skin was on fire. She couldn't hold on to a body with such little blood left in it for much longer…

Her blood covered Falco. His hands were pushing hard into the wound. He was crying too… "You're going to be fine, my love."

She wanted to close her green eyes, but she couldn't… He looked at her in a way that was all-consuming, so fixated was his stare, so full of love and history, that she couldn't look away. He continued to hold her gaze, and just as she thought she was truly dying, she felt the sinews of her flesh begin to rejoin.

Falco could feel it too; he knew he was healing her. A tear fell from his cheek and landed on her own. He held her tightly, concentrating as he fixed a wound that would have killed her, that should have killed her, that was intended to end her life. She knew she shouldn't have felt surprised by Kohl's actions, after all she had done to him, but she couldn't help it… He had claimed to love her, and he had tried to murder her. She felt, ironically, deeply betrayed… so betrayed that she might have killed him herself if she had the strength.

Everyone and everything comes second to the Lord Hunter. Before all else comes Hydo Jesuin.

She remembered Falco's words well, and no matter how many times she repeated them in her mind, she still couldn't believe it. She watched his gray eyes, brimming with tears.

"I love you, Falco," she smiled up to him.

"And I love you, Jessop," he whispered.

They were the last words she heard before descending into darkness.

* * * *

When Jessop woke, Falco was there, stroking her hair. She moved to sit up, but found the motion to be agonizing. He stilled her, resting his hand against her shoulder. "I have healed you, but that was nearly a fatal wound. Your body needs time to recover fully."

She tried to speak but her lips were dry and her throat ached. He reached for something and she saw it to be a glass of water. He held it at her lips and let her sip slowly. When he put the glass down, she spoke.

"He tried to kill me..."

Falco nodded, reaching over and stroking her face. She knew they were still in the Blade, but they weren't in her quarters. They were in a much larger room, with a gray seating area, a glass table to eat at, and woven rugs on the floors...Falco looked tired. He had bathed, his dark hair still damp, and he had changed his clothing. She wondered how long she had slept and what had happened in that time.

"He did. And I'll kill him for that," he spoke, his voice low.

She noted the future tense of his threat. Kohl had survived. "He... He's gone?"

He looked at her darkly, and she knew things had not gone according to plan. "Mhmm... Many of them are. While I was healing you, he grabbed Hydo. They leapt into the bullet. Hanson and a handful of the others too. They escaped."

She lurched up, forgetting her wound, and immediately found herself in excruciating pain. "The Blade of Light?"

He lowered her back down against her pillows. "Safe. They escaped with their lives, nothing more."

She sighed, relief washing over her, but only for a moment. If they escaped they could be anywhere...

Terror seized her chest and she shot Falco a look. He immediately knew her concern. "Don't worry," he spoke, and stood from the bed. He left her there and walked through a doorway. How could she not be worried? Did Falco know where Kohl and the others had escaped to or what their plans were? She tried to follow him with her gaze, but her movement was too restricted. After a long minute, Falco reappeared, and in his arms was the sleeping body of their two-year-old son.

Jessop began to cry. Falco brought him to her quickly, and laid him down beside her, so that his dark head of hair was grazing her chin, his small, snoring face resting against her arm. She tightened her lips to silence her soft cries and ran her hands over her son's back. She marveled at how he had grown and changed in the time that she had been away from him. Jeco was bigger, his face somehow less round, his hair darker like his father's. Falco took her hand and she squeezed it tightly; he kissed Jeco's head as he crawled over them. It may have been Azgul, it might have been the Blade, but with her husband and son present, it was home.

* * * *

That night, with Jeco sleeping between them, she and Falco spoke. He caught her up on everything. He told her who amongst the Hunters had chosen to stay—including, to her surprise, Urdo Rendo—and who had fled when they could. He spoke of whom he trusted to be loyal, such as Teck Fay, and who would need to be tested further. She listened and gave her knowledge of each Hunter, and when they were done talking and planning, and developing contingencies, they lay in silence.

In many ways, they had been victorious. The Blade of Daharia was theirs, the Glass Blade under their rule, and many Hunters had aligned with them... But Hydo still lived, and so did Hanson and Kohl O'Hanlon. She knew there had never been three people who would want her family dead more than those three, and never had there been three who were so viable a threat.

"They will come for us, like never before. Hanson, Hydo, Kohl... they will be back for their Blade, for our lives."

Falco fixed his stormy gray eyes on her. "Let them try."

If you enjoyed *The Glass Blade*, be sure not to miss the second book in Ryan Wieser's Hunters of Infinity series.

A Rebel Base e-book on sale October 2018.

About the Author

Ryan Wieser completed her B.A. in Sociology and Socio-Legal Studies before going on to complete her MSc. in Experimental Psychology. Having been raised in Africa and educated across multiple countries, Ryan has a passion for travel and an interest in diverse cultures. She currently resides in Wyoming with her husband, Sam, where she is writing her next book. For more, please visit www.ryanwieserbooks.com.

Printed in the United States
by Baker & Taylor Publisher Services